READERS SAY...

"This was a good women's fiction romance. There is an overarching series mystery for this series, but each book also has its own mystery. I am enjoying getting to know these sisters and their histories. I'm loving piecing things together and making guesses (and I'm really striking out on guessing whodunit in this series). This book has a second chance romance with a single dad. The daughter is adorable." ~Michaela, Amazon Reader

"This is a second chance love story. It's so good. Alex and Sam are best friends in elementary school until they graduate. Years later Alex moves back to where they grew up. Will they get their second chance." ~Angie, Amazon Reader

"What happens when "We've both had fears and misconceptions about each other."? Read the story of Sam

and Alex. Can they get beyond these and find the truths that can set them free?" ~Rhonda, Amazon Reader

"After she losses her job Dr Alex Stafford returns home to confront the past and start over. This is a second chance love story with a mystery added in. Can't wait to see what happens next." ~Gale, Amazon Reader

"Her life is about to change when she is let go from her job. She will go home but there are bad memories there and she is about to meet him again. He now has a daughter and a widower, she will learn there are secrets about her parents death. Someone will stop at nothing to stop her learning the truth." ~ Tanya, Goodreads Reviewer

THE VINEYARD NEIGHBORS AND FRIENDS

MELODY ARCHER

WANT TO READ MORE SWEET & CLEAN ROMANCE?

Eliza and Daniel Stevenson's Love Story is *waiting for you!* Simply, click the link below to grab your copy of this FREE Sweet and Clean Romance :)
Go here: www.memorablefictionbooks.com/pages/free-book

For my son Saejal.
Your love of family and your love of helping others, inspired
me to write this story.

PROLOGUE

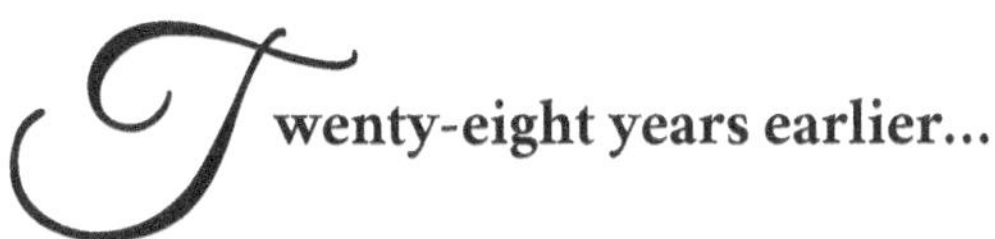*Twenty-eight years earlier...*

A PRIMITIVE FEAR lodged in her throat.

Panic flooded her veins.

Her heart raced.

Alexandra Stafford continued to run.

Her gangly teenage legs ached and strained from the effort.

Turning her head, she caught a glimpse of the man in a blue baseball cap chasing her.

She forced herself to run faster.

Her vision blurred and she could no longer see her assailant.

She ran down the abandoned road, her eyes darting to the right and to the left trying to find a way to safety.

A red-tailed hawk flew above her head and began to circle above a large field filled with tall, broken trees.

The predator's piercing screech filled the air.

Shivers flew up her spine. The warning sound vibrated throughout her body.

Dark clouds formed in the evening sky, a sense of foreboding setting her nerves on edge.

All of a sudden, a deluge of rain poured from the night sky.

The soil became wet and slippery.

She needed to keep going. She needed to escape.

Could she lose him in the thick foliage?

With no time to lose, Alex turned towards the ditch and began to run through the thick trees.

It was difficult to run through the tangled web of the foliage.

But she didn't have any other option. The road that had been her favorite place to run, had now become deadly.

Alex's heart pounded violently in her ears.

Fear squeezed tight knots in her belly.

Panic caused her throat to close in on itself.

The crunching of the man's shoes on the leaves could be heard behind her.

Night was closing in around her and she couldn't see the man's face.

She didn't know who he was, but she was determined to do whatever she needed to do to escape.

A sudden windy gale blasted another onslaught of rain against her body, soaking her clothes.

The heavy weight of her drenched clothing made it even more difficult to run.

Her legs were beginning to tire.

Her lungs burned.

Her body shivered from the icy cold.

Branches stabbed at her arms and legs as she hurried through the dense crop of trees.

How had her daily evening run suddenly turned so wrong?

She glanced behind her.

With the darkness crowding in, this time she only saw shadows.

But the loud stomping sounds of his feet carried on top of the wind.

His long strides were closing the gap between them.

Turning back around, she tried to run faster but tripped and fell to the ground.

Scrambling, she hurried to get back on her feet.

A large rock's sharp edges cut a deep gash in her leg.

She spotted a large stain of blood on the corner of her grey sweatpants.

Forcing herself not to think about the pain, she hurried on.

Her legs — now bruised and bleeding — strained with the pressure.

Without warning, she tripped and fell on an old tree whose roots stuck up out of the ground.

In the distance, she could hear the church bells echoing across the island. It must be seven o'clock. Grams would worry if she didn't return home soon.

Taking a deep breath, she struggled to get back up on her feet.

But, just then, strong hands grabbed her shoulders.

His fingers dug into her skin.

She winced in pain.

"Let go of me!" Alex cried out.

But her attacker only gripped her arm tighter.

Alex struggled to get free, but she couldn't escape from him.

Without warning, something hard hit the back of her head.

Then everything went black.

SLOWLY, her eyes opened.

She blinked, but couldn't see anything.

Everything was dark.

A sulphuric-like smell filled the room.

She nearly gagged.

Thick cotton wrapped around her head, it's tight thickness causing her not to see anything.

It was a blindfold.

She tried to reach up to pull it off, but her hands wouldn't budge.

Somebody had tied her hands behind her back.

Stark fear coiled in her belly, weaving its way upwards where it clung to her throat.

Who was this man? Why did he attack her — what did he want? Where was she?

Her head hurt as more questions crowded in.

She tried to reach up to rub the soreness at the back of her head. But her hands were bound by a strong rope.

Panic gripped her.

Her thoughts raced.

Memories of what happened haunted her. She had been on her usual evening run, enjoying the quiet evening. Then, without warning, there was a man who chased her. He caught up with her and hit her head with something.

She had blacked out.

Then, later in the night, the beastly man had violated her.

Alex bit her lip as a sob escaped.

Her heart pounded as fear flooded her.

What would this horrible man do to her next?

The rope chafed at her skin as she struggled to free herself from the tight bonds.

A thousand thoughts raced through her mind at once.

Why did the man chase her and attack her? Who was this madman? What did he want from her? Where did he bring her — what was this place?

Panic hit her and she tried once more to pull her hands free.

The rope only tightened.

Fear tightened its grip on her throat.

Dread filled her belly.

What would she do now? What was going to happen to her?

Most of all, how could she escape?

Alex bit her lip as her thoughts swirled.

All of a sudden, she thought of her grandmother. She had always been a very wise woman. What had Grams told her? *Whenever you get into a tight spot, don't give up. Have faith. Then sit in silence, say a prayer and wait. You'll be surprised how you'll begin to get ideas and solutions that will help you.*

Alex forced herself to be still and slowed her thoughts down.

Grams was always reminding her to have faith like a mustard seed. She prayed for a way that she could break free from her captor.

Feeling sore, she moved her body a little. Her hands scratched at something that poked out of the wall.

Her finger gingerly touched it again.

It felt like a sharp nail.

An idea formed. Would it work if she used the nail to try to cut through the rope?

She had to try.

With determination, she began to rub the thick rope forcefully against the edge of the nail.

She could hear the fiber as it rubbed against the sharp steel end.

A long time passed, but she continued to work at it.

Touching it with her fingers she could tell her efforts were working. The rope was fraying at the ends.

She was nearing the end of her efforts.

Maybe it wouldn't be long until she would be rid of the rope that bound her altogether.

Suddenly, heavy footsteps drifted to her ears.

The man was getting closer.

She continued to work the pressing need even more urgent now.

Alex fingered the rope again. It was thinning. As she touched it, it seemed almost thin enough now.

She stopped rubbing the rope against the nail when she heard footsteps stop in front of her.

The man was here.

Her heartbeats accelerated.

A popping sound echoed through the air as he bent his knees to crouch near her.

She stiffened at his closeness.

She wanted to escape, but her movements remained constricted.

Suddenly, his rough hands touched her hair.

At the touch of his cold hand, she jerked back.

His low voice emerged in a raspy whisper, "So, my pretty Alexandra. I've caught you in my lair. My mother will be so happy for me. Both my mother and grandmother always thought I'd amount to nothing. But now that I have you, they will both be proud of me. Finally, a girl from the island's well-known Stafford family will be mine."

Alex stiffened at his words.

This stranger knew her name – and the name of her family.

She shivered in fear.

He touched her face and hair, grabbing her shoulders to pull her closer.

All of a sudden anger erupted from deep inside of her.

"I'm not yours to own. Get away from me!" Alex shouted at the man.

He grabbed her tightly by her slender shoulders.

"You *are* mine. Don't fight me, or it will go far worse for you." The man's low voice had a harsh edge to it.

Alex moved her torso, trying to get away from him. She pulled against the rope, trying again to free her hands from the constraints.

The man gripped her shoulders hard.

His fingers touched the angel necklace she wore around her neck.

"I want this angel necklace. I must have it. It will remind me of you — my angel." His low voice was hoarse.

He started to tuck at the silver chain to pull it off her neck.

Alex struggled to free her hands. Finally, this time, when she tugged her hands against the rope, it finally gave way.

Her hands were free at last.

With all her might, Alex pushed against the stranger, and cried out, "No! This necklace is mine. You can't have what's mine!"

He grabbed her, quickly turning her so that his arm was around her neck in a chokehold.

She wanted to take off the blindfold, but she was too busy fighting against him.

"So you think you're clever do you? You figured out a way to untie your hands. But I'm far stronger than a weak girl like you. You'll never be able to get away from me." His raspy chuckle mocked her.

Anger flooded every cell of her body.

She grabbed his arm and pulled with all her strength.

The man resisted. She couldn't get him off of her.

It was time to resort to drastic measures.

She bit his arm and pushed him away as hard as she could.

He yelled in pain, quickly yanking his arm away from her neck. Once more she pushed against him with all her might.

She could hear his feet stumble against the wood floor.

As he fell, her fingers grabbed something and pulled it off his arm.

His watch.

Yanking the blindfold off her eyes, Alex turned to see her attacker. His face was hidden by a black ski mask.

All she could see were hate-filled brown eyes.

He clutched his leg with one hand. Did the fall hurt his leg?

The man struggled to get back on his feet.

Panic flooded her at the determination she saw in his eyes.

She needed to escape.

Alex realized she only had a few seconds to make her getaway.

She ran out the door.

She hurried to get away, focused on finding safety.

She had to trust her instincts because she was lost. She didn't recognize any familiar landmarks.

Alex continued to run.

"You scarred my arm and stole my watch!" Alex heard his loud voice, out of breath, as the man shouted from behind her. "I won't forget what you did! I will hunt you down, if it's the last thing I do! You hear me?"

Fear made her run even harder. With all her strength, she ran.

The one thing on her mind was that she needed to escape.

She intended to run as fast as possible to get to safety.

CHAPTER ONE

lex

A CHILLY WIND blew across the ocean as the ferry made its way across the blue water to Martha's Vineyard.

Staring out at the rolling white-capped waves, nausea began to churn in Dr. Alexandra Stafford's belly.

Swallowing quickly, she shifted her focus.

Thunder rumbled from the darkening storm clouds in the sky above.

She shivered.

Alex caught her first glimpse of the island in the distance.

Fear gripped her heart.

Memories that haunted her for years spun through her mind like a pack of vultures circling their prey.

She was going back to the place of her life's most painful moments.

Agonizing experiences flooded her thoughts. Her twin sister's death, her parents' deaths from a boating accident a few years later and then the terrible attack from a stranger when she was a teenager still haunted her memories.

Alex's throat closed in on itself and panic swelled in her chest.

How would she be able to handle living here again?

The island was the one place she'd vowed never to return.

In a twisted turn of events, she was coming back to stay.

Alex fingered the St. Michael's pendant she wore around her neck.

She wore the treasured necklace every day. At night was the only time she removed it.

Her mom and dad had given Alex the necklace for her birthday the year after her twin sister, Anne, died.

Her twin had always loved to hear the story of their great-grandfather Captain Henry Stafford and how he had saved the life of the young princess.

Anne had always dreamed of finding the tiara with the pink diamond someday.

She was grateful her parents commissioned a custom designed necklace. It had a warrior angel figurine — like the angel on the Saint Michael's pendant — and, as a surprise, they added a small pink diamond.

The pendant was made of gold and the jewel was a truly authentic, rare pink diamond.

It looked like the angel was holding the pink gem in one hand.

For Alex, the angel was a symbol of protection and a source of comfort against the dark and evil forces in the world around her.

The pink diamond reminded Alex of her twin sister's dream to one day find the missing tiara. Last year, Lizzie found the tiara in the secret room at the beach house, but the pink diamond was missing.

Warmth flooded her as memories returned of her parents and the people she'd known from her childhood.

There were a few islanders that were long-time friends. Dr. Grace Waverly and her best friend from childhood, Becca Featherstone.

Becca had called a few weeks ago. The two of them talked regularly throughout the years, ever since Alex left Sweet Beach Cove.

In fact, her friend was the person she called whenever she needed encouragement or advice.

The day Alex called to tell Becca she was moving back to the island, she had been excited.

"Alex, this is the best news I've heard all year," Becca gushed over the phone line. "I've always wanted you to live nearby again so we could have coffee and chat together like we used to."

"Becca, I'm glad. I'm a little nervous about returning to the island. There are too many unknowns. Will it work out to get the children's medical clinic going? Will I be able to reconnect with friends from years ago without it being awkward?" Alex questioned.

"You're thinking about Sam Chadsworth aren't you?" Her

friend asked. "I see him around the island often with his young daughter. I think he looks lonely."

"I hurt him years ago when I refused his marriage proposal, Becca. I don't know if Sam will want to talk to me," Alex explained.

Becca sighed. "I know you have regrets, Alex. But I still think you should try talking to him."

"Maybe."

Her best friend had been one of her biggest supporters throughout the years since she moved away from the island.

There were other friends and mentors. Dr. Grace Waverly was both. She was the woman who inspired Alex to become a doctor. It was Dr. Waverly who took care of her after that stranger's attack when she was a teenager.

However, it was the friendship she'd once had with Samuel Chadsworth — the one man she'd never forgotten — that had been the most on her mind.

Last year, Alex talked with Sam briefly when she'd joined her six sisters for the test weekend at Lizzie's inn.

Her former high school sweetheart from long ago was as kind and handsome as she remembered.

He had briefly shared about the death of his wife. Later on, he talked happily about his young eight-year old daughter, Zoe.

Alex couldn't help but notice he was guarded in his conversation with her.

She didn't blame him.

Memories surfaced of that day years ago when she had refused his proposal of marriage. They had been childhood friends. As they continued to get to know each other, they became more than friends.

The two of them started to date soon after Alex's sophomore year in high school.

It was at that point that something happened that changed her life forever.

It was during the weeks after the start of Alex's junior year, she was brutally attacked by a stranger.

Everything shifted from that day on.

Alex began to put more distance between her and Sam. Yet he continued to pursue her. He wanted the two of them to continue to remain close.

Later, when Sam visited Alex during her first year of college, he proposed.

Alex had quickly refused his marriage proposal.

Her fears of getting close to a man — any man — were very real.

Her refusal not only ended their dating relationship, but it had also ended their childhood friendship.

Ever since that day, there had been a big hole in her heart.

A big part of the trauma she had suffered was a secret that hardly anyone knew — except two women. Dr. Waverly and her late grandmother.

Alex never told anybody because of the deep shame and anguish that flooded her soul each time she remembered.

There was something about her now — that would make Sam reject her if he ever found out the truth.

Regret clung to her like a deep wound that wouldn't heal.

Somewhere deep inside, she longed to restore her friendship with Sam again.

Now, if by some miracle Sam wanted her back in his life — she would never be able to give him what he'd always longed for — a family.

It was something she had yearned for, for a long time.

But time had forced her to give up on that dream.

Yet, Alex couldn't help but long for a fresh start and healing of old wounds from the past.

Would that old house she'd inherited from her grandmother become a place of heartache or healing?

The shuffling sound of feet near her interrupted her musings.

A man wearing a yellow raincoat leaned his elbows on the ferry's rail beside her.

"I couldn't help but notice your bright purple t-shirt with the yellow handprints. Looks like a combination of fun and sunshine. Perfect for the beach," the man spoke in low, even tones.

Briefly, Alex looked down at her shirt.

What in the world inspired her to put this old t-shirt on today?

Silently, she shook her head, upset with her choice of clothes.

Memories returned of that day years ago. It was during the summer festival that Sam had the idea for them to create matching shirts. Together, they dipped their hands in yellow paint and placed both palms on the purple t-shirts.

Warmth flooded her as she remembered all the laughter and fun they'd had that day.

Alex shoved down the longing that rose up inside her whenever thoughts of Sam swirled in her mind.

"Thanks." She didn't know what to say to this stranger's comment.

He continued talking. "Is this your first time visiting Martha's Vineyard?"

Alex turned to him. "No, it's not. I grew up on the island. Now, I'm returning to stay."

Her voice sounded flat to her own ears.

"You used to live here?" One eyebrow lifted with curiosity as he waited for her answer.

She nodded, taking a moment to really look at the man beside her.

He looked like a man of Native American heritage. His light brown skin, black, wavy hair, and large, dark eyes reminded Alex of one of her friends from childhood.

"Yes. My sisters and I grew up on the island," Alex replied. It frustrated her that this man looked vaguely familiar, but she couldn't recall where she had seen him before.

"Sounds like there's a story there." His easy going manner made her want to blurt out her life story.

She nodded and sighed.

"I'd love to hear it. I love stories." He grinned. "But first let me introduce myself. My name is Chesmu Sagamore."

He held out one hand in greeting and she shook hands with him.

"Your name sounds familiar." Alex paused, trying to remember. It slipped her mind. "My name is Alexandra Stafford. But my friends call me Alex."

His smile grew wide, revealing even white teeth. "Nice

to meet you, Alex. My name might sound familiar because I go to different events, singing songs and sharing stories about my people, the Wampanoag tribe."

"That's probably where I heard your name then." Alex nodded.

She would mention this man's name to her sisters. Perhaps they would remember Chesmu.

Looking back out at the ocean, she replied, "To answer your question, my decision to return to the island is a long and painful story. It's too boring to get into the details now. But for now, it looks like I'm back on the island for the foreseeable future."

"What made you decide to return?" He leaned on the railing, turning to her, a warm light in his eyes.

His friendly smile invited more conversation.

"I was recently let go from my position at Mercy Children's Hospital in Boston. The administrator cited budget cuts when I was given my notice." Alex sighed heavily, still stunned at the way she had been quickly forced out of her position.

She was convinced her former colleague Dr. Ross had a hand in convincing the administrator that Alex should be let go. Ever since she had refused to date him, Dr. Ross had held a grudge.

"Sorry you were let go. That must have been difficult. But Martha's Vineyard is a great place to be when you're in the middle of change."

"I guess time will tell if that sentiment will hold true for me." Alex swallowed back frustration.

"It will."

The confidence in his voice was a little unnerving.

Alex couldn't allow herself to believe his words.

She had plenty of reasons to become jaded over the years.

The island had swallowed up too many people she loved.

First her twin sister, Anne, died when she was six. When she turned ten years old her parents died in a boating accident. Later, when she was in high school, she was attacked by a stranger when she'd been out jogging one evening.

She'd come home bruised and bleeding, her innocence lost.

After her narrow escape, she ran back to Grams' house.

Her grandmother took care of her, insisting she go see the doctor.

In recent years, she'd told her sisters what happened that night long ago, but they'd been sworn to secrecy.

Alex had never told Sam about the attack that night.

It was because of that terrible attack and her focus on medical college that she had refused his marriage proposal.

Alex had made the decision not to trust any man to get close to her again. Being vulnerable wasn't safe.

Years ago, that choice had cost her the only man she'd ever loved.

It had been a very costly mistake.

In the end, Sam had married someone else.

She shook her head, trying to shake free from the memories.

Turning to Chesmu she asked, "What about you? You live on the island?"

"Yes, I spent my childhood with my family here. My people are of the Wampanoag tribe in the town of Aquinnah on Martha's Vineyard. My family ancestry dates back thousands of years," Chesmu stated, a shimmer of pride in his eyes.

"That is truly inspiring. A great legacy to pass onto your children," Alex commented.

Longing stirred in her for a family of her own. But she pushed it down. It was a yearning she realized that was forever out of reach.

It was too late for her.

"It will be. Someday, I will meet the right woman who will help create that legacy." He chuckled.

Alex sent him a wistful smile. "It's good you still have your dreams, Chesmu. Sometimes, it's too late. We have to accept what's been lost."

He shook his head, a sadness in his dark eyes. "Alexandra, I don't believe that's true for you. You just need time to heal from old wounds and the freedom to believe in yourself and your dreams again."

"I'm not so sure about that." Alex pondered his words, amid the loud crashing of waves against the ship.

"Time will have to convince you then." He chuckled. "Do you have plans when you arrive?"

Alex nodded. "I've inherited my grandmother's house. My plan is to start a medical clinic for children."

"That's wonderful. You're a children's doctor?"

She nodded. "I am. It will take a bit of time, but I'm

hoping to get the medical clinic up and running in a few weeks."

"The island needs a good doctor for children." He looked like he was about to say more, when a woman's voice interrupted them.

It sounded like the woman's voice was from the other side of the ship.

"Chesmu, come over here," she called again, "I want you to see something."

The man beside her grinned. "That's my stepsister. It looks like I need to be going. I'm glad we could meet, Alex."

Alex smiled warmly. "It was nice to meet you as well, Chesmu."

He nodded before he hurried away.

She turned to see him walk over and hug a woman with dark hair, but lighter coloring than him. Once again, a sense filled her that she had met the woman somewhere before.

The vague memories were sure to come back to her at some point.

Turning her head, she stared at the familiar sights of the island which were now closer and in plain view.

Alex noticed the clouds above, darkened to a grey-black.

A shudder rippled through her body.

As she continued to look up, she spotted a red-tailed hawk flying overhead. The familiar sight reminded her of the terror she still felt from that night long ago.

A red-tailed hawk had flown in the sky above her that

horrible night, as she tried to make her desperate escape from the man who chased her.

Without warning, the predator's loud cry filled the air.

Alex inhaled a quick breath.

A foreboding flooded her at the bone-chilling sound.

She shivered as the memories tried to force their way into her thoughts.

Pushing them back, she swallowed quickly.

Readjusting the shoulder strap of her blue tote, her grip tightened on the bag.

With her other hand, she clung to the railing as the ferry began to dock at the island's port.

A crease formed between her brows.

As she turned her head, her gaze swept over the large parking area near the docks.

She stopped suddenly when she spotted a man and young girl walking their bicycles on the side of the area, near the trees. A dark brown dog trotted happily beside them.

The man looked familiar.

When the little girl turned and pointed at the ferry, the tall man turned to look at the large ship.

Alex sucked in a breath.

She recognized that face.

Samuel Chadsworth.

The man looked at the incoming ferry, with his daughter by his side.

His eyes stopped when they found her at the ship's railing.

Did Sam recognize her?

He stared for a minute longer, a frown forming

between his brows. Without warning, Sam suddenly turned to his daughter. He spoke to her quickly and then they turned and rode away.

Alex stared after them, biting her bottom lip.

Her heart plummeted in her chest.

If Sam recognized her and didn't respond, what sort of welcome would await her now that she was back to stay?

Thoughts of her old boyfriend from years ago wasn't her only worry.

Fear circled around and around in her head. Questions surfaced that had gnawed at her for years. Would she finally discover who her attacker was when she was a teenager?

What about her parents' deaths in the boating accident? Would she learn more details about what had happened to them?

Alex wanted answers.

Panic filled her chest again.

Breathe in. Breathe out. Have courage. Those thoughts swirling her head were the voice of reason amid all her fears.

Alex longed to be free of the fears that had haunted her all her life.

What she really wanted was for the nightmares from the past, to finally stop.

What she really wanted was to be left alone.

What she really wanted was peace.

She remembered Chesmu's words. *You need time to heal from old wounds. Then you'll have a new freedom to believe in yourself and your dreams again.*

His words swirled around and around in her mind.

Pain and heartache had paralyzed her for years.

She had allowed fear to trap her for far too long.

Maybe if she let go of the past, she would gather courage to face the future.

Problem was, she didn't know how.

 *am*

SAMUEL CHADSWORTH SLIPPED the front wheels of his bicycle inside the wooden rack.

His thoughts spun round and round.

The woman he'd seen on the ferry earlier today was the same woman he'd loved and lost.

Sam breathed out her name with his next breath.

Alexandra Stafford.

He still remembered everything about her.

The reason he believed the woman he saw was Alex, was because of the shirt she wore.

He never forgot that day years ago.

The summer before their junior year, the two of them went to a hand painting booth at the summer festival.

That's when they decided to be creative and make their own unique t-shirts.

They chose purple t-shirts and, as they talked and laughed together, they dipped their hands in the yellow hand paint and stamped their hand imprints on the front and back.

They'd had so much fun that day.

He smiled wistfully at the memory.

That day was the last time he'd heard Alex laugh. A few weeks after they started their junior year, she changed drastically. She hardly said two words to him or anyone else at school.

It seemed like the joy of living had been ripped away from her.

He had been shocked at the change in his girlfriend.

Despite asking questions, he never did learn the reason Alexandra kept him at arm's length.

But they continued to spend time together. Eventually, Sam asked her to marry him during her first year of college.

Alexandra had refused.

It took a few years to heal from the pain of losing the only woman he had ever loved.

Then, a few years later, he met Alice. She was calm, quiet, and a healing balm to his troubled heart.

They had only been married for a couple of years before their daughter came along. Sadly, in only a short amount of time, Alice was diagnosed with cancer and was swiftly taken from them.

Sam swallowed. There had been too much loss.

Love brought too much pain and heartache.

He decided he never wanted to fall in love again.

From now on, it would just be him and his beautiful little girl.

That would have to be enough love for him.

His eight-year old daughter loudly called his name, shaking him out of his silent musings.

Sam shook his head, forcing himself back to the here and now.

"Daddy, it was fun to ride our bicycles. Just you and me." Her smile grew wide as she removed her helmet.

"I agree. I love when it's just us together, sweetie. And it's really great that you were home early from school today. It's a perfect way to start the weekend with plenty of time to play outside." Sam slung his head gear over the handlebars and grabbed his little girl into a big hug.

Zoe giggled. Squirming out of his arms, she ran inside the house.

He chased her across the front porch and into the house, where he grabbed her again kissing her cheeks.

Zoe laughed out loud. "Daddy, you're the best."

"Aww. I happen to think you're the best too." He hugged his daughter again until their dog tackled the two of them.

The brown lab started to jump up and down, his gruff bark reminding them he needed attention too.

"Milo, let's give you a quick rub down." Sam began to pet their dog's thick brown hair.

Zoe giggled. "Milo wants some hugs too."

His daughter showered their dog with hugs and kisses.

Then, just as quickly, she jumped to her feet.

"Daddy, I'm going to my room to get my sketchpad. I

saw some new flowers in the backyard and I want to try to draw them." She waved and hurried down the hallway.

"Alright, beautiful." He grinned as she ran off to her bedroom with her dog running after her. He was thankful she was now back from the hospital from her bout with a bad cold and flu.

His daughter was now her energetic self again.

He pushed back the constant worry that tried to plague him.

As a dad, he was determined to do everything he could to keep Zoe healthy and well.

Sam rubbed his forehead, deep in thought.

Even with all the loss he'd had in his life, he was very thankful for the one female in his life who filled his days with love and laughter: *his daughter.*

That would have to be enough for him.

THE SEA AIR enfolded Alex in a familiar cocoon of salt water and warmth, whispering in the breeze as she got out of her car.

The dark clouds above had shifted a little. The warmth of the sun pierced through with welcome rays shining through the dark haze.

Motionless, she stood beside her black, compact car on the driveway of her grandmother's old home.

It was an old, Georgian-style house, built with stone. There were a total of six bedrooms, a living room, parlor, and a large kitchen. Behind the large home stood an old-style carriage house.

On both sides of the house, green vines had grown tall enough to reach the weathered shingles.

When her parents were still alive, she remembered Gramps had hired a contractor to build a porch with a roof that extended to the outer walls.

The large, stately porch columns reminded her of the grandeur of days gone by. Through the years, this house continued to stand tall and majestic.

For a few weeks, one summer in her early teenage years, Gramps and Grams and her sisters had all moved to this old house while the cottage by the beach was being cleaned and renovated from unexpected water damage.

Alex stared at the porch that was empty now, but still held the best memories of laughter and sweet iced tea.

Quickly, she wiped away a stray tear as memories enveloped her.

The house looked as resilient as it ever was, in spite of the unpredictable storms that had engulfed the island and the Stafford family over the years.

The shrill ringing of her phone jerked her back to the present.

"Hello, Alex." Jane's cheery voice was just what she needed. "I thought I'd check how it's going, since it's your first day back on the island."

"Hey, Jane. Thanks for calling. It's going well. I made it back here, so that's something." Alex chuckled. It was good to hear Jane's voice and to catch up with her sister. "How have you been?"

"It's going okay. I've been busy planning weddings, so that's always interesting." Jane sighed. "But lately, when I help to plan the happy couple's big day, I always feel a twinge of longing. "

"I think that's a good sign, Jane. Maybe you've had a chance to heal from your old boyfriend. Maybe you're ready to meet the right guy."

"Yeah, maybe," Jane said. "The trouble is, I've been a little gun-shy ever since I dated Devon."

"I'm not surprised you're hesitant. I would be too if I found out the man I thought I was married to already had a wife in another state." Alex was still shocked that Jane's ex-husband had fed her such a massive lie. "But I have no doubt you'll find the right guy for you."

"I hope so," Jane said. "But enough about me. How are you?"

"I'm doing alright. I'm back and trying to find the courage to take the next steps." Alex grinned sideways. "It was nice to see you at Lizzie's wedding."

"That was a fun weekend." Jane chuckled. "I can't believe Lizzie invited our old boyfriends."

Alex grimaced. "I believe our dear older sister was trying to play the matchmaker."

"So, it would seem. But I did have a good talk with Wade Hampton. It felt like the years fell away and we were back to being the good friends we were years ago." Jane paused. "But how about you, Alex? I noticed you and Sam Chadsworth had a chance to talk."

Alex swallowed at the mention of Sam's name.

He was still one of the most handsome men around. His brown, wavy hair had some silver streaks in it now, but it only made him more attractive.

Those large, hazel eyes had smoldered with intensity

as he looked at her. For the first time in a real long time, she wanted to feel his arms around her again.

"Alex?"

At her sister's voice, Alex was pulled out of her memories. "I did have a good talk with Sam. Life has matured him. But he is still as kind and compassionate as I remember."

Nostalgia wound its way around her heart.

"Maybe you should have coffee with him now that you've moved to Sweet Beach Cove," Jane suggested.

"I don't know. His wife died a few years ago and now he has a little girl to take care of. I don't think that would be a possibility." The walls around her heart began to close in on themselves.

"Why not?" Jane exclaimed. "His wife passed away. Perhaps the man is lonely. Maybe he's looking for a good conversation with an old friend."

"Yeah, maybe." Alex's fingers toyed with her watch.

Jane continued, "Maybe Sam would like to talk to someone he can trust about his daughter."

Alex nodded. "When we talked, Sam said he was grateful he could work from home so he could be there for Zoe. There have been a few times she's been sick."

"That's so sad." Jane sighed. "That reminds me of our sister Anne. When Anne died suddenly from pneumonia at six years old, it was a very sad time for mom and dad and all of us."

Alex's eyes misted with unshed tears. "I struggled for years with Anne's death. She was my twin sister. We did everything together. There were some days when I was convinced we could hear each other's thoughts. However,

Anne's death as a child was the reason, I wanted to become a children's doctor. I wanted to do what I could to help sick children to get better so they could live long, healthy lives."

"Did you ever tell Sam about what happened to Anne?" Jane asked.

She paused, fear forming a fist in her stomach. "No, I never did. I always held back the deepest part of myself from him."

"Why?"

Alex hesitated, then, with a shaky voice, said, "I was afraid of getting too close to Sam. I believed — foolishly — that he would take over my life and then I wouldn't be able to fulfill the promise I made to my twin."

Jane whispered, "I remember. You promised Anne you would work hard to become a doctor so that children wouldn't have to suffer like she did."

Alex pushed away a lone tear that trailed down her cheek. "Yeah, I did. I still miss her."

"I know you miss Anne. I do too," Jane whispered. "But you have fulfilled your promise to Anne. You've already helped a lot of children get well."

"I've had a few good years. However, a lot more children still need help." Alex sighed.

"Well, I want you to know I think the work you're doing to help children is admirable," Jane said. "And now you're here, standing at the very home you'll remake into a children's medical clinic."

Alex chewed on her lower lip nervously. "Yes. I'm back."

A few months ago, their grandmother passed away.

After the funeral, when the lawyer read the will, each of them learned they had inherited something substantial from their beloved Grams.

Alex stared at the old house she'd inherited from Grams. It was located near the heart of the Sweet Beach Cove community.

Grandmother had written in the will that she hoped Alex would turn this old stone cottage into a medical office.

"You sound nervous or unsure about this new step in your life, dear sister. Are you holding back because you are worried about living close to Sam?" Jane's question poked at her insecurities and fears.

"I think there is a little fear about living so close to the man I once loved."

Alex didn't add that she still had trauma from the attack when she was a teenager.

Jane added, "A lot of years have passed since you two were best friends in middle school and high school. He has changed and so have you."

"I suppose." She hesitated. "I remember that I broke his heart when I said I needed to stay in college to finish my medical degree. He wanted us to marry. I don't think he's ever forgotten that. I regret that I didn't explain myself better back then." Alex sighed heavily.

"Dear Sis, that's why you need to talk to him." Jane's words were filled with wisdom — but it was easier said than done.

"You're right. I do need to talk to him and explain." Alex sighed.

"Good. It would help clear up the past between you two."

Alex mumbled, "But that doesn't mean it wouldn't be a difficult conversation."

"That's true. But you would have a better relationship afterwards. It would be worth it," Jane said.

Alex didn't say anything. She hoped that would be true.

"It would be lovely if the rest of us sisters ended up moving to the island. Maybe that's what Grams had in mind all along." Jane chuckled.

"Maybe. Grandmother knew what she wanted, that's for sure," Alex replied.

"She did." Without warning, a loud noise in the background interrupted them. "Sorry, my son, Noah, is calling for me. I've got to go. I'll talk with you soon, Alex.".

"Sounds good. Bye, Jane." Alex ended the conversation and slipped the phone in her pocket.

Alex slowly walked towards the front porch.

Thoughts of Sam Chadsworth swirled in her head.

Maybe what Jane said was true.

It had been so long since she had any kind of close relationship with a man. It terrified her.

She had always needed complete control of her life. Would she find the courage to let go — even a little?

At the loud thump of a car door closing, Alex turned her head.

"Sis, you made it here at last." Lizzie hurried over, pulling her into a close embrace.

She grinned. "Hey, Lizzie. It's good to see you. You look radiant and beautiful."

Lizzie sighed happily. "That's because I'm in love, Alex. Completely and totally in love. I can't believe Jonathan and I have been given a second chance for love in our older years. I feel like I'm living in a dream."

"I'm happy for you, Lizzie. That's really amazing."

"Thanks Alex." Her sister grabbed her hand. "Maybe it's finally your turn to fall in love."

With an unsteady hand, Alex tucked a strand of blond hair behind one ear. "I don't know about that, Lizzie. Maybe, it's too late for me. So far there hasn't been a man in my life that I could spend the rest of my life with."

"It's not too late for you, Alex. Look what happened to me." Her sister slipped her hand on the curve of her arm. Slowly, they started walking the long driveway towards the house. "And as far as finding the right man, have you thought about Samuel? You and Sam used to have a close relationship."

The image of the man and the little girl she'd seen from the ferry surfaced.

Had it been Sam?

If it had been, his quick departure seemed like a sign that Sam might not want to renew their friendship.

Alex shook her head. "That was years ago, Lizzie. When I briefly talked with Sam during the weekend at your inn last year, he was kind, but I sensed he was stand-offish with me."

Lizzie stopped and turned suddenly. "You think it's because you refused his proposal of marriage when you were in college?"

Alex nodded and scuffed the gravel with her tennis shoe. "Yeah. I have to admit to feeling the sharp sting of hurt for years that Sam gave up on our friendship. But the truth is, I have only myself to blame. After all, years ago, I chose medical college over him."

"I'm so sorry, Alex." Her sister looked into the distance for a moment, before she spoke again. "Maybe he was hurt back then, just like you were."

"Yeah, maybe. I still regret how I treated him."

Her oldest sister persisted, true to her nature, "I think you should talk to him. Whenever I've seen Sam around town, I can't help but sense he's lonely. Reach out to him, Alex."

"Jane told me the same thing. I suppose I could have coffee with him and we could start talking." Alex sighed her thoughts heavy with doubt. "We'll see. He might not agree to it, but I guess I can try."

"I'm glad Jane agrees with me. Give Sam a chance." Lizzie slipped her arm around Alex's waist giving her a light hug.

Alex shrugged, not convinced. But maybe she should try and see what his response would be to her invitation.

They had reached the porch of the old stone house.

Together they stopped and stared at the house in silence.

Her gaze swept across the front of the dilapidated house. Alex's shoulder drooped with the weight of all the work ahead of her.

"It looks rather dismal and dreary, doesn't it?" Lizzie glanced around, noticing the dirty porch, scraped windows, and cracked wood door.

"Yeah. It looks like I've got a lot of work ahead of me,"

Alex murmured, thinking it through. "And I must say it still feels strange to be back here. I didn't expect to ever come back to the island to live. But since I was let go from my position at the hospital, I've needed to make some changes."

"That's understandable. I can relate to difficult changes. It's how I felt last year when my late husband died suddenly. I was out of options and out of money. I was forced to move back here. But Grams' cottage has been a wonderful new beginning for me." Lizzie rubbed her hand along the strong column. "You'll be alright, Alex. Besides, now you have family nearby if you ever need help."

Alex nodded. "That is a comforting thought. I have a feeling I'm going to need it."

With a shaky hand, she tucked some stray tendrils of blond hair behind one ear.

Knots formed in her stomach as fear flooded her. She wondered if she had bit off more than she could chew, at trying to re-make this house into a medical clinic?

Worry had flooded her thoughts ever since they let her go at the children's hospital.

Fear was her constant companion at this sudden move back to Martha's Vineyard.

Alex knew she would need to adjust to this new change.

Now she was here.

The island was the one place Alex thought she'd never return.

Stepping close to the door, her hand shook as she slipped the key into the lock.

This place was now hers. This old stone cottage was now her home.

Her hand twisted the rusty knob on the cracked oak front door.

The door creaked and the hinges groaned from lack of use.

Her sister followed her, standing motionless beside her.

The entryway was brown and barren.

Patches of holes were scattered throughout the linoleum floor. Along the cream-colored walls long scratches remained from the people who had rented the house before she inherited the place.

From the front door she could see the living room, the kitchen, and the hallway.

Her heartbeat accelerated as she looked around the barren place.

Overwhelm and stress flooded her.

It was difficult to arrive at her new home and see so much work waiting for her.

Alex sighed heavily and set down her things.

"Let's go look around. Show me this house you inherited from Grams."

"Sure," Alex half-whispered, in automatic response.

Together they walked down the hallway.

A washroom was on one side of the hallway. On the other side were three bedrooms and at the very end a large bedroom.

All the rooms were a dingy beige.

"Looks like there are lots of rooms for you to put to use. Do you still want to renovate and turn this old house into a medical office?" Lizzie asked.

She nodded. "Yes, I do. But, look at this place, Lizzie. There's so much work that needs to be done to fix it up."

Alex looked at the old windows and wood panelling on the walls in the last bedroom.

Her heart sank.

Lizzie reached for her hand. "Don't give up, Sis. We'll take it one step at a time. You should draw up the ideas you have and show them to Jonathan. He's restored a lot of older homes on the island."

"You're right. I'll write down my ideas today. Maybe Jonathan will know how to make this into a workable office space." Alex turned, sending her sister a small smile.

"Good. Then why don't you stop by for dinner tonight?" Lizzie asked.

"That would be lovely. Thanks."

Together they walked back towards the front of the house, they stopped at the kitchen.

"It might be a good idea to make one space into a small kitchenette. Like a break room for your employees," Lizzie commented.

"Yes. That's a good idea," Alex agreed. She jotted down notes on her phone.

Lizzie looked at her watch. "Well, I should get back. I need to cook lunch for all the guests at the inn. See you tonight around seven o'clock?"

"Of course. I'll be there." Alex smiled as she watched her sister drive away.

It would be good to take a break and have a meal with her sister and her husband tonight.

Being surrounded by family again would help her find

the strength to face this familiar, but very different, world where she now found herself.

ALEX STAFFORD hurriedly brushed her blond hair, letting it fall in gentle waves to her shoulders.

Her movements were jerky.

It was almost time to go to Lizzie's for dinner. She didn't want to be late.

Looking down at her wrist to check the time, she realized she'd forgotten to slip on her watch.

Turning to her dresser she grabbed her watch.

Suddenly, haunting memories returned.

Her breaths quickened and her heart raced.

With shaky fingers she touched the black leather strap of her watch.

Her whole body shivered.

It was the memory of another black watch that haunted her. It was the reason for so many sleepless nights — nightmares Alex had suffered since she was a teenager.

Years ago, when she went to the police, the island's old police chief Elias Hart had peppered her with questions for which she had no answers.

Who was this man? I don't know.

Did you see his face? No. He wore a black ski mask. But I did see his dark brown eyes.

Why did he chase you — what did he want? I don't know. He just went on and on about how proud his mother and grand-

mother would be proud of him, because he had one of the Stafford girls.

When the questioning had finally ended, the police didn't arrest anyone. They couldn't find the evidence they needed to charge and arrest anyone.

At the time she was questioned, Alex had lost the attacker's wrist watch. So, she didn't mention that small detail to the police.

She figured that black watch must have fallen out of her pocket when she raced home.

It would have been better if she still had that watch — then she could give it to the police.

Alex shuddered.

She would never forget the crazed look in her attacker's dark eyes or his low, raspy voice.

Those vivid images had gone round and round in her head for years.

Alex walked over to her bed and sat down.

She clutched her soft, brown teddy bear — nicknamed Buttons — the same cuddly bear she'd kept from childhood.

Pressing the tattered fur to one cheek, a rush of comfort engulfed her from the softness.

Stop it. She whispered to herself firmly. *You're not going to rehash all the same ugly memories.*

Setting Buttons back on the bed, Alex stood up, her legs shaky.

With determination, she clutched her purse tightly and hurried down the stairs and out the front door.

Tonight, she would enjoy spending time with family at Lizzie's place.

She would let go of her worries and fears for one night and try to have fun.

CHAPTER THREE

lex

ALEX KNOCKED on the wooden door at Lizzie's place.

A bird call drifted through the trees.

It sounded like, *cheer, cheer cheer.*

She turned to see a large Northern Cardinal.

Fond memories returned of Grams telling her about the unique island birds.

This one, with its bright scarlet feathers and bright red-orange triangular-shaped bill, was a male bird.

For some inexplicable reason, his bird-song lifted her spirits.

Cars filled Lizzie's parking area behind *The Vineyard Inn.* A sure sign the inn was filled with guests.

Her sister had made her business successful.

It was encouraging to see all of Lizzie's hard work start to pay off.

Alex couldn't help but admire her oldest sister. She had bravely faced one of the most painful times of her life after her husband of twenty-six years of marriage suddenly died.

Still reeling from her loss, Lizzie somehow found the strength and courage to move on with her life.

With a lot of hard work, she had turned Grams' old beach house into an inn.

Her sister was an inspiration.

It gave Alex hope that perhaps her plans of turning Grams' old house into a medical clinic would come to fruition.

She hoped so.

Alex knocked a second time.

Without warning, the door swung open.

Annie's wide smile flickered in the dim evening light.

"Aunt Alex!" Her niece grabbed her hand.

Annie pulled her in close with a warm embrace.

Alex's heart melted.

It had been far too long since she had been close to any of her relatives.

"Annie, how wonderful to see you. It's so good to be with my family again." Alex smiled as her niece loosened her arms and stepped back.

"Come on in. Mom's putting last minute touches on dinner." Annie's green eyes, so similar to her mother's, sparkled with mischief.

"It smells good." Familiar scents of chicken, sea salt mixed with the familiar smell of pine wood flooded Alex's senses welcoming her back to her grandmother's old beach house.

As Annie opened the double doors, she stepped into the familiar dining room.

The normally sun-light room emerged darkened with shadows.

She thought it was strange that the normally busy room was dark and empty.

The place echoed, its vastness dark and silent as a tomb.

"Where is everybody, Annie?" Alex whispered, her voice trailing off as she stepped forward.

Her sandaled feet echoed against the wooden floor. A breeze from the sea brushed lightly against her cheek in the shadowed room.

All of a sudden, bright lights flooded the room.

Alex blinked.

"Surprise!" A chorus of loud voices erupted, flooding the room and echoing off the walls.

Looking around the room, Alex's eyes grew wide at the sight of all the familiar faces.

People she knew from her childhood were scattered throughout the large dining room.

A large sign hung on the wall at the far end with the words: *Welcome Home, Alex.*

She stood motionless for a minute, overwhelmed.

"Well, did we manage to shock you?" Her sister Charlie spoke after the clapping ended.

"You did. Especially Lizzie here, who didn't say one word when she stopped by to chat this afternoon." Alex eyed her oldest sister with a raised eyebrow.

Lizzie grinned as she walked towards her. "We really wanted to make this a special surprise, Sis." Lizzie looked over the crowd with a warm smile.

"I think we did it, everyone. Alexandra is at a loss for words. That's a sure sign we've well and truly astonished her."

Everyone in the crowd laughed.

Many called out in loud voices, "Welcome home" towards Alex.

She stood motionless, a smile tugging at the corners of her lips.

"Lizzie's right, you all have managed to overwhelm me. Thank you for such a warm welcome back, I appreciate it." Alex smiled, still trying to process it all.

The crowd clapped. Alex was grateful when Lizzie spoke again, "Pastor Tim, if you would be willing to say grace, then we'll get everyone started filling their plates at the buffet."

The minister was a gray, haired man and the lead pastor at the Sweet Beach Cove community church.

He'd been Grandmother's pastor for many years.

"Let's give thanks to the good Lord that another one of Elizabeth Stafford's family has returned home to the island." Pastor Tim stood beside Lizzie and Alex and said a prayer for the meal.

Alex swallowed back emotion, touched that Grams' old pastor would refer to her moving back to the island as a reason to give thanks.

Her grandmother would have been pleased.

As soon as the pastor finished saying grace, Lizzie spoke to the gathering, "If you all could form a line at the buffet table. Our waiters are happy to serve you. Also, one more thing. It looks like the weather has cleared up and the sun is shining once more. If you prefer to eat outside on the deck, please do that and enjoy the sunshine."

ﻬ

ALEX STEPPED toward the buffet table, the savory scents teasing her senses.

Her late grandmother's old friends surrounded her as she stood in the line to get her food.

The Cantrell family, including their sons and daughters, had joined Lizzie's welcome home party of people. She also saw Bobby Sutton, his wife, Susan, Jerry Hart, his wife, Linda, and their twin sons, Ryan and Dylan Hart.

It looked to be a busy night.

Ted Cantrell leaned close. His weathered face broke into a smile that crinkled the corners of his eyes. "Alex, I must say it's a privilege to have you back on our island again. You've been away for far too long. It's always good to see one of Elizabeth Stafford's granddaughters return back home. Don't you agree, mother?"

Ida Cantrell stood next to her son. Her silver hair was up in its usual bun and she wore a stylish hat. Most folks considered her the matriarch of the island. "Alexandra Stafford, I remember you from your reckless teenage years."

Alex took Ida's comments with a grain of salt. She knew from past experience the older woman was known throughout these parts as a woman who spoke her mind, whether good or bad.

Her daughter Vera Cantrell had inherited Ida's stubborn traits. However, Vera had added the offense of putting action behind her stubborn and evil intentions.

Now Vera was serving a prison sentence for setting fire to Lizzie's beach house.

That crime still shocked Alex, considering how the Cantrell's had been friends with the Stafford family for generations.

"Yes, those were wild days back then." The direction of this conversation was a little unnerving. Alex wasn't surprised some islanders still judged her for what happened years ago. "I suppose it's a good thing I grew up."

A crease formed between the old lady's brows at her reply. She adjusted her wire rimmed glasses, her steely gray eyes peering as if making an assessment of her character.

It was a long time before she spoke again.

"Humph. We'll have to see if that's true," Ida remarked, a wry twist to her lips. "What work will you do now that you're here?"

Her son turned to Ida. "Mother, Alexandra is a children's doctor."

"Well, you made something of yourself after all. At least that's something." The matron noted with a rare hint of approval. "Did you move into your late grandmother's old stone cottage?"

"Yes, I did. I moved in and started cleaning today. It will take a bit of work to get that old house back in shape."

"I'm sure that's true. Will you be working at the

hospital then?" The old matriarch leaned closer, pushing her eyeglasses up on her nose.

"Some of the time. However, I want to renovate Grams' old cottage into a children's medical clinic."

"Well, that sounds like a near impossible task, I'm sure. Fixing that old stone heap will take a miracle." The matriarch leaned heavily on her wooden cane. "Think you can manage all the work?"

Alex gave a curt reply, "I believe I can."

Ted spoke, "Mother, Alex has always been a hard worker. She'll do fine."

"Maybe. We'll need to wait and see. Time will tell," Ida commented, her words laced with doubt.

Alex exhaled slowly, shaking off the sting from Ida's words.

She was determined to prove her wrong. She must.

AS SOON AS her plate was filled with her favorite foods, Alex turned to walk towards the doors that led to the outside deck.

For a moment, she stood motionless against the deck railing. The salty breeze tugged at her blond curls, wrapping her in its familiar warmth.

In the distance, the blue water touched the evening sky looking like it had been painted with brushstrokes of orange, pink, and gold.

Many people were standing on the deck talking with one another. A few folks walked along the freshly cut grass.

Alex spotted Sam talking with an old friend of his, Ward Hampton. Ward was one of the top anchors for a popular Boston news network and had been for years.

Lizzie must have invited both men to tonight's party.

Ward and Jane used to date when they were in college. Alex wasn't sure what happened or why they broke it off between the two of them.

Alex turned to see Sam's handsome face. He had a chiseled look with a square jawline, high cheekbones, and generous full lips.

A warmth flooded her belly as Alex remembered his lips on hers.

Sam's kisses had always been tender. He'd always been gentle with her. But after she'd refused his marriage proposal, he disappeared from her life.

Regret clung to her like a leech, sucking out every inch of happiness. Was it too late for them to talk? Would Sam even listen to her explanation or apology?

She wouldn't blame Sam if he never wanted to talk to her again.

Her eyes continued to look around the large room.

She saw Sheriff Hart, his wife, Linda, and their twin sons, Ryan and Dylan.

Ryan spoke to his twin brother, and then Dylan turned to look at her.

Noting the two men's continued glances her way, she sensed they were talking about her.

For a long moment, Dylan stared at her, his dark eyes held an intense but secret expression.

He had always seemed so strange. Both of the Hart twins had always been an enigma to her.

"Alex, I'm so glad you're back home." Becca Feather-stone snuck up from somewhere behind her. "You're staring over there with a frown. What's up?"

Alex sighed heavily.

"Dylan Hart is staring at me. His eyes look like they're boring holes into my skull." Alex turned to her friend a crease deepening between her brows.

"Dylan? He's always been a little strange. But he's always been that way." Becca chuckled. "Don't worry about him, Alex. He's harmless."

Alex shrugged off the uneasy feeling, realizing she must be letting her imagination run away with her again.

"I'm happy to see you, Becca."

Becca's brown, wavy hair reached down to her shoulders, matching the cute, brown rimmed glasses she wore.

"And I'm very glad we can talk face to face," Her friend added.

"I agree. It's so much better than a phone call."

"It is." Becca took a bite of finger food, a wide grin on her face. "Are you glad to be back, Alex?"

"In some ways. However, it was necessary after I was unceremoniously let go at the children's hospital." Alex sighed remembering the shock of it all. "It might take me some time to adjust to living back on the island."

"You will adjust, Alex. If anyone can tackle the unex-pected, it's you." Her best friend's confidence in her surprised Alex even after all these years.

"Thanks, Becca, I appreciate you saying that." Alex grinned. "I'm surprised at the number of people who showed up to the party tonight."

"I'm not surprised. You, my friend, have a lot of islanders who think the world of you."

Alex shrugged. "Perhaps some. But Lisa Cane came tonight. I'm never quite sure where I stand with her. And Slater Williams is here too — he never seemed to like me much. I'm surprised they showed up."

"Well, Lisa always loves a party. But as far as where you stand with her, I think it's obvious that she was always jealous of you. Don't you remember in middle school when she cheated off of your test paper. You were always so good in science and Lisa wanted to get good grades like you."

Alex sighed. "That was years ago, Becca. Lisa's grown up since then."

"Maybe." Becca added, "Lisa also latched onto Slater during our sophomore year — as soon as you broke up with him and told Slater you didn't want to date him anymore. But Lisa and Slater didn't last long."

Alex took a sip of her iced tea. "I do remember that. But all of that is history. It happened when we were kids, Becca. I really don't believe Lisa's the same person anymore. I think she's changed."

"I hope that's true." Becca shrugged and turned to look over at Slater. "However, Slater always had a thing for you, Alex."

Alex glanced over to where her friend was looking. She spotted a slender man, who now sported grey-blond hair. It was Slater. He had more age-lines on his face now.

She turned back to her friend. "Slater was angry when I told him we were through. But it's been years. I hope he's moved on from that after all this time."

Becca nodded. "I hope he has moved on too. I see Lisa is talking with Slater. I've seen them together once or twice around town. But Lisa never seems to stay with one guy very long."

"I just hope Lisa knows what she's doing." Alex shrugged. "Anyway, how are you and your family doing, Becca?"

"We're good." Becca smiled. "Colin is often gone since he got that job in sales last year. It's good money, but our three children and I miss him. But he has some time off coming up in a few weeks, so that will be good."

Her friend had always been a homebody and loved spending quality time with people.

"When I began to help Mrs. O'Connor with her annual Sweet Beach Cove Quilt and Craft Day last year, it really helped me to get to know more folks in our community. I'm not quite so lonely anymore. And my children are helping out too."

"That's great, Becca. I'm sure you've made some beautiful quilts." Alex's smile widened. "How are your children?"

"They are just great." Becca beamed as she talked about her children. "You remember our oldest daughter Amanda married Kurtis O'Reilly last summer?"

"Yes, I do." Alex nodded.

"Well, Amanda is now nine months pregnant and due to have her first baby in a few weeks." Becca grinned from ear to ear.

"How wonderful. I'm so happy for you, Becca." Alex hugged her friend. "You will make a fabulous grandma."

Becca chuckled. "Oh, I hope so. I can't wait to hold our first grand-baby."

Alex couldn't help but be very happy for her friend. There were many ways they differed from one another, but they had always appreciated their strong friendship.

Becca continued talking about her children, "Our two youngest children are doing great. Brendan is a senior and will graduate at the end of this school year. And our youngest, Kaylee, loves all her friends at school. She also works in the book shop and cafe."

"You have a wonderful family, my friend." A pang of longing hit Alex like a stomach punch.

She yearned for a family of her own.

Fears held her back.

It would mean finding a man to marry. It would mean being vulnerable with a man. It would mean finding a man she could trust.

Swallowing back pain, she realized how impossible it would be to have a family of her own.

Quickly, Alex switched the direction of their conversation. "You said you were working on a quilt with Mrs. O'Connor. I would love to see them."

"You can, Alex. In a few weeks we're going to have a baby shower for Amanda at Mrs. O'Connor's quilt shop, *Yarn Around The Cove*. I'd love it if you would come and join us." Becca named the date and time.

Alex nodded. "I will. Thanks for the invitation."

"Anytime, my friend."

A light tap on her shoulder caused Alex to turn her head.

An old school friend Lisa Cane stood beside her with a grin.

"Here you are, Alex." Lisa Cane approached her. "It's been too long since I've seen you back on the island."

Next to her was Slater Williams. "Alex, this is a real surprise to see you back."

Becca winked at her and whispered, "I'm off to get another drink."

Alex smiled and turned to Lisa and Slater.

Lisa's silky black hair was now in a pixie cut. Slater's once handsome face looked more like a roadmap between wrinkles now. Time had aged them all.

"Hello, Lisa. Hello, Slater. Yes, it has been far too long. How have both of you been?" Alex asked, leaning against the deck's railing.

Lisa chattered on, "Busy, but good. Ever since my divorce last year, it's felt like my life has been in chaos. But in the last couple months I feel like I'm finally finding my footing again." Lisa chewed on a celery stick her dark brown eyes pensive.

"I'm glad. Slater, how's life treating you?" Alex turned to the man. His grey eyes studied her necklace.

Hearing his name, Slater looked up at Alex. "I'm good. I've been focused on getting in shape. My work at the magazine forces me to sit most of the day, so I need the extra exercise."

"You look like you've been working out." Alex nodded. Slater had been a fitness guy ever since she'd known him years ago.

"I'm happy you noticed, Alex. You're looking good

too," Slater commented and Lisa turned to him with a frown.

Alex was tempted to chuckle, but she forced a neutral expression.

Right then, someone called Slater's name, and he hurried away.

"Lisa, you mentioned changes. How's your daughter doing with them?" Alex asked.

"It's been hard on Avery. But she's a trooper. Now that she's graduated high school, she wants to go to college in New York. She insists on being close to her dad. It's so far away. I don't know if I'm okay with that." Lisa sighed heavily.

"I'm sorry. I guess that's what happens when your children grow up." Alex started with a small smile. "My sister Lizzie went through something similar when her children finished high school."

Lisa sighed. "Good thing you didn't marry and have children of your own, Alex. You don't have to deal with the loneliness and sadness of when your children leave the nest."

"I suppose that's true." Alex swallowed back the bile that rose in her throat.

Horrible memories from the day she survived the attack from that stranger. Only two people knew the full extent of what happened to her. Dr. Grace Waverly, who had examined her after the incident, and her beloved grandmother.

Only recently, did she tell her sisters. But Alex had sworn them to secrecy.

Grams had taken the knowledge to her grave.

She lightly touched the pendant that hung around her neck. It was a reminder to focus on faith instead of her fears.

Lisa's eyes moved to her neck and her eyes widened.

"I see you still wear that angel necklace." Lisa stepped closer to get a better look. "I always liked it. The figurine of the tough-looking angel alongside the pink diamond is a beautiful touch. It's like extra protection somehow. Is that why you wear it?"

"Something like that," Alex replied quickly, nervous about the sudden turn in the conversation.

Quickly changing the subject, Alex spoke again, "Tell me about what you're up to these days, Lisa."

Lisa turned her head to stare over at the flower garden, nibbling on her sandwich before turning back to Alex. "Since the divorce, I've needed to work a lot more hours in order to keep up with the house payments. So besides being a long-time receptionist at one of the local hotels, I also have part-time work in the evenings at a local restaurant, *Comfy Cove Cafe.*"

"Good for you, Lisa. Sounds like you're busy."

A hint of steel was in Lisa's tone. "Well, I do need to work hard and save my money. I wasn't born with a silver spoon in my mouth, Alex."

Alex didn't know what to say to that. She remained silent.

But her heart sank a notch at hearing her friend's struggle.

A memory returned of when the two of them were in grade school together. A couple of times Lisa voiced the fact that Alex's family had money and her family did not.

It was her grandparents that had money, not her and her sisters. Grams taught them to work hard for a living.

They grew up working to pay for things they wanted or needed.

What her friend didn't seem to realize was that Alex would give all the money away just so she could bring her parents back from the grave and have them in her life again.

Alex was about to reply, when a friend of Lisa's interrupted and began to talk with her.

"Sorry, Alex, it looks like I need to go. Nice to see you back on the island again." Lisa quickly waved before she walked away with her friend.

Alex turned to look around the room. She spotted Sam looking over at her from the other side of the room.

She offered him a friendly smile.

Chesmu Sagamore walked over to talk to her.

"Dr. Alex. It's nice to see you again so soon." Chesmu's dark eyes were filled with humor.

Alex grinned. "It's good to see you too. I'm happy you came tonight."

"I am too. My step sister asked me to join her." Chesmu looked around. "From the crowd gathered here tonight, I can see your family knows a good number of islanders."

"Yeah. The Stafford family has lived here for over a hundred years. So, my sisters and I know most folks in the Sweet Beach Cove community." Alex grinned. "But I never expected such a big turnout. It's nice to see so many friends from my childhood."

He smiled easily. "It's good to be appreciated, Alex.

Enjoy it. I feel the same way whenever I return to my community of Aquinnah."

"Are you happy to be back, Chesmu?"

He nodded. "Thrilled. I'm always grateful to enjoy time with my people. And I have already begun to plan storytelling events in my community of Aquinnah. You should come to one of my storytelling events, Alex."

"I would be happy to. Thanks for the invitation."

Chesmu grinned. "Of course."

Alex was thinking about Chesmu's invitation when her sister Jules tapped her arm.

"Alex, Dr. Grace Waverly wants to talk to you." Jules smiled wide.

Alex turned to see a familiar face walking her way.

"I should talk with her." Alex turned to her sister. "But before I go, Chesmu, I should introduce you to my sister Julianna. You two should talk. You'll find you have a lot in common. You're both storytellers." Alex's grin widened as she overheard them getting to know one another.

She walked over to her friend and mentor.

Dr. Grace Waverly.

Her childhood doctor had aged gracefully.

Her familiar brown wavy hair had turned into a lovely halo of white. Smile lines had formed deep lines beside her eyes over the years. She had grown older. "Alexandra, my dear, it's so good to talk to you in person again."

She chuckled. "It's wonderful to see you again, Dr. Waverly."

Grace Waverly studied her in silence before she spoke again. "I am so glad that you decided to move back to the island again, Alex. Since we had that chat a few weeks ago,

I've been so relieved. I'm thrilled that you've agreed to take over the care of my younger patients. Now, I'll be able to retire from my medical practice without worry."

Alex's smile widened. "I'm glad that it worked out so well. Did you find another doctor willing to take over the medical care of your older patients?"

"I did. In fact, I see her now." Dr. Waverly eyed someone who was in the crowd of people and waved at her.

The woman began to walk towards them.

Her olive-colored skin tones and black hair looked familiar.

Alex recognized her as the same woman she saw on the ferry.

She was the stepsister of Chesmu Sagamore.

"Hello, Dr. Waverly. Good to see you again." The woman shook the older doctor's hand.

"You as well, Mika. I wanted to introduce you to the doctor who will be caring for my younger patients. Dr. Mika Sagamore, this is Dr. Alex Stafford." Alex shook the woman's hand,

Suddenly, she realized why Mika looked familiar. "Mika, it's nice to see you again," Alex explained.

Grace Waverly looked between the two of them, her eyebrows lifted in surprise. "You two seem to know each other already."

"Yes, we do, Dr. Waverly. Mika and I went to school together growing up. Much later, we both took similar medical classes during our first year of college," Alex explained.

The older woman nodded. "Why, that's wonderful.

And to think you've both come back here to the island. This is good news indeed."

Alex smiled slightly and looked over at Mika.

Mika's lips had tightened. For a moment, her features seemed frozen and she didn't respond.

Woodenly, Mika replied, "It's good you will take over caring for the young patients from Dr. Waverly's practice, Dr. Stafford." Dr. Sagamore's cool tone was unmistakable. "I'll make sure to have the patient files sent over."

Mika's unfriendly attitude was very off-putting. Alex should have expected it, but she couldn't help but be taken aback.

She had never liked Alex when they were in grade school or in college. Alex had always wondered why this woman held a grudge against her.

She swallowed back emotions and forced herself to speak in soft, polite tones, "Thanks, Dr. Sagamore. Dr. Waverly speaks very highly of you."

"Thank you," Mika's reply was clipped and guarded.

Dr. Waverly addressed them both, "Two excellent doctors. My patients will be in good hands. I will be calling each of you with a final update on patients and their care before my official retirement."

"Thank you, Dr. Waverly. I appreciate that." Mika nodded. "I need to be going, but thank you for keeping me updated."

With a quick nod to both Alex and Grace, Mika excused herself and walked away.

Alex turned back to Grace Waverly. "I am looking forward to getting to know the patients you've transferred into my care."

Dr. Waverly commented, "Good. I'm glad."

Just at that moment, a young girl ran and hugged the older doctor.

"Excuse me, Dr. Waverly? I wanted to tell you I'm going to miss you when you go." The eight-year old sniffled and wrapped her thin arms around the doctor's waist.

"Oh, my dear. I'll miss you too." Dr. Waverly embraced the little girl. For Alex it brought back fond memories of how gentle the older doctor had been during her own childhood doctor visits.

"Zoe, would you like to meet the doctor who will look after you when I retire?" Dr. Waverly turned to see Zoe's dad was now standing near them.

"Yeth, I would." The little girl's lisp was adorable.

Dr. Waverly looked at Alex. "Your new doctor is here. Zoe Chadsworth, meet Dr. Alex Stafford."

Alex recognized the little girl's last name. So, this was Sam's little girl. She should have recognized Zoe from when she saw her with Sam at the fall festival last year.

Zoe had grown up, she definitely looked like her dad.

The little girl's eyes widened. Alex grinned and crouched down until she was eye-level with the girl.

"You're going to be my new doctor?" Zoe asked, her brown eyes big and round.

All of a sudden, Alex glanced to her right and noticed a large pair of leather Oxford shoes standing next to her.

Without missing a beat, Alex replied, "I will be your new doctor, that is — if your dad agrees?"

Alex glanced up to see Sam looking at her, his eyebrows lifted in surprise.

The years had only made him more handsome. His

square jawline was sculpted into even more distinct lines. A few strands of silver had been added to his brown waves and his dark brown eyes remained as ever — steady, deep, and constant.

Was Sam surprised to learn that Dr. Waverly's younger patients would be transferred to her care?

"Can Dr. Stafford be my new doctor, Daddy?"

"That would be good." As always, Sam's voice was even toned, reflecting none of his emotions.

"Then, I'm happy to be your new doctor, Zoe." Alex smiled as the little girl hurried towards her and wrapped her arms around her.

A bittersweet warmth flooded her at the little girl's excitement.

To feel the warmth from the love of a child was something that Alex had longed for — for years.

When the stranger attacked her as an innocent teenager, the end result had stolen her dream of having her own family, forever.

Moisture filled her eyes as she continued to hold the little girl in her arms enjoying the closeness.

The moment Zoe removed her slender arms, Alex couldn't help but feel a momentary sadness at the sudden loss.

At least she would still see Sam's little girl as her doctor. She was happy about that.

Grace Waverly who started to speak and Alex stood to her feet, turning to her friend and mentor.

"Good. I'm glad we have that settled. Zoe will be in good hands with Dr. Alex as her doctor." Dr. Waverly smiled at Alex.

A wave of warmth flooded Alex at the admiration and respect she glimpsed in her mentor's eyes. "Thank you Dr. Waverly. Your encouraging words mean a lot to me."

"It's the truth. I believe all the young patients here will be very well taken care of with you as their doctor, Alex." Her mentor grinned, then hurried on. "But, I have a few more people to talk to before the evening is over. So, I'll see you later Alex, Sam, and Zoe."

With a quick wave, Dr. Waverly walked away from them.

Alex waved back at her mentor, pleased to have seen her again.

One of Zoe's friends ran to the eight-year old and tugged on her arm. The two little girls scampered away, leaving Alex and Sam alone.

When Alex looked hesitantly over at Sam, a thoughtful look burned in his brown eyes and he continued to study her.

"Walk with me?" Sam's invitation was a welcome one.

"Sure. That would be nice." Maybe they would finally get a chance to have that talk.

CHAPTER FOUR

am

TOGETHER, they walked down the weathered wooden stairs that led to her sister's beautiful garden.

Sam rested his hand on the small of her back as they walked.

His voice was low as he asked, "Are you back on the island to stay?"

A big part of him hoped Alexandra had come back for good.

"Yes, I am."

Sam expelled a breath. "That's good to hear."

A slow smile lifted the corners of her lips.

Tingles spread up his arm as he touched her.

His mother had taught him from a young age that it was important to be a gentleman to all ladies.

He was offering her protection, but for some reason, with Alexandra, his wayward heart seemed to offer much more.

He could feel a slight trembling in her body.

Forcing himself to refocus, he asked, "What happened to your job in Boston?"

Alex grimaced. "I was unexpectedly let go. Budget cuts. At least that's what I was told."

She shrugged. "It definitely shook things up in my life."

"And the island beckoned you back?" He couldn't resist teasing her.

She sighed heavily.

"I had a chat with my sisters," Alex explained. "They reminded me of my inheritance from my late grand-mother. The old, stone cottage I inherited is rather worn down and desperately needs new life. Sort of like I do, I guess. Maybe it's optimistic to think I could turn it into a children's medical clinic, but I feel like I must try."

Alex released a long breath.

"That's quite an undertaking. But if anyone can do it, you can, Alexandra." Sam tried his best to offer encour-agement.

Her beautiful blue eyes widened.

The expression on her features told him she was surprised. But why would Alexandra be surprised by his belief in her ability?

"Thanks, Sam. That means a lot to hear you say that." Alex shifted on her feet. He sensed this woman was still nervous around him after all these years. "It'll mean a lot of expensive and time consuming repairs to get the house fixed up."

"There are a few good construction contractors on the island," he offered.

"Is there somebody you recommend?"

"Jason Harper," Sam responded without hesitation. "He has two men who work for him, and he has a good reputation around these parts."

He watched as Alex quickly jotted down Jason's name and number as Sam read the information from his list of contacts.

They continued to walk together through Lizzie's flower garden. The beautiful oasis was farther away from the house, amid thick shrubs and trees.

A sweet scent of roses filled his nostrils.

Birds chattered from their perch in the shade trees above.

They walked slowly among the pink, purple, and blue flowers.

Turning his head, Sam watched as Alex plucked an invisible piece of lint from her shirt.

Long ago, when they were dating, he remembered Alex would pick at her clothes whenever she was feeling a little nervous.

He glanced at Alex, her profile softened by the dusk.

She turned to him, and, seeing him studying her, her cheeks turned a lovely shade of pink.

Alex stuttered a little as she asked, "How are things going for you, Sam?"

The lilting sound of her soft voice was nearly his undoing.

"I'm keeping well. At the moment, I'm working on my newest computer software design. It keeps me busy." His gaze flickered towards the house where his daughter played with her friend. "But of course, my daughter comes first. I juggle my schedule around her."

Sam had always found it easy — too easy — to tell Alexandra the details of his life.

"Of course, I understand. Your daughter is a wonderful girl," Alex commented as they began walking slowly back to the inn.

"Zoe is my biggest blessing." He swallowed at all the times he had worried over her health. "Speaking of my daughter, that brings up something I wanted to talk to you about. Since you'll be taking over Zoe's care, there are details you should know."

"What is it?"

Unconsciously, Sam ran a shaky hand through his hair.

"Zoe has asthma. She's also just returned home after a week-long stay in the hospital — bronchitis. My daughter has suffered from lung problems since she was a small child." Worry and fear colored the edges of his words. "I just want to see her get well."

Alex paused and turned to him, concern filling her big blue eyes.

"Sam, I promise to do everything I can to care for your daughter. Now that she's in my care, I'll do my research and see how we can get to the root of your daughter's health problems." Determination was evident in her voice. It was just the reassurance he needed.

Sam exhaled a long breath of relief. "Thank you for helping Zoe, Alex. My daughter is the most important person in my life. She's all I've got."

They walked in silence for a little longer, reaching the edge of the garden.

The scents of sea salt, earth, and flowers mingled around them.

Alexandra whispered, "I understand, Sam. I will do everything I can to help her. You have my word."

Sam knew when Alexandra gave her word, she bound herself to it.

That was all he needed to hear.

He could breathe easy again.

This woman — the same woman he loved years ago — would be watching closely over his daughter.

Once again, his life was being weaved together with this sometimes stubborn but always beautiful and compassionate woman.

Sam decided he would need to be careful not to let himself get taken in by her beautiful face and compassionate nature.

He'd already done that once before — and had been rejected.

He didn't think he'd be able to handle the heartache of loving and losing her a second time.

ALEX NOTICED Sam looking towards the house, a crease of worry etched the deep lines between his brows.

"Maybe we should start walking back to the house," she offered. Most likely he was worried about his young daughter.

He nodded and, once again, placed a gentle hand on the small of her back.

Emotion flooded Alex at the familiar gesture.

Her heart betrayed her and a longing stirred deep inside for more between them.

Alex's logical mind didn't believe Sam would ever want a second chance with her. She had hurt him years ago and she didn't deserve it.

Still, she desperately hoped he would forgive her — someday.

Gravel crunched beneath their shoes as they walked towards the inn. Bright lights shone in the windows, laughter and chatter mingled together in the evening air.

The soft rustle of leaves whispered in the night.

Low voices unexpectedly cut through the quiet night.

"Dr. Alex Stafford. Welcome home." Sheriff Hart stood in front of them, flanked by his two sons, Dylan and Ryan Hart, and another officer Miles Carter. Both Ryan and Miles were police officers. She thought Dylan was a handyman years ago. She wasn't sure what he did now.

Despite being dressed in civilian clothes, both Ryan's and Miles' rigid posture offered a reminder of their profession as cops.

"Your folks would be glad to see you back on the island, Alex."

"Thanks, Sheriff." Alex forced her voice to remain steady despite the many emotions that flooded her at the memories of her parents. "Yes, I think they would have loved this party."

"Well, it's a real shame they're gone." Sheriff Hart's eyes flickered for a moment. Was that regret she heard in his voice? "They would have liked seeing you return to the island."

"I think so too. Sadly, they are no longer here with us." Alex hesitated then decided to speak her mind, "What my sisters and I would like is to get answers on the details surrounding our parents' boating accident. My sister Lizzie told me she talked to you about some new information we found in our late grandmother's journal— which brought up questions concerning our parents' deaths. Have you considered reopening the investigation?"

Sheriff Hart chuckled. "I took a look at those pages Lizzie sent me. It seemed to me like the ramblings of an old woman — a woman who most likely had started to lose her mind before she died."

Alex's heart sank, hope deflating like a balloon pricked by a thorn. She tried again, "But I really think if we renewed our efforts with the investigation…"

"The case is closed, Alex." There was an almost fatherly tone to his dismissal. "Sadly, accidents like this happen all the time."

Alex sighed, heavily. The word accident seemed wrong when applied to her parents' deaths.

The screeching cry of a hawk could be heard overhead, mirroring her frustration.

She searched the sheriff's face for any sign of concession. His clenched jaw and unrelenting beady eyes were like a steel cage.

He spoke again, finality in his tone, "It was determined by the police years ago that your parents died from a boating accident. So, I won't reopen the investigation unless I have a very good reason to."

Alex's shoulders slumped slightly, the weight of unresolved history pressing down on her.

A single green leaf fluttered down to the ground between them — a silent witness to the conversation and the unchanging verdict.

Miles Carter stepped closer, speaking in a low drawl, "Face it, Alex. The unexpected deaths of your parents was a terrible tragedy, but an accident all the same. There's nothing new to find."

She tilted her head to one side, considering his words.

A slight breeze carried a scent of cigarette smoke that she hadn't smelled in years.

Anxiety flooded her at the smell. The pungent aroma — similar to burnt coffee — reminded her of something, but she couldn't remember what it was.

Alex reached one hand up to her necklace. Her fears soothed as her fingers traced the familiar edges of her St. Michael's pendant.

She looked up to see the sheriff's eyes looking at her with concern. The other three men were staring at the tight grip she had on her necklace.

Alex turned towards Miles.

Miles quickly moved his eyes from Alex's necklace, upwards to meet her gaze.

Alex forced an even tone, pushing back fear, "I'm not so sure about that. We haven't finished reading the rest of my grandmother's journals. Who knows what we'll discover?"

The corners of Miles' lips tightened for a moment. He gave her a curt nod and turned his head to Ryan and Dylan.

Ryan stepped into the fading twilight, his long shadow imposing.

His eyes met hers, staring her with a steely gaze. "Digging into the past — into a decades old case that was closed a long time ago — won't get you any further in your search." The firmness in Ryan's voice didn't match the mood of the evening. "For your own good, Alex, you should leave it alone."

The statement swung through the air — like a gauntlet thrown at her feet. Alex's jaw tightened, a soft ticking sound in the quiet evening.

She held Ryan's eyes, searching.

Ryan only stared at her with a hard, impassive stare. His words were a challenge to her resolve.

Sheriff Hart nodded once. "See you later, Alex and Sam."

As if in silent cue, all four men turned and walked away.

Their footfall was like soft thuds on the grass, growing fainter as they distanced themselves from her.

Only a trail of unease remained.

Alex stood motionless, the tension in her body palpable.

Sam's presence was a comfort. A reminder she wasn't facing the dark shadows of the past alone.

She turned to him.

Sam looked over at Alex, his eyes calm and steady as he waited for her to say something.

Alex swallowed the unease she still felt from Ryan's words. They simmered like hot lava in her throat.

"What do you make of that conversation?" A quiver of

doubt laced her voice. "Do you think Miles Carter and Ryan Hart were doing their best to strong-arm me from searching for answers to what happened to my parents?"

Sam's jaw tightened as he watched the four men retreat.

He shook his head, uncertainty in his eyes.

"I'm not sure," he admitted, his voice low and filled with concern. "To me, it sounded like some kind of warning."

Sam looked at her, seeing right through her. In that moment, it was as if he reached through the years.

A quiet understanding was reached between them.

"But you won't stop trying to uncover the truth about your parents' deaths, will you?" He didn't even bother to frame it as a question.

Sam understood her, he always had.

Alex squared her shoulders, a new resolve forming in her heart.

She inhaled deeply of the briny air of Martha's Vineyard.

"You know me all too well, Sam." Her words cut through the air, crisp and certain. "My sisters and I are determined to continue our search. I think we might be surprised by what we find."

Alex paused for a moment, trying to sense his reaction.

He was quiet as he rubbed the stubble on his chin. His dark brown eyes stared out at the water behind Lizzie's beach house.

He turned to study her, a crease forming between his brows. "Is that a good idea, Alex? You might bump up against unexpected enemies in your search for answers."

The fading light from the sunset cast long shadows between them.

Between them there had always been this unspoken bond forged by the years they had spent growing up together on the island.

Warmth flooded her at his protectiveness. Sam had always looked out for her. Even after all this time — even with the strained relationship they had now — he was still willing to watch over her.

She couldn't help but appreciate him all the more.

"It's a risk I need to accept if I want to learn what happened to my parents." Alex sighed.

Sam's dark eyes searched hers for a long time before he nodded.

It seemed he had come to accept her decision, despite his worry for her safety.

An idea formed in her mind.

It was a risky question — but she would ask Sam anyway.

"What would you say if I were to ask you to help me search for answers, Sam?" Her voice shook with the question, but she needed to know.

A smile tugged at the corners of Sam's mouth.

The smile reached to his eyes, softening the lines etched into his face as he looked at her.

"Just like the good old days?" His grin broadened, reflecting shared memories. "Despite my misgivings — especially in light of today's subtle scare tactics from our local law enforcement — I'll do what I can, Alex. I'll help you try to solve this mystery."

Alex released the breath she'd been holding. She hadn't

realized how important his answer was to her, until this moment.

He was right. It would be the two of them working together to figure it out, just like the old days.

Years ago — during their middle school years — the two of them had solved little island mysteries together.

Alex had read the entire Nancy Drew Mystery series and she'd been inspired to be a detective.

Together, she and Sam had learned the whereabouts of Mrs. Dillon's tabby cat and brought the animal back to her house.

They had also uncovered the mystery behind the disappearance of newspapers down their street.

It seemed one of the neighborhood dogs had been taking them and burrowing newspapers inside his kennel. Mr. Ben Larkin had been surprised when they told him what happened. To his credit, Mr. Larkin put his dog on a leash whenever the newspapers were delivered after that.

Side by side, they had solved minor mysteries.

Now the two of them were much older.

Doing a deep dive into the past, would be both heady and dangerous for the two of them.

But they could do this.

Together they would be unstoppable, despite the veiled warnings of those who warned them to leave the past alone.

"Thanks, Sam. You have no idea how much it means to me to have your help." Alex tucked a tendril of blond hair behind one ear.

He nodded. "I just hope we don't end up regretting digging up the past."

"I understand. But I believe this is too important. I need to find out the truth, Sam," Alex replied.

"I know." Sam ran his fingers through his hair, studying her for a long minute.

Then he said, "Well, I need to get going. It's getting late. I should probably get Zoe home."

Alex nodded. "Of course. I think I'll stay outside and enjoy the view of the water from my sister's beautiful garden. It's a nice quiet spot to think."

Sam briefly turned to look over at the row of flowers that separated Lizzie's backyard from the beach and blue water beyond.

"Don't stay out here too long, Alex. It's getting late." Sam looked at her, waiting for her reply.

"I'll only be a little while longer, I promise. Go find your daughter, Sam. Don't worry about me." Alex smiled, forcing a bright smile she didn't feel inside.

With a quick nod, Sam hurried away towards the bright lights of the inn.

Alex turned and slowly walked towards the tall trees and flowers that graced the edge of the well-manicured lawn. Lizzie had set up white mini-lights along the trees and bushes that added a beautiful glow to the garden area.

Looking around, she noticed quite a few people were starting to leave the party. Looking at her watch, she noticed the time was almost ten o'clock in the evening.

Sam was right. It was getting late.

But she still had time to enjoy the beautiful view of the beach and water from her sister's backyard.

Moving close to the edge of the bushes that bordered

the path that led down to the beach, she stared out at the water.

Orange and red hues from the sunset skipped across the waves, spilling a white glow across the dark blue water.

The salty scent of sea water flooded her nostrils and surrounded her with the feeling of being home.

As she remembered her conversation with Sam, she smiled. It had been a long time since there had been someone she could trust who was willing to help her.

It surprised her that Sheriff Hart wouldn't reopen the investigation into her parents' boating accident. And even more shocking was listening to police officers Ryan Hart and Miles Carter discouraging her from continuing her search for answers.

A knot of worry formed in her belly.

She reached up, her fingers curling tightly around the warrior angel pendant. The necklace was a comfort when anxiety began to creep into her thoughts, as it so often did.

Her thoughts returned to the questions that shuffled through her thoughts about her parents' deaths.

Searching for answers about the boating accident was more than simply discovering what happened.

Uncovering the truth was a step towards justice.

Uncovering the truth was a step towards learning the history of her parents and their family.

Uncovering the truth was a step towards finally having peace and healing from that awful tragedy that had thrown her family's lives into a tailspin years ago.

She was grateful Sam was willing to help, despite his misgivings about their safety.

As she thought about growing up on the island, memories returned of the days she spent with Sam. He had always been so kind and thoughtful.

Even after that terrible attack from the stranger, he had been patient with her.

Suddenly, the crunch and snap of branches nearby cut through the night air.

The silence was broken.

Alex turned her head at the sound.

In the fading light, a stranger dressed in black ran towards her.

As soon as he reached her, his black gloved hand reached out and yanked at the gold chain that circled her neck.

The chain scraped against her delicate skin as the stranger viciously grabbed it.

"No! That's my necklace!" Alex yelled, reaching up to stop the stranger. She glimpsed a black ski mask as she reached over to stop him.

But it was too late.

In a flash, the stranger was gone. He ran down the path and towards the beach.

"Stop! Give it back!" Alex yelled again. Kicking off her high heeled shoes, she started to run after the man who stole her necklace.

However, running in the tight skirt proved very difficult. She chased him for about a mile, then gave up, exhausted.

She stopped. It was impossible to catch up with him.

Her breath came in short gasps.

Alex watched as the robber suddenly made a sharp left turn. The stranger ran in between some tall bushes and disappeared from sight.

Shock, fear, and anger each competed for the number one spot in her emotions.

With shaky fingers, Alex touched her bare neck.

The most memorable piece of jewelry she'd ever been given, was now gone. Her parents' gift to her, was now in the cold hands of a cruel stranger.

Who was this horrible person? What possible reason could they have for stealing her necklace?

The more she thought about it, the angrier she became. How could someone randomly steal her most treasured possession?

She refused to believe the most important gift she'd ever received was gone for good.

No. There had to be a way to find the robber who stole her necklace. She had to get it back.

Perhaps this wasn't a random stranger after all. Did someone deliberately target her?

It was time to get some answers.

Reaching into her pocket she pulled out her phone and dialed the number.

"You've reached 911. What is your emergency?"

"I've been attacked by a stranger. He stole my necklace. The police must find him. I must get it back," Alex responded, anger at the injustice still in her voice.

After she explained more details about what happened — including her location — she was assured the police would arrive shortly.

Alex hurried down the beach towards Lizzie's house.

Tension crawled up her spine. A massive ball of fear and anxiety knotted in her belly as questions rose to the surface.

Would the police be able to find the stranger?

Was it impossible now to retrieve the most important piece of jewelry she owned and get it safely back into her hands?

CHAPTER FIVE

lex

"You say the stranger stepped out from behind the bushes in Lizzie's garden, ripped the necklace off your neck, then ran towards the beach?" Detective Jonas Sullivan questioned Alex.

Alex's six sisters, Jonathan, Will, Jake, and Officer Miles Carter were all seated in Lizzie's Great Room at *The Vineyard Inn.*

Alex nodded. "Yes, he did. However, I didn't get a good look at this guy. He wore a black ski mask."

The detective was busy writing, making notes of all the details. She was grateful that she was being questioned by Detective Sullivan instead of Officer Miles Carter.

She knew the Sullivan family and had grown up with

Jonas Sullivan. He was an honorable man who valued truth and honesty.

His parents, Cormack and Nora Sullivan, had been good friends with Alex's parents years ago.

She hadn't been surprised to learn Jonas had been promoted to the rank of detective. He'd always been a hard worker who enjoyed serving others.

He was one of the trustworthy cops on their island. Honest as the day was long.

But she could freely admit she didn't have those same feelings of trust with Police Officer Miles Carter.

When she was eighteen, Alex began hearing comments from her grandmother of how she thought the police gave up too soon, looking for answers to her parents' deaths.

At that time, Officer Carter had discouraged her from looking for answers to the mystery. The officer's actions prompted a little mistrust on her part.

It bothered Alex that she felt that way.

"Can you describe this necklace?" Detective Sullivan questioned.

Quickly, she switched off her rambling thoughts to focus on the present moment.

Sighing, Alex nodded. "Yes. It was custom made for me and given as a birthday gift from my parents. The pendant has the figure of a warrior angel holding a sword in one hand, over his gold breast plate. Located in the middle is a pink diamond. It has similarities to a St. Michael's pendant."

The detective nodded. "And the necklace has a gold chain?"

"Yes. And the pendant itself is gold. It's quite valuable.

I've got a photo of it here." Alex opened her phone and showed him a photo of her standing with her sisters.

In the picture, the necklace looked clear, the pink diamond glimmering in the sun.

"It would help me to see it up close, to know what we're looking for. If you could email me the photo, that would help," Detective Sullivan suggested.

"Sure. I'll send it to you now."

"Thanks, Alex." The detective wrote more details down.

Lizzie spoke up suddenly, "Alex, do you think this might have been the same guy that attacked you years ago?"

"I doubt it. The person who stole my necklace tonight was quite slender and wiry looking. That other guy years ago, was heavy with hairy arms." Alex turned to her oldest sister as she tried to describe what she remembered from years ago.

Detective Sullivan suddenly turned to her. "What's this? I didn't know you were attacked before. When did this happen?"

"When I was sixteen." Alex told him the short version of what happened years ago.

She was glad Sam wasn't in the room at the moment.

Alex had never told him what happened to her years ago. Deep down, she hoped the need to speak about it to Sam would never arise.

The detective asked, "So you went to the police and they found nothing?"

Alex nodded. "That's correct. So, that's why I don't think it's the same person."

"But you said the man who attacked you years ago and the man tonight both wore a black ski mask over their faces." Jonas Sullivan was good at asking questions that brought the details into the open. "Which means, you don't know their identity."

"That's true." Alex sighed.

Detective Sullivan ran a hand through his dark hair. "Well, that's not very helpful. And tonight's attacker wore gloves, correct?"

"Yes." Alex grimaced.

"It's likely we won't find fingerprints either." Jonas Sullivan wrote down some more notes. "Sounds like this person who stole your necklace — and your attacker from years ago — were very careful to cover up their identities."

Alex swallowed and nodded.

Her six sisters and Jonathan were all seated on the sofas around the room, listening in rapt attention.

Just at that moment, she spotted Sam.

He stopped in the doorway and stared at her for a long time. His expression was unreadable, which was normal for Sam.

The only tell-tale sign of worry was the noticeable rising and falling of Sam's chest, and his slow release of a heavy sigh.

Was it a sigh of relief that she was safe?

Alex gave him a hesitant smile, hoping to relieve his worries.

Sam walked over to the sofa where she was, and sat beside her.

He turned and whispered, "I'm glad you're alright."

"Thanks, Sam. I'm okay. Lizzie must have called you," Alex whispered back.

"Yeah, your sister called."

Alex murmured, "Sorry for interrupting your evening because of this."

"Alexandra, I was happy to come over. As for interrupting my evening — that's the least of my worries. I'm just glad nothing worse happened to you." Sam rubbed the back of his neck, the crease between his brows deepening.

Sam had been worried about her. She couldn't help but feel somewhat pleased knowing this.

Perhaps he wasn't as unaffected by her as he let on.

Officer Sullivan interrupted their conversation with his next question, "I just want to clarify the details of this person who stole your necklace. Did you notice anything at all that would help in our search?"

"All I can tell you is I noticed he or she was slender and taller than me by a couple of inches. But not much else. Everything happened so fast."

Officer Sullivan nodded and wrote down more notes. "When this person ripped off your necklace, they ran away. That's when you chased them down along the beach?"

Alex swallowed her voice strained. "Yes. But I couldn't run fast enough to catch up with the thief. It's very difficult to run in my skirt."

A heavy weight pulled on her chest as she thought of all she'd lost.

"That's too bad. One more question, Alex. Can you think of anyone who would want this necklace so much that they'd resort to stealing it from you?"

A deep crease formed between Officer Sullivan's brows, his dark eyes intense as he studied her.

Alex thought back to the evening. "No, not really. I mean tonight there were quite a few people who took an interest in my necklace. But that's nothing new. Folks have always taken an interest in it."

"Do you recall the names of people who seemed interested in your necklace tonight at the party?"

"Yes. I remember some of their names. Ida Cantrell, Ted Cantrell, Lisa Cane, Slater Williams, Dr. Mika Sagamore, and Dr. Grace Waverly. Later in the evening I talked with Sheriff Hart, his two sons, and Officer Carter here."

"Everybody, I just mentioned, are folks who noticed my necklace, but I'm finding it difficult to believe any of them would try to steal it."

"Why do you think none of those people would want it?

Alex shrugged. "I guess it's because I've known most of them all my life. I don't remember any of them attacking me before."

Jonas Sullivan studied her for a long moment deep in thought. Then he nodded. "Thanks, Alex. I think we have what we need for now. Officer Carter, do you have questions?" The detective turned to his fellow police officer.

"Yes, I've got a few," Officer Carter began.

He looked at Alex and shook his head. "Unfortunately, your testimony isn't much for the police to go on, Alex. But we'll do our best to find the culprit who stole your necklace."

Alex sighed heavily. It didn't sound like he was giving her much hope to recover what she'd lost.

Miles Carter turned to Sam. "Sam, I'm glad you're here. There are a few questions I want to ask you as well."

"Go ahead." Sam turned to the officer.

"Is it true that you had just finished talking with Alex, only minutes before the necklace was stolen?" Officer Carter raised an eyebrow.

Sam nodded. "It's true. We were talking in the garden. Our conversation ended when I realized how late in the evening it was. I went inside Lizzie's house to find my daughter and leave for home. It must have only been ten or fifteen minutes after I got home that Lizzie called to let me know a stranger had stolen Alex's necklace."

"Hmm. So, you didn't see this person?"

"No, I didn't see them. However, the ugly red welt that I can plainly see on Alexandra's neck — as well as the missing necklace — shows me someone did aggressively steal her necklace from off her neck."

"Maybe." Miles Carter shrugged and took some notes.

Both officers stood to their feet.

"Will you be able to find the culprit?" Alex asked.

"We'll do our best. But I can tell you right now, from your story and from what others have said, we don't have a lot to go on to try to find this stranger." Officer Carter. "We'll let you know what we find, Alex — if anything."

Wide-eyed, Alex stared in disbelief at the officers as they left Lizzie's house.

"I'm sorry, Alex. They didn't give you much hope of finding this guy." Lizzie walked over to Alex and gave her a hug. Her other sisters nodded in agreement.

Sam stood to his feet. "I asked the teenager across the street to care for my daughter. She offered to look after Zoe for a few hours. I must return home soon."

Alex nodded. "Of course. Thanks for coming, Sam."

She followed him to the door.

Sam whispered, "For what it's worth, I hope they find this stranger, arrest him and return your necklace to you. I'm sorry this happened to you, Alexandra."

"Thanks, Sam. I appreciate it." She swallowed back emotion. His concern for her was touching.

"One more thing. From my perspective, it seems like you were deliberately targeted by someone. The question is, was it only because they wanted your necklace, or was there some other reason?"

Long after Sam left, his questions circled around in Alex's thoughts. After she got home, she stayed up late trying to come up with her own answers to his questions.

No answer came immediately to mind.

However, one thing was for sure. She wasn't going to stop until she found out who did this.

THE SHRILL RING of his phone woke Sam the next morning.

"Good morning, Sam." Ward Hampton's sunny voice on the other end of the phone line was annoying. "I wanted to call about the security software you were talking about last night. My boss told me they would like to purchase it for the newsroom."

Sam yawned and said, "Good morning, Ward. Thanks

for letting me know you are interested in the software. Just a minute. I'll go to my office computer."

His friend had always been up at the crack of dawn with his job as anchor for a popular Boston news network.

They had been good friends since high school. Their personalities were opposite of one another, but they still got along well.

Ward had always been an extrovert, with a lot of friends. Sam, on the other hand, was an introvert who had always preferred a small group of close friends.

"You sound tired. Didn't you sleep last night?"

"Not real well." Sam stifled a yawn and turned to put the coffee grounds into the coffee maker. "I didn't get home until past midnight last night. I'm brewing my morning java now. Hopefully that'll help wake me up."

His friend chuckled. "Were you up late because of a woman? Are you dating someone, my friend?"

"Not dating. But, yes, it was because of a woman who's in trouble." Sam poured himself a cup of the hot brown liquid, and sat at his kitchen table.

"What sort of trouble?" Concern was evident in the low tones of Ward's voice.

Sam stirred cream into his mug of coffee. "You might not have heard, but a stranger stole Alexandra Stafford's necklace last night. Anyway, I was up late in the evening, answering Detective Sullivan's questions."

"Stole her necklace? Is she alright?" Ward asked.

Sam nodded. "Yeah, Alexandra is shook up, but she's okay. She was really scared last night."

"I'll bet," his friend continued, "If I remember correctly, years ago, you two were an item."

Sam rubbed the back of his neck. "That was years ago, Ward. All I'm doing now is trying to help her solve the mystery of her parents' boating accident. And I suppose now, I am answering questions about her missing necklace. There's nothing going on between us."

"But there could be, if you wanted more than friendship with her, Sam," Ward encouraged.

Sam shook his head as he found the link he was looking for on his computer. "I don't think Alex is interested. She's very independent, smart, and likes to be in control of every aspect of her life. Besides that, she sometimes seems a bit stand-offish with men."

"Sounds like a challenge for you, Sam," his friend said thoughtfully. "You should use this time of searching for answers together to get to know the real Alexandra. Protect her and let her know you're there for her. Most of all, let her know she can trust you. Who knows, you might decide you were meant for each other."

Sam shook his head. "Nice try, Ward. But it's not going to happen." His friend was silent on the other end of the phone line.

Sam quickly wrote a short email with his website link inside. "I sent you the email with the links to purchase, and videos on how to install the software. You can forward the information to your boss. If there are any problems, let me know. I'll take care of it."

"Thanks." Ward paused, and then spoke again, "And, Sam?"

"Yeah." Sam set his mug of coffee down on his desk and waited.

"Think about what I said. I noticed Alex watching you at the welcome party. I believe she still has embers that burn for you. All you need to do is fan them into flame," Ward encouraged softly before he hung up the phone.

As he sat and drank his coffee, Sam's thoughts whirled as he pondered his friend's words.

It was impossible for him to believe that Alex was still interested in him.

He couldn't see any evidence of it.

She had always been stand-offish with him. Ever since that one summer when she came back to school — she seemed nervous and on edge.

That's when she began to create distance between him and her. Looking back, it still seemed so strange.

Sam thought about the upcoming weeks.

It was true, he would be spending more time with Alex.

By necessity, they would be forced to join forces.

Would he be able to get past the thick shell she had placed around her heart? Was it possible for him to persuade her to finally let down her walls around him?

He didn't think so.

However, perhaps Ward was right. He should at least try.

CHAPTER SIX

lex

ALEX YAWNED as she carried the large pitcher of sweet iced tea to the front porch.

Last night she hardly slept.

She was jumpy and nervous about the stranger stealing her necklace at the end of her welcome party.

In the couple hours she managed to sleep, Alex had awoken from one of her terrible dreams.

It was the same nightmare she'd had over and over again for years.

In her dream, the same guy who attacked her years ago was chasing her.

He wore a black ski mask just like last time.

But this time the guy found her, tied her in ropes, and locked her up in his cold, dark, cabin-like house.

This time she couldn't get out.

She was forever abandoned and alone with no way of escape.

Her deepest fears of being vulnerable, trapped, and all alone, had surfaced again.

Her hand shook as she carried the pitcher of sweet iced tea.

For a minute she tossed the idea around that the guy from years ago and last night's guy who stole her necklace were the same person.

But as quickly as the thought entered her mind, she dismissed it.

It was impossible.

The person last night had been very slender and only slightly taller than she was. However, the stranger years ago was taller and quite heavy-set.

The differences between the two attackers were much too glaring. There was no way they could be the same person.

Unanswered questions churned in her mind and begged the question: who was the thief from last night?

Fear and worry continued to plague her thoughts.

Stopping at the doorway, Alex took a deep breath.

Stop thinking about all your fears and worries, Alex. Your sisters have stopped by to see you. Enjoy time with them.

She was going to focus on her family.

They had come to her house to offer their support.

She was grateful for them.

After the mental pep-talk, Alex pushed open the screen door and stepped onto the wide, open porch.

Looking around at her siblings, she smiled warmly.

"I'm grateful you all could stop by before you headed on home." Alex yawned as she poured sweet iced tea into their tall glass cups.

Settling down on a nearby chair, she sighed.

The effects of sleeplessness ran through her body. Her thoughts raced in a million different directions.

This morning, being together with her sisters, helped calm her nerves. It was wonderful to enjoy some time, sitting together on the front porch before they each left the island.

"We felt it was the right thing to do, Alex." Jane's brows drew together, a crease of worry forming. "We needed to double check that you were alright, Alex," Jane spoke with sincerity.

Moments ago, when they arrived at her house, each sister had embraced Alex in a warm hug.

"I'm alright, but still in shock."

Jane's mouth thinned with displeasure. "That's understandable."

Her sister Charlie shifted in her chair, turning to Alex. "We're sisters, Alexandra. Where else would we all be, but with you?"

"Charlie's right." Jane took a sip of her cool drink. "We're not only here to double check that you're alright, Alex. I feel like each of us has been separated from each other's lives for far too long. Now is our time to catch up."

Jane reached over and squeezed Alex's hand. "Now we'll finally get the chance to learn how to be real sisters again — a true family. Grams would be pleased."

"It's good," Jules smiled. "Just like the good ol' days with Grams and Gramps. This is wonderful, Alex."

"Thanks, Jules. It brings back fond memories for me too," Alex replied as she refilled her sister's glasses with Grams' sweet iced tea. Alex placed the pitcher on the deck's wooden side table.

"So, Alex. About last night, we couldn't help but overhear that police officer who was talking with you. He didn't offer much hope of finding your necklace," Torrie commented.

Alex closed her eyes for a minute, feeling utterly miserable. She still couldn't believe her necklace was missing.

Finally, she opened her eyes, staring at her sister. "It's true, Torrie. But somehow, I can't accept that. I'm desperate. I must get my pendant back."

"I believe you will get it back, Alex. Why? Because I know you, Sis. You're like a dog-on-a-bone when you're determined to find something." Torrie shrugged matter-of-factly.

Charlie jumped in, "I agree with Torrie. And we'll be right by your side. Right, sisters?" Charlie looked around the room at her five sisters, who all nodded in agreement. "You're not alone in this, Alex."

Alex rigidly held her tears in check. Her voice cracked as she replied, "thank you so much, Charlie and all of you. I didn't realize how much I needed to hear that — especially after everything that's happened."

Jane scooted her chair closer to Alex and held her hand. "We're here for you, Sis."

Alex squeezed her hand. She was becoming more and more thankful for her sisters the more they spent time together.

"Thanks so much, Jane. I really am grateful for all of you. But the police are looking into it. Detective Sullivan assured me he'd be calling me soon with an update." Clearing her throat, Alex hurried to switch the topic away from herself. "Anyway, enough about me. Let's talk about something a little happier."

"Alright. Well, I have something I want to say. It's completely off topic," Torrie whispered, a secretive smile pulling up the corners of her lips. "Jonas Sullivan sure has grown up into a handsome man."

Alex grinned wide and chuckled. "You forgot to mention – single. Are you interested, Torrie?"

The youngest of the seven sisters had already been engaged three times before. Alex didn't know the reasons why her sister had broken three engagements to different men.

But it was good to hear Torrie was back to her old fun-loving ways.

"Maybe." All the sisters couldn't help laughing at Torrie's response. She grinned. "I just needed to say it."

"He's available, Sis. But you might need to move back to the Vineyard if you want to date him," Alexandra prodded.

"I suppose. I promise I'm seriously thinking about it." Torrie grinned. "But Alex, I want to know more about you. I couldn't help but notice you were having a good chat with Sam. Care to tell us?" Torrie raised one eyebrow, a secretive smile playing around the corners of her mouth.

Heat stained Alex's neck, moving swiftly to her cheeks at her sister's hint of a romantic relationship between her and Sam. "We did have a nice talk. Sam told me about the software he's working on and talked about his daughter, Zoe. Sam is a very devoted father."

"That doesn't surprise me at all," Lizzie commented. "Even when you two were dating in high school, Sam always seemed like a faithful guy and protective over people he cared about."

Alex swallowed as memories washed over her.

She nodded. "He still is. That hasn't changed."

"Maybe you'll get back together with Sam now that you've moved back to the island, Alex," Jules commented. Julianna was the sister that always longed to see a happy ending for people.

Jules was a romance writer always looking for a happy ending. Her many fans definitely seemed to thrive on the love stories she created between her hero and heroine.

"I doubt that will happen, Jules." Alex was ready to change the conversation. "But Sam did agree to help me research the mystery surrounding our parents' deaths."

"Oh my. So, you've decided to dig into that can of worms. I got a lot of push back the last time I brought that subject up with Sheriff Hart." A crease formed between Lizzie's brows and she shook her head.

"I am going to tackle that subject, Lizzie. As sisters, I feel like we need answers. I just need to figure out a plan on how to learn what happened." Alex sighed, her mind swirled with ideas on how to do this.

"I'm glad Sam has decided to help you," Jules piped up, a grin on her face.

Alex sighed. "Yes, but I don't think Sam is too excited about the idea though. Especially when we got what sounded like a warning from both police officers Ryan Hart and Miles Carter."

"Oh? What did they say?" Charlie asked.

"Just that it wouldn't be a good idea for me to try to find out more about the mystery surrounding our parent's deaths. They told me I should leave it alone." Alex sighed and rubbed her forehead in frustration.

"I've been thinking about last night's attack on you, Alex. Do you think someone is trying to scare you away from digging into the past?" Lizzie asked.

"Possibly. But if that's true, I think it's even more important to keep searching for answers. How ridiculous they are to believe they can stop the Stafford sisters from searching for what happened to our own parents." Jane's voice was tinged with indignation and anger.

Alex nodded. "I agree."

"From reading Grams' journals, I believe she wanted us sisters to try to find out the truth." Lizzie nodded. "So, I think what you're doing is great, Alex. Maybe we can come up with ways we can be of help to you."

Alex smiled at her oldest sister's support. "Thanks, everyone. Now, it looks like I'll need to find who took my necklace and continue the search for answers about what happened to our parents. Anyway, I really appreciate your support in this."

"We're sisters, Alex. Grams wanted us to do what we could to learn more about what happened to our parents. So, where do we start?" Charlie asked.

"We need to go where the people are that could have the answers we need," Jane answered. "This would be the old timers on the island who might remember when our parents were still alive. Places like Mrs. O'Conner's quilt and craft shop. And perhaps the local book club. I remember Grams mentioned something about that. I think an older widow — Mrs.Vickle — runs the book club. We could talk to her."

"Those are great ideas, Jane. I wonder if Miss Sadie's would be another place to chat with islanders. Folks from the Sweet Beach Cove community love to gather and talk at her diner," Lizzie commented.

Alex nodded, taking a sip of her sweet iced tea. "Those are great ideas. I'll make a list. I wonder what we'll discover?"

"Hmm… I'm curious to find out," Charlie murmured. "I hope Sam helps you get your necklace back."

"Perhaps he will help me." Alex turned to her sisters. "If the police don't learn anything new, I hope to enlist his help."

Charlie nodded. "That's good."

Shaking her head, Alex tried to shake off the sinister questions that plagued her mind.

"Anyway, enough about me. Tell me about you all. Torrie, how's it going at your veterinary clinic?" Alex turned to her youngest sister, Victoria. Torrie had been unusually quiet and she wanted to learn more about what was going on in her life.

"It's going well. Small pets continue to come into the clinic for treatment. We're busy. However, lately I've been having some disputes with another veterinarian. I hope our disagreement will get resolved soon." Torrie sighed woefully.

"That's the joy of co-workers sometimes." Charlie

grimaced. "Maybe that's a good reason for you to think about moving back to the island. Grams did give you ten acres of farmland in her will. Perhaps you could start your own veterinary clinic on the island."

Torrie nodded. "Yeah, I've been thinking about it. I still have a little bit of time left on the contract I signed when I started working there. After that, I'll have the freedom to make changes."

Alex commented, "That's great, Torrie. How about you, Katie? How are you doing?"

"I've been enjoying all the paintings that have recently arrived at the Art Museum. Art has always inspired me. My work as a historical art preservationist is very rewarding."

"That's great to hear, Katie." Alex smiled warmly. It was wonderful to hear Katie was doing work she loved.

"Maybe, soon, you can take a look at the art that Lizzie and Jonathan discovered in that secret room behind the den in Grams' beach cottage," Jane suggested.

"I will do that. I want to make sure all that artwork is taken care of properly. Then, of course, we'll need to see what each piece is valued at in case we want to sell any paintings." Katie's eyes brightened at the thought.

"That's a good idea. I'm still surprised at what Lizzie and Jonathan found in that secret room after the fire at the inn."

Lizzie nodded. "All of the valuable items are still there. We fixed up the den, and the secret room behind it, and took photographs of everything. Soon, all of us sisters will need to go through it and decide what we want to do with those historical items."

"True. I'm quite interested in the historical books that were discovered in that secret room. But I suppose no one here is surprised by that." Jules grinned as she looked over at her sisters.

"No, we're not surprised." Charlie grinned. "Books are definitely your thing. Speaking of books, how's it going with your writing?"

Julianna's smile widened. "Really good. My beach romance series has been optioned to become a television series. I'm excited about that. And I am almost ready to publish the last book in my second romance series too. I am looking forward to seeing where the coming years will take me."

"That is exciting, Jules. We're all proud of you." Alex grinned. "And how is your daughter doing?"

Jules' husband had left her for another woman when their daughter was only three years old.

Since the divorce Jules had remained single, raising her daughter alone.

"Emma's doing great. She has two good friends from her school and they have all sorts of fun play dates together. I'm grateful I can work from home and write. It's a lot easier to take care of my daughter." Jules sighed.

"Do you think you'll return to the island and to the small cabin you inherited from Grams?" Alex was curious about Julianna's plans. She'd always been the quiet sister who never shared a lot of details of what was going on in her life.

Jules nodded. "I'm leaning more towards the idea. I was thinking I should do that soon so the transition isn't too hard on Emma."

"That's probably a good idea, Jules. I think the same is true for my twin boys," Charlie began. "Waylon and Dutton are active teenagers, and I'm seriously thinking of moving onto that waterfront property sooner rather than later. You all know I love the fact that Grams gave me those two boats and the ten acres by the waterfront in her will. My boys love being near the water, like I do, so they might be alright with a move to the island."

Jane nodded. "I think your boys would love it, Charlie. I've been talking to Noah and he's finally open to the idea of moving here. I think I'd be interested in finding a place near the water, but we'll have to see."

Alex nodded. "It would be so good to have you and Noah nearby, Jane. If you moved back to the island, you would definitely have your hands full with event planning. There seems to be no end of events on Martha's Vineyard."

Jane nodded. "After folks would get to know and trust me, then I hope I would have enough business to keep me busy. Thanks for your support, Alex."

"Of course. We're family." Alex took a sip of her sweet tea, turning to Lizzie as she spoke.

"I'm glad all of you are open to the idea of moving back to Martha's Vineyard. There's nothing I would love more than to have my sisters and nieces and nephews back here." Lizzie sighed with a smile of contentment. "Grams wrote in her journal that she wanted each of us to return to the island."

"I remember that." Charlie nodded. "Sometime soon we should all read more of what our grandmother had to say, Lizzie. I love listening to the stories Gram wrote in her journal."

Lizzie grinned. "Well, you're in luck."

She opened up her handbag and brought out an old leather journal." I brought along Grams' journal, thinking if we had time, we could read the next part of the book together."

Alex stood to her feet and walked to the side table.

"Maybe we each need another tall glass of sweet iced tea before we get started." Picking up the large pitcher she walked to each one of her sisters and poured the cool liquid into their glass cups.

As soon as Alex returned to her chair, Lizzie began to read, "Last time, we read the story of our great-grandfather Captain Henry Stafford. He received a tiara with a pink diamond from the king when he saved the princess's life." Their oldest sister turned the brown weathered page. "Here's Grams' next journal entry."

Lizzie began to read, *"Our artist friend Lucca — who had a little help from his teenage son, Lucca Jr. — just finished the painting of our beach cottage. We hung that piece of art in the den.*

The beautiful blue colors and sun shining on the waters and the house, are reminders that there are still sunny days ahead for our family, despite losing my son and his wife a year ago.

Our seven granddaughters think it's a lovely painting. The smiles on their faces — after so much sadness — makes this project all worthwhile.

It's been a difficult time for our family this past year.

Ours isn't the only family that has gone through heartache.

A couple weeks ago at the supermarket, I was reminded that our family wasn't the only family that suffered loss.

While there, I talked with Jean Bellanger. Her son, Matty, was my son John's best friend. Matty died the day when John and his friends went diving to search for treasure in that old shipwreck when they were teenagers.

I told her, "Since my son and his wife died in that boating accident a year ago, I have a better understanding of the horrible loss you suffered from the loss of your son, Jean."

A tear squeezed out of the corner of her eye. "I'm sorry you had to deal with this kind of suffering, Elizabeth. In the years since I lost Matty, I have found some small comfort when I discovered photos and a journal that my son kept. It helped me understand him better."

"I'm glad." I sighed. "I don't know if John or Anne kept a journal. If they did, I hope one day we'll find it. We do have family photos that have been a comfort to all of us."

"You should search to see if John or Anne wrote a journal. You might be surprised by what you discover." Jean squeezed my hand.

"Maybe." As I thought about my friend's idea, I didn't even know where in the world I'd start looking. I had already cleaned up the cabin where my son had lived with his family, there was no journal found.

Jean asked, "Tell me, how are you and William and those lovely granddaughters of yours doing, Elizabeth?"

I told her some days were harder than others. Then I asked her, "Does losing someone you love get any easier as time goes on, Jean?" Jean was quiet for a long time before she spoke, "When you lose someone you love, you'll always feel the sting of loss, my friend. But, after a while, the anger begins to fade until all you're left with are wonderful, heartwarming memories. I've found that remembering the good things about your loved one, helps to get through the sad days."

I took Jean's words to heart that day. As I walked home, I began to make a list in my head of all the wonderful memories I had of my son, John, and of his wife, Anne. Then I asked our young granddaughters to draw pictures of good memories they had of their parents.

"I remember that day," Charlie whispered, her eyes glistening with unshed tears. "I drew a picture of me with dad in our wetsuits standing on the deck of his boat. Those were some of the best memories I had with dad."

Jane pulled a tissue out of her purse and blew her nose. "I remember drawing a picture of all of us at a big party. It was mom and dad's anniversary and we invited all our family and friends. That was one of my best memories."

The sisters nodded, each of them had a faraway look in their eyes as they recalled their childhood.

"Our grandmother was always thinking of ways to make us smile. Gramps was too," Alex whispered. "I remember I drew a picture of all of us. Dad, mom, all us sisters, and Gramps and Grams we were all having a picnic on the beach together, enjoying time together. Those were special memories to me."

Lizzie sighed. "I'm grateful for all the good memories."

Alex nodded. "Please, read on, Lizzie. I want to hear what else Grams had to say."

Her sister continued to read the journal, *"William and I decided to try Jean Bellanger's idea. We began to search the beach cottage as well as that old cabin where John and Anne used to live. We were both disappointed when we didn't find any photos or journals anywhere. I guess our son and his wife didn't leave anything else for us to find. It looks like we must be content with the memories we do have."*

Lizzie looked up at her sisters. "That's the end of that entry. The next page begins a new journal entry. We can save that for next time."

"Sure. That's a good idea, Lizzie." Charlie sighed. "I must admit, I'm disappointed Grams and Gramps didn't find any other photos or journals that our parents left behind."

Jane nodded. "But it sounds like they searched that old cabin, but they didn't search everywhere. Alex, maybe you should take a look inside this old stone house. In the early years, our grandparents lived in this house. You never know what you'll find."

"That's true, Jane." Alex's mind swirled with possibilities. "I hadn't thought of that. I'll make time to do a thorough search. We'll need to clean things up anyway because I have Jason Harper's construction team starting renovations at the start of next week. Who knows what we'll find?"

lex

Out of breath, Alex slowed her run into a slow walk along the sandy beach.

Since she moved to the island, she continued her daily jogging routine.

Lizzie had been happy to offer her private beach, in front of the inn, for Alex's use in the mornings.

Most of the guests at *The Vineyard Inn* didn't venture outside until after ten in the morning — most days.

It was these quiet jogging times that Alex loved.

The small breeze that had begun the day had now picked up speed and strength. The windy gale swung like an untied sailing mast along the ocean water.

White capped waves and the cloudy sky above whispered a warning of incoming wind and rain.

Hurrying a few blocks to her house, she grinned at the sight of Harper's Construction truck parked on her driveway.

They had arrived early. Good.

She would be happy when the renovations on Grams' old house were completed. The sooner the better.

Opening the door to her house, she saw the three men busy working in the newly torn-down kitchen area.

"Alex, do you have a minute?" Jason Harper turned from where he was working on some paperwork on an industrial sized wood bench.

The construction team had been tearing down old kitchen counters and peeling off old wallpaper for the past two weeks.

It had been a noisy couple of weeks, but Alex had gotten through it.

She spotted Dylan Hart and his co-worker Troy McCade measuring the walls.

Alex turned to Jason. "Of course."

A smile hovered over the corners of her lips as she walked towards the owner of the construction company.

It was like walking through a jig-saw puzzle to maneuver her feet in between the array of tools on the floor.

"I wanted to let you know what we're up to." He began by explaining, "We've finished tearing down old counter-tops and that one bedroom wall you wanted removed. Now we'll begin building. It will likely be loud at times, just so you know. However, we'll cover the area with plastic to keep the dust from getting away from the main construction area. That way it shouldn't bother you upstairs."

"Thanks for that. Too much dust and I will start sneezing." Alex grinned.

"That's usually what most folks tell me." Jason nodded.

"Now you're ready to start building?"

He nodded. "Yes. Does that sound good to you?"

Alex nodded. "Yes, it does. That sounds really good. How long do you think the building process will take?"

"Four weeks. That's my best guess. It does depend on suppliers, but most of the wood and tools we'll be using for this project are readily available, so I can't foresee any problems." Jason grinned.

"Sounds great. Thanks for letting me know. Maybe I'll disappear when it gets too loud if I can get away. Thanks again. I'll see you all later." Alex grabbed her keys and waved at Jason and the team of guys who stood behind them.

Troy McCade and Dylan Hart nodded in her direction. While Troy grinned, Dylan had his usual brooding look firmly in place.

She shrugged. He'd always been a quiet guy, not saying much. Ryan was the outgoing one — Dylan was the quiet one. He'd been that way for as long as she could remember.

She shook off uncomfortable feelings and forced a smile and waved at them, before hurrying out the door.

As she pedaled her bicycle towards her friend's coffee shop, Alex thought about the laborers Jason had working for him.

Alex remembered Troy came from a family who loved to work with their hands. She remembered his father liked to make small things with wood. It seemed like Troy had inherited his dad's passion for woodworking.

Dylan, the other worker, was the twin brother of Ryan Hart. Ryan was one of the police officers searching for the person who stole her necklace. Ryan had always been an extrovert, whereas Dylan had always been the quiet one in the Hart family.

Perhaps it was much like the differences between her and her sisters.

She shrugged off the strange thoughts that weaved their way into her mind.

Within a few minutes, she arrived at her friend's small book and coffee shop.

Happily, she slipped the wheels of her bicycle in the wooden rack and opened the door to *Beans With Books.*

Spotting her friend behind the counter with a customer, Alex browsed one of the book aisles while she waited for her friend.

She was learning through the pages of a new beach romance when Becca appeared beside her.

"Hey, you. I'm glad we could have coffee together today." Becca pulled her into a quick hug. Her best friend had always been affectionate. It was one of the things she appreciated.

"It's slower right now, so I thought we could sit at one of the tables and have coffee and chat."

"I'd love that." Alex followed Becca past a few book aisles to a quiet area. Four tables were located in a small alcove near the large window.

Becca walked to the corner table. "My daughter Kaylee is looking after customers, so I have lots of time to chat. But, before I sit down, I'll quickly get each of us coffee."

"Sounds wonderful, Becca." Alex leaned back in her chair looking around the small room as her friend walked towards the kitchen.

Looking at the rows of bookshelves and the small but adorable kitchen where the coffee and pastries were made, Alex couldn't help but smile.

Her friend had dreamed of owning her own bookshop and coffee house for years. When her grandparents passed away last year, Becca had finally been able to begin her business.

Becca returned and set a steaming mug of coffee in front of her.

"Thanks. It smells delicious." Alex smiled as Becca sat across from her. "You have a wonderful little spot here, my friend. This is a perfect location on one of the adorable cobblestone streets of the Sweet Beach Cove community."

"Thanks. I agree." Her friend grinned. "I'm grateful my grandparents left me a little money as an inheritance. That's how I was able to put a down-payment on this building and start a business I love." Happiness bubbled over in her friend's voice as she talked.

Alex's smile widened in response. "I'm so happy for you."

"Thanks, Alex. It's a lot of work, but it's work I love." Becca sighed with contentment.

"That's perfect." She looked around at the tables and fireplace that helped to create a cozy coffee shop atmosphere. "Do you get a lot of customers each week?"

Becca sipped her coffee. "It has taken a little time, but now we're getting more customers. I think it simply took people a bit of time to adjust to a new bookstore and coffee shop in the community. The good news is that when we added the book club, we began to attract many new faces."

"You started a book club?" Alex raised an eyebrow.

Becca shrugged. "Well, I wasn't the one that started it. An older widow, Mrs. Elsa Vickle organizes and runs the book club. But we've opened up this space in the cafe for the members every week on Tuesday evenings. There are about seven ladies and two men that show up for it so far. They choose a new book each week to talk about."

"My goodness, you really do have a lot going on. Tuesday evenings, huh? I might show up and see what it's like."

"You should come to the book club. Mrs. Vickle tells me that new members are always welcome."

Alex nodded. "I will. It sounds like it would also be a chance to see more folks from the community."

"That's true." Becca grinned. "But enough about my coffee and book shop. I want to hear more about what's going on with you, Alex. Are you still determined to dig into the past to find out what happened with your parents?"

Nodding, she set her mug down on the table.

With a heavy sigh, she explained. "I am. I just feel like there might be details the police might have missed years ago. Our beloved grandmother thought it was important enough to write this down in her journal. Her dying request was that all of us, as her granddaughters, would search for more details of what happened to our dad and mom. I feel a duty to do this for Grams."

Becca nodded. "I understand. Are you going to do be searching for answers by yourself?"

"No, I have help." Alex smiled. "My sisters will help when they can. But, at the welcome party, Sam agreed to help me in my search."

"Wow. I'm impressed." Becca leaned closer and whispered, "But I'm not surprised. I believe Sam still has a thing for you — even after all these years."

Alex shook her head. "No, I don't think so. He's more distant with me than he ever was. But I'm grateful for Sam's help all the same."

Becca tucked a strand of brown hair behind her ear, deep in thought.

"Maybe he's just biding his time."

"I don't think so." Alex thought about the conversations she'd had with Sam in the past week. "Sam did seem a little protective the other night, but that's because my necklace was stolen. He was worried."

Her friend's eyes widened in alarm. "Wait — what? Somebody stole your necklace?"

"Yes."

"Alex, you didn't say a word about it to me. Now you must tell me everything that's happened." Becca had suddenly turned into a drill sergeant, demanding answers.

"Becca, I didn't tell you because I didn't want you to worry. You have enough on your hands with your family and your business."

Her friend sputtered. "Well, your habit of keeping things from me ends today. I must insist you tell me all the details."

Becca leaned back in her chair, her dark eyes like laser beams— pointed and unrelenting.

"Alight, I will." Alex chuckled softly at her friend's insistence. She explained everything that had happened the night of the welcome party.

"So, you have no idea who the stranger is who stole your necklace?"

Alex sighed heavily and shook her head. "I'm afraid not. I gave the police all the information I could think of, but they didn't give me much hope that they would find anything."

"This is ridiculous. And stolen off your neck in plain view."

Alex nodded. "I'm afraid that's true. It was after that happened that Sam acted a little more protective of me."

"Well, I'll bet he was. I'm not surprised. Since learning this little bit of news, I must say I'm feeling a little protective of you right now too," her friend sputtered out the words.

"I'll be fine, Becca. I'm okay." Alex ran a finger across the top of her mug. The nervous pinch in her stomach belied her confident words.

"Alex, I can't help it. I'm worried about you." Becca Featherstone stared across the table.

A crease had deepened between her friend's brows as they talked.

Alex ran a finger along the edge of her coffee mug, deep in thought. "I know you're worried. I have to admit, ever since my necklace was stolen, I've had a lot of sleepless nights. I still can't believe it's gone."

Alex sighed heavily.

Her best friend shook her head. "It shocks me that something like this could happen anywhere on our peaceful island."

"I agree. But I keep wondering, does someone on the island want only the necklace, or do they also intend to scare me away from my search into my parents' deaths?"

Becca gripped her mug with both hands. Her voice shook as she whispered, "Maybe they're trying to do both."

"You might be right." Alex nodded and swallowed back fear that tried to consume her.

"Alex, I don't think you should handle this on your own." Becca sighed. "Talk to Sam. Make a plan on how you'll work together on this, promise me?"

"I promise, Becca."

Alex looked at her watch, noting that she still had details to organize and phone calls to make.

"Sorry, I need to run. I'll see you in a few days for the book club." Alex stood to her feet.

Becca followed and squeezed her in a tight embrace. "Sounds good. I'll see you then. And, Alex?"

She turned, waiting in silence for her friend.

"Keep me updated on your progress with the necklace and your search. And remember to tell me if you get into trouble." Becca made the sign of the cross, a hint of her Catholic upbringing. "I mean it."

"Okay, my friend."

Alex grinned as she walked to the front door. Becca followed and, just as she opened the door, she leaned close whispering, "Oh, and don't forget — I also want to hear all the details between you and Sam. You two will be working closely together, so you never know what will happen."

Alex released a slow breath. "There is nothing going on."

"So, you say, right now. But if anything changes, tell me, alright?"

Alex sighed. "Sure, Becca."

With a quick wave to her friend, Alex got on her bicycle and rode away.

Thoughts of Sam flooded her mind — brought on by the talk with her best friend.

She wanted Sam to be her friend again, but she didn't think they were even at that point yet. He was still hurt by what happened between them years ago, she was convinced of that.

Not to mention, she had her own fears and worries.

A day didn't go by, for the past almost thirty years, where she didn't tense whenever she was in close proximity to a man.

Nightmares continued on a regular basis of the man who attacked her years ago.

Try as she might, she couldn't put it out of her mind.

But, of course, Sam didn't know anything about that. She hadn't wanted to tell him.

Alex couldn't help but wish things were different between them.

In the end, the reality was that there wasn't anything going on between her and Sam.

Most likely, there wouldn't be ever again.

Then why did her heart beat faster whenever thoughts of Sam Chadsworth swirled in her mind?

ALEX FINISHED the last of her business phone calls and sighed in relief.

She was in the process of getting details organized for the transfer of Dr. Waverly's younger patients to her clinic.

Grams' old house needed to be renovated into a children's medical clinic and ready to accept patients within the agreed time limit.

Many details had already been finished.

Alex began writing down a list of the details that had been completed.

She had her medical license. She had set up her business with an accountant. And she had set up insurance.

She was grateful that the mortgage on her condo in Boston had already been paid off by the time she sold it. Thankfully, the realtor had been able to sell it at a good price.

She was thankful for a little extra cushion in her bank account.

At least half of that money had been used to purchase

the costly medical equipment that she would need for the new clinic.

And now she would need to get the website designed and hire a receptionist and two nurses.

Alex was going to start small. If the time came when she needed to expand, she would do it at that time.

Taking out a pen, she put a checkmark by tasks she'd already completed.

The other detail she needed was the approval from the board of selectmen to operate the medical clinic as a business in the Sweet Beach Cove community.

The deadline was only a few weeks away.

The construction workers continued to create a loud racket, but from her bedroom upstairs she could still make phone calls.

Alex was grateful for that at least.

Her last phone call of the day was Sam.

"Hello, Sam? It's Alex." There was a nervous flutter in her voice. Annoyed at her own weakness, she pressed on. "Do you have time to talk?"

"Hello, Alexandra. I do have time. But it would work better if you stopped by my house. We can talk here." Sam explained further, "I'm in the middle of helping Zoe with something and it's difficult to hold the phone and talk at the same time."

Surprised, Alex replied, "Of course, Sam. I'll be there soon."

Hurrying out of her bedroom, she stopped suddenly.

She saw Dylan and Troy sanding the stairway railing and she asked, "I didn't realize you were working upstairs? It was my understanding that you were all working downstairs in the main rooms. That's where most of the renovations are needed."

Troy replied, "Jason asked us to sand the railing. But we'll be back downstairs to continue the renovation as soon as this is done."

"Oh, I didn't realize that. Thanks for letting me know." Alex scurried around the workers, thinking she would need to talk to Jason and ask why he insisted his crew do other work on the stairway.

She really didn't want more noise close to rooms where she worked upstairs. It was difficult enough to focus with all the hammering she heard downstairs every day.

Alex hurried out the door. Taking her bicycle, she began the short ride to Sam's house.

It was a sunny day, perfect for riding her bicycle. Hopefully, the exercise would help get rid of her nervous jitters.

She could hear a dog's loud bark in the back yard as she set her bike in the bicycle rack.

Knocking on the front door, she waited. After a few minutes, when no one opened the door, Alex hurried around the side of the house to the gated fence that bordered the backyard.

"Sam, are you here?" Alex rested her hands on the gate and looked around, her voice carrying on the wind.

"Milo, quiet down." She heard Sam's low voice before she saw him. He walked towards the gate, wearing brown short pants and a royal blue t-shirt.

He grinned at her as he opened the gate. "Welcome to our little oasis, Alexandra."

A brown dog rubbed against her hand as she walked beside Sam into the backyard.

Beautiful green trees and flowers grew along their fence, giving the backyard that peaceful feeling of a safe harbor.

A small trickle of water flowed from a fountain and slipped into a small stream of water that followed the path of wildflowers.

"Wow, Sam. You've created a beautiful secret garden in your own backyard." A peaceful contentment flooded Alex. She came to a stop looking around the colorful sanctuary.

"Thanks, we love to spend time out here. Don't we, Zoe?" Sam's smile widened as he turned to his young daughter.

Zoe turned from her drawing and exclaimed, "Dr. Alex, you're here. Let me show you what I drew."

Her heart flooded with warmth at the eight-year old's eager response. Walking towards Zoe, Alex replied, "I would love to see what you drew."

Bending down into a crouched position near the little girl, Alex looked over to where her finger pointed at the easel that stood on sturdy wood legs.

On the canvas, Zoe had painted the water fountain and the trickling stream surrounded by flowers and green shrubs. A broad expanse of blue sky seemed to reach its long arms to embrace the secret garden.

In the painting, her dad and their furry dog stood like guards watching over the land.

"This is so beautiful, Zoe." Alex turned to look at the

little girl and whispered, "I didn't realize you were an artist."

Zoe beamed over at her. "Thanks, Dr. Alex. My dad's been teaching me how to draw and paint."

Alex turned to look over at Sam, who was studying her intently. Turning back to Zoe, Alex whispered, "When your dad and I were kids, we went to school together. Sometimes, at lunch time, he would show me his drawings. Some were funny sketches of people and others were beautiful drawings of different places on the island. Your dad is a very talented artist, just like you are."

"Thanks, Alexandra." Sam smiled. "I remember you used to whittle faces of animals and people on wood. Do you still do that?"

Alex nodded. "Yes. Being a doctor, I'm comfortable wielding a knife and trying to carve things. It helps me relax."

"Wasn't it your grandfather who taught you how to do that?" Sam asked.

Alex grinned. "I wanted to spend time with Gramps so badly, that I decided to learn what he was good at. Whittling on wood."

"What is whiting, dad?" Zoe asked.

Sam chuckled. "It's Whitt-ling, Zoe. Sound it out, pumpkin."

Zoe tried again, "Whitt-ling."

The eight-year old still stuttered over the long word, but she was getting it.

"Whittling is taking a piece of wood and carving something from it."

Zoey shifted her head to the side, a curious expression in her eyes. "Like what?"

"Like an animal, a person's face, or another type of object," Sam explained to his daughter.

"Hmm, that sounds like fun. I'd like to learn to do that," Zoey suggested.

Alex thought about it. "If your dad is alright with it, I could begin to teach you how to whittle, Zoe."

Sam grimaced. "Well, if Dr. Alex is by your side when you learn, I think that would be okay."

"Thanks, dad. And thanks, Dr. Alex." Zoe grinned. "Dad, you didn't tell me that you two went to school together." Zoe turned to her dad with a smile hovering on her lips.

"Well, now you know," Sam replied with a grin.

"I want to hear more stories," Zoe pushed as only an adorable little girl could.

Sam shook his head. "Some other time, Zoe. Right now, I think it's time for you to call your grandmother. Remember you said you'd call her back later today."

"You're right, I did. Okay, I'll go call Grams. See you later, Dr. Alex," Zoe stood to her feet and quickly hugged her.

"See you later, Zoe. Thanks for showing me your painting," Alex replied, standing to her feet.

"Come back again and I'll let you see another one." Zoe grinned.

Alex nodded. "I'd like that."

The little girl waved quickly before running inside the house.

"Your daughter is a whirlwind." Alex smiled and peered over at Sam.

He nodded quickly. "That she is."

"It's pretty great that she spends time talking with her grandmother. Growing up, I appreciated any chance to talk with Grams. She had a lot of advice to offer when I needed it most. I hope it's the same for Zoe," Alex commented.

"It is good that my daughter talks with her grandmother. My mother has struggled with depression ever since my father left, so I think Zoe cheers her up." Sam ran a hand through his hair, a crease forming between his brows. "Anyway, you didn't come here to talk about Zoe or my mom. Let's head over to the patio table to talk. I need to get you out of the sun."

A warmth flooded Alex at his continued concern for her. Maybe that was one of the reasons she trusted Sam so much.

She followed him as he led the way to two cushioned chairs that were next to a wooden patio table.

A large umbrella hovered over the table, shading the two of them from the heat of the sun.

Sliding down onto the cushioned chair, she turned to Sam. "Thanks, Sam. It does feel a little cooler in the shade."

"I'm glad. Tell me what's going on?" He leaned his elbows on the table, his dark eyes probing as he studied her.

She shifted in the chair, feeling the heat of his gaze.

CHAPTER EIGHT

am

SAM'S EYES lingered on Alexandra's beautiful face, enjoying the view.

He had always thought she was captivating, even back in high school.

Her expressive, blue eyes were framed by wavy, blond hair and dark brown eyebrows. Her nose had always been small and straight with a little upturn at the end, which only added to her appeal.

Full lips rested under her delicate nose.

He remembered their sweetness.

Would he have the chance to hold her in his arms and kiss her like he'd done many years ago?

"Sam?"

"I'm sorry, Alex. I was distracted. What did you say?" Heat rushed up his neck to his cheeks.

Sam leaned back in his chair and rubbed the back of his neck in a nervous gesture. What was he doing thinking about Alex in that way? He forced those emotions downward, hoping they wouldn't suddenly erupt again and surprise him.

"I was saying, we should make a plan as to how we'll search for more information about my parent's deaths." Alex studied him, confusion evident in her eyes. "And my stolen necklace as well."

"That's a good idea." He nodded, then asked, "Have you heard anything more from the police?"

Alex sighed heavily. "Detective Sullivan is supposed to call me back sometime today with more information. So, I guess we'll see if they've found anything."

"Sounds good. Well then, let's focus on what steps we should take to find answers to your parents' deaths years ago." Sam hoped Alex's search wouldn't lead to answers that would bring more trouble for Alex or her sisters.

Clearing his throat, he asked, "Where do you think we should begin?"

Alex tucked a strand of hair behind one ear. Throughout their childhood, it was a familiar gesture that meant she was nervous about something.

"I was thinking it might be a good idea if we could start talking with some of the older folks on the island who might know more about what happened back then," she explained.

"That's a good idea. We should start where the older islanders usually get together," he suggested.

"My thoughts exactly. My friend Becca told me the book club meets weekly at her cafe, *Beans With Books.* They meet at seven on Tuesday evenings. We could join them this coming Tuesday."

"A book club? I don't normally do that sort of thing." Sam sighed, it was a crazy idea. "But I guess I'll go. Who knows what we'll find?"

Alex's smile widened as he agreed to her plan.

"Thanks, Sam. I think we'll be surprised by what we learn. Folks often love to talk about memories they have of days gone by. So, who knows what we'll find out?" Alex shrugged. "Maybe sometime later, after we've talked with folks at the book club, we can go to Mrs. O'Conner's new shop, *Yarn Around the Cove.* What do you think?"

Sam didn't want to go to all these places and talk with so many people. He was an introvert after all. Crowded places made him uncomfortable.

But the hopeful look in those beautiful blue eyes forced him to smile and agree. "Of course, Alex. We'll go and see what we learn. Maybe we should put together a list of questions."

Alex nodded. She was about to reply, when the loud ringing of her phone interrupted them.

Hurriedly, Alex answered, "Hello?"

She took a deep breath. "Detective Sullivan, it's good to hear from you. Do you have any news about the identity of the thief?"

Alex clicked the button to turn on the speakerphone.

The two of them listened intently to what the detective had to say.

"No, I'm sorry, Alex. We questioned several people

who were at your sister's house that night. They were all dead ends. We tried, but we haven't been able to ferret out the person who stole your necklace." Detective Sullivan sighed. "And we did a search of your sister's backyard. We didn't find anything there to help us. I'm sorry, Alex. I know that's not the news you were hoping to hear."

Sam observed her closely and saw her shoulders sag in response to the detective's words.

"I'm sure you did your best. Thanks for trying, Detective."

"You're welcome. However, if you learn anything new, give me a call."

Alex nodded. "I will. Thanks."

Her hand shook, and she hung up the phone and slipped it into her pocket.

"I can't believe the police didn't find anything." A sheen of moisture glistened in her blue eyes.

"Maybe they didn't have much evidence to go on," Sam suggested. "I think we should search Lizzie's backyard ourselves. It's possible the police missed something."

"That's a good idea. We should do that." Alex nodded silently. Suddenly, she stood to her feet. "But, right now, I should go. Thanks for talking with me, Sam."

Alex started walking quickly towards the garden gate.

Sam stood to his feet. He remembered how important that necklace was to her. She wore it all the time during their school years together.

Losing that angel necklace was sucking the life out of her.

He hurried after her. "Alex, don't go. We need to talk about this."

She stopped and turned towards him.

A few stray tears trailed down her cheeks.

He stepped closer.

With a hoarse voice, she whispered, "There isn't anything else to say. The police didn't find my necklace — or the person who stole it."

Sam's chest clenched with an undefined ache. "I'm so sorry, Alex."

He stepped closer and with one hand gently wiped the tears away from her cheeks.

"I remember you telling me years ago how your parents gave that necklace as a birthday gift. You called it your warrior angel necklace. You told me, when you wore it around your neck, you felt safe. You said the necklace gave you strength to be brave." He looked deeply into her upturned face.

"It's true. But, now with the loss of my heirloom I can't but feel like I've lost my parents and twin sister all over again." She reached up to touch her bare-skinned neck. Her voice cracked as she whispered, "And I'm afraid I no longer believe I'm brave."

"I'm sorry, Alexandra." He pulled her into his arms and held her close to his heart. She clung to him as sobs shook her shoulders.

It was difficult for Sam to believe that after all these years, he was finally holding this woman in his arms.

He leaned his cheek against the softness of her blond hair.

When she finally quieted, he whispered, "I know you think your warrior angel necklace is what makes you brave, honey. But it's not the necklace, it's you. You are brave. You have a warrior's spirit inside of you."

Alex pulled herself away from his chest.

Her big, blue eyes, like two pools, looked up. "Do you really believe that about me?"

"I really do, Alexandra. You can't help being brave — it's one of the things I admire the most about you." Sam found himself mesmerized by this woman.

With gentle hands, he pulled her closer. Her eyes widened as she looked up at him.

Her strawberry pink lips beckoned to him, and he couldn't resist.

Leaning his head down, he gently touched his lips to hers. She tasted sweet, like strawberries, and he needed more.

He pulled her closer, pressing his lips to hers, caressing her mouth more than kissing it.

Sam's emotions whirled and skidded and the blood pounded in his brain.

"Dad, are you out here?"

Sam jerked back at the sound of his daughter's voice calling his name.

Thankfully the two of them were hidden behind a large bush, located just before the garden gate.

Hurriedly, he loosened his arms from around her and stepped back.

A soft gasp escaped her lips.

"Alexandra, I don't know what I was thinking. I'm sorry," Sam whispered. When his daughter called his name again, he turned to look towards the house. "I'm coming, Zoe."

Turning back to her, Sam whispered in a shaky voice, "I shouldn't have kissed you. Forgive me. It won't happen again."

Alex simply nodded, her expression unreadable.

Finally, she whispered, "Your daughter needs you. And I must be going." As her gaze met his, he noticed a sadness in her big, blue eyes. "See you later, Sam."

Turning, she opened the garden gate and hurried away.

As he walked back towards the house where Zoe waited, a mixture of emotions flooded him.

Regret. Worry. Fear.

He regretted allowing his emotions to sway him. Memories of being rejected by Alex years ago flooded his thoughts.

No, he couldn't allow his heart to be vulnerable a second time.

His belly tightened into a knot.

Panic rioted inside him at the thought of being on the receiving end of another broken heart.

He was convinced he wouldn't be able to survive it a second time.

BECCA, *I'm so confused about my feelings for Sam.*

Alex texted her best friend later that evening.

She lay down on her bed, glad all the noise from the construction builders was gone.

Now she could focus again.

Only a short time later, Becca's reply appeared on her phone.

Spill it. What happened between you two?

Alex explained that when she was talking with Sam at his place, Detective Sullivan called telling her the police search didn't find anything.

I was devastated by the news. As you know, that pendant is more than simply a necklace to me. It's my most valuable treasure and keepsake.

Becca immediately replied. *I know. Until recently, I don't ever remember seeing you without it. Tell me what happened.*

She sighed remembering her promise to tell Becca if there was anything new that happened between her and Sam.

After that, I began to tear up. I started to walk away, so I wouldn't cry all over Sam. He asked me to stay and told me he realized how important that angel necklace was to me — Sam remembered I'd told him one time that wearing it made me feel brave. He said it wasn't the necklace that made me brave. That I was brave. I was surprised when he admired that most about me. Alex texted quickly, emotions bubbling up as she remembered.

Oh, my goodness. Becca replied instantly. *Did he kiss you?*

Alex paused. *Yes. To say I was shocked is an understatement. But it felt like one of those kisses that your soul can melt into. It was sweet and heartfelt, just like Sam. Only a minute later, his daughter called and Sam quickly pulled away. He apologized for kissing me, telling me it won't happen again.*

Becca quickly texted back. *I'm sure he believes that, but I have no doubt Sam will kiss you again.*

Alex hesitated, staring at her friend's bold statement.

Then she hurriedly replied. *Becca, what do you mean? He regrets kissing me.*

After a short while her friend responded.

Alex, don't you see? Sam is pulling away from you because fear is holding him back. He's afraid to let his heart be vulnerable with you again. However, Sam won't be able to get away from you. Simply because both of you are trying to solve this mystery and are forced to spend time together. So, I believe another kiss between the two of you will happen sooner than you think.

Her mind burned with the memory of Sam's kiss. He had gently gathered her into his arms and held her snugly against his chest. His kisses were sweet.

Even in remembrance she felt the intimacy of his kisses. The touch of his embrace was almost unbearable in its tenderness.

Was that why she hadn't pulled away in fear? Ever since the stranger attacked her at sixteen years of age, she'd been too afraid to let herself get close or be vulnerable with any man.

Somewhere deep inside her heart, the truth was laid bare. Alex realized she had always remembered Sam Chadsworth as a man she could trust.

He was kind. He was protective. He was safe.

She trusted him.

With the exception of that unexpected kiss, Sam had been distant with her.

Her heart hammered with the truth. With fearful clarity she realized Sam didn't trust her. She really wanted Sam to trust her again.

Finally, she texted back. *Maybe. I doubt it, Becca. I'm*

convinced that ever since I broke Sam's heart years ago, he's held himself back from me. He doesn't trust me anymore. Maybe he never will.

It didn't take long for her friend to reply. *I hear what you're saying, Alex. But I believe that as you continue to be a friend to Sam, his heart will soften towards you. He'll forgive the past and start to trust you again. You need to give it time.*

A heaviness centered in her chest.

She paused a moment before replying. *You're right. With some time spent together, perhaps he'll begin to get to know the real me. I long for Sam to trust me again like he used to, Becca. I know it'll take time. Waiting is something that's difficult for me.*

Her friend replied. *I know, but believe in you. You'll persist. I have a feeling it won't take as long as you think for Sam to begin to trust you again.*

Alex sighed. *I hope you're right.*

I am. Becca replied. *I've got to go, my friend, but keep your head up. It's going to get better. I'll see you on Tuesday, for the book club.*

See you then. Alex clicked the button and hung up the phone.

Turning out her night light, she lay back on her pillow and thought about Sam.

Regret still clung to her like splattered mud. She'd been so scared to commit to marriage to a man — even if he was her best friend.

Would Sam ever truly forgive her? Could he ever trust her again?

Just as she was beginning to doze off, suddenly, she heard a loud thump.

The sound came from the downstairs front door.

Slipping out of bed, she hurriedly put on her blue housecoat.

Flicking on the light switch on the stairwell, Alex raced down the stairs.

Was somebody at her front door?

Bracing herself, she swung open the door.

At first, she looked both ways, but couldn't see anybody around.

However, the lingering smell of stale cigarette smoke wafted up her nose.

She shivered.

The stale odor of strange smoke was somehow familiar. A rush of anxiety and fear flooded her at the bitter scent.

Why could she detect the smell of cigarette smoke?

There was only one explanation.

Somebody, who'd been smoking a cigarette recently, stood on her front porch.

Looking around once more, she saw no one.

She started to close the door when a folded piece of paper fell to the porch landing.

With a shaky hand she reached down. Opening up the letter, she read the bold writing.

Alex, I know you're back on the island. Your welcome party was quite quaint. But you need to leave this island. The necklace is just the start of what I'll take from you if you don't stop your search for answers about your past. You've been warned.

Her heartbeat accelerated.

Hurriedly, she closed the door and turned the deadbolt.

Resting her head against the back of the door, she shuddered.

The handwritten note was from the robber who stole her necklace.

Why would the robber want her to stop searching for answers about her past?

Refolding the paper with shaky hands, Alex exhaled slowly to try to slow her racing heart.

She tried her best to shake off the fear.

Despite this new threat, she couldn't give up.

There was no way that somebody was going to get away with stealing one of the few heirlooms that meant the world to her.

CHAPTER NINE

lex

THE NEXT DAY, Alex walked into the Sweet Beach Cove police station, still unsettled by the threat she'd received last night.

Last night she tossed and turned.

It seemed a good night's sleep had abandoned her ever since the night of the robbery.

Worried over this unexpected threat, she had called Detective Sullivan.

He'd asked her to stop by the station.

After the officer at the front desk checked the appointment with the detective, she was shown the way to his office.

Alex walked down the long hallway towards the detective's office.

She had just reached the door, when she heard loud voices.

A rather angry and loud conversation seemed to be coming from Sheriff Hart's office.

The male voices were so loud, she could hardly help but overhear their words.

"Dad, I'm the one who has been following your orders and doing all I can to put a stop to people nosing their way into our family problems. I did what you asked. It's not fair that Ryan should get the important tasks," a male voice said.

"Dylan, you aren't part of the police force. So, it's natural that you only get the leftover tasks."

"Shut up, Ryan."

An older male voice spoke in low tones, his words sounding firm and final, "Boys, stop arguing. Dylan, I can count on one hand the times you've followed through and finished what I asked you to do. If it seems like I give Ryan important tasks, it's because Ryan has proven he can be trusted to finish the job I give him."

There was silence for a moment before the voice continued, "Dylan, you have never shown that you are committed to doing what I tell you. All along, you've been lazy and incompetent. Why can't you be more like your brother?"

A small gasp escaped Alex at the conversation she was overhearing. It seemed that Sheriff Hart was angry at his sons. Well, one son in particular.

She was suddenly anxious to escape.

Turning, she swiftly knocked on the detective's door.

"Come in."

Hearing his words, Alex walked into his office and closed the door.

"Alex, I'm glad to see you." Detective Sullivan stood from behind his desk and walked towards her. "Did you bring that note?"

"I did." Alex nodded. Slipping her hand into her pocket, she pulled out the note. She'd tucked it inside a plastic bag.

Handing it to him, he read it again.

The detective shook his head. "Sorry you're being threatened, Alex. I'll get this note over to my team to take a closer look. We'll see if we find fingerprints or anything else that would help us uncover who wrote it."

She sighed. "That would be good. But I won't hold my breath that they'll find anything."

Detective Sullivan looked over at her, a flicker of sympathetic understanding in his eyes.

"I can understand your doubts, Alex. But I can't afford to be skeptical. It's my job to press forward until we find the answers we need."

Alex nodded. "I appreciate that, Detective. Well, thanks for everything. I should be going."

She walked to the door, but, with her hand on the doorknob, she turned, "You'll let me know if you find anything?"

"Of course."

Alex left the police station, glad that that threatening note was in the detective's hands.

As she drove away, she spotted Ryan and Dylan walking out of the police station.

The conversation she overheard earlier still rattled her. She couldn't help but feel a tiny bit of compassion for

Dylan, who seemed to get the brunt of his father's criticism.

&

"Dr. Alex, do you think we could try whittling the face of my dog Milo onto a piece of wood?" Sam's daughter had arrived on her doorstep.

She was happy to redirect her thoughts and focus on the little girl.

"Of course. That's a great idea, Zoe." Alex realized the young girl would be more motivated to work on a carving of her beloved dog.

They walked upstairs, into her spare room.

It was the room she used when she wanted to work on her wood projects.

Setting up two chairs side by side, Alex reached over and grabbed the safety gloves, small carving knives and two blocks of wood pieces.

"Zoe, do you want to draw a picture of your dog, so you have something to help you focus as you whittle?" She smiled at the little girl, who nodded with a big smile.

Giving Zoe a blank piece of paper and a pencil, it didn't take long before she drafted a beautiful likeness of her dog.

Sam's daughter was a gifted artist. Her attention to detail amazed Alex. It was definitely a gift that should be encouraged in one so young.

"That's perfect. It looks just like Milo." Alex encouraged. "Now we're ready to put on our safety gloves."

Zoe, eagerly slipped on the gloves.

Alex was grateful she had been able to find protective gloves that were for small hands.

"Alright, we'll start slow. I'll show you how to begin carving into the wood." She sent the little girl a warm smile.

The two of them sat side-by-side, while Alex's hand covered Zoe's small one. They began carving the face into the wood.

All of a sudden, Zoe asked, "Can I sit on your lap, Dr. Alex?"

Her smile widened.

"Of course." A thrill of happiness flooded Alex at the trust she saw in the little girl's eyes.

As Zoe shifted comfortably on her lap, Alex wrapped her arms around her small body.

She couldn't stop herself from pondering, what it would be like to be permanently part of Sam and Zoe's lives?

As she held the small girl in her arms, a yearning rose on the inside that only intensified.

What would it be like to have a family of her own — a place to belong, to be accepted and loved?

ALEX PARKED her car on the main street of Sweet Beach Cove, near *Beans With Books.*

Her friend's coffee and book shop was a beehive of activity.

Despite hardly sleeping last night, she was glad to be here tonight.

Alex hoped she'd be able to relax enough to enjoy the book club.

Behind her, she could hear women's voices.

Turning, she saw ladies walking towards the bookshop and cafe, with a copy of the week's book in their hands.

The book cover image was a man kissing a woman.

The novel was a romance.

Memories filled her of the other night.

Her mind burned with the memory of Sam's kiss. A shiver rippled through her body.

Sam's kisses curled her toes. Being held in his arms this time was far better than the memory of their first kiss.

It had been the summer just before their junior year of high school.

The two of them had spent the afternoon together exploring the island and then went to the beach for a picnic.

As the evening drew to a close, Sam had pulled her close and kissed her.

He had left a burning imprint on her.

Yesterday's kiss had been more breathtaking than that first time years ago.

Unbidden memories rushed in and her blood soared.

Suddenly, she looked up and spotted the man who filled her thoughts riding his bike down the street towards her.

Her sandaled feet shifted from one foot to the other as she waited.

Nervousness flooded her at seeing Sam again.

Alex rubbed her clammy hands on the sides of her jean shorts.

"Hey, Sam," her voice shook slightly as she greeted him. He slipped the bicycle tire into the wooden bike rack and slipped the chain and lock in place. "I'm glad you came."

Sam turned to her, a pensive shimmer in the shadow of his dark eyes. "Of course. Did you think I wouldn't show up?" He paused for a moment and studied her. "I promised to help you get to the bottom of this mystery."

She nodded quickly. "I remember. And I'm grateful. Thanks."

"I hope things between the two of us are alright?" His voice drifted into a hushed whisper, "Again, I'm sorry for letting things get out of hand yesterday."

Things. Sam meant he was sorry for kissing her.

She, on the other hand, wasn't sorry.

But, as she peered up into Sam's dark eyes, she could see his face was clouded with uneasiness.

He hesitated, measuring her for a moment.

She could sense his disquiet.

Maybe Becca was right after all.

"It's okay, Sam. Everything is good between us," she said softly, her eyes unwavering on his handsome face.

He spoke again, relief evident in his tone, "Good. That's really good."

She was beginning to realize there were depths to this man that she had yet to uncover.

And she was determined to uncover those depths — to learn more about who Sam really was.

A muscle clenched along his jaw. He looked into the

distance for a moment, almost like he was in another time and another place. Pain was carved into his face — she caught a glimpse — before it swiftly faded.

"Sam?" Alex asked.

"What is it?"

Little did he know, she was desperate for his help in more ways than one.

She swallowed. "I would like to ask for more of your help."

"Of course. What is it?"

Hesitant, Alex explained, "I need to tell you. Last night somebody left a threatening note by my front door."

"What did it say?" Sam asked.

"Basically, the note said I'd better stop asking questions about the necklace, or more items will be taken away from me." Alex swallowed nervously.

"Did you show it to Detective Sullivan?" Sam asked.

"I did. He's going to get his team to analyze it for fingerprints to see if they can find out who wrote it."

Sam nodded. "Good."

He rubbed a hand through his hair. "I admit I'm really worried about this, Alexandra. What if these threats don't stop?"

"I can't stop, Sam. I'm desperate for answers," her voice was firm, final. She drew a deep breath and forbade herself to tremble. "I must find out who stole my necklace and I must know what happened to my parents."

He paused, his hand rubbing the back of his neck. A crease of worry formed between his brows. "Alright then. So, what do you need help with?"

Biting her lip, she looked away for a moment. Her

emotions were high whenever she thought of her dead parents, twin sister, or her attacker.

Turning back, the words rushed out of her lips as she tried to keep fragile control over her raw emotions.

"Would you help me continue my search? I would totally understand if you wanted to stop. But the truth is, I can't stop. I'm desperate to have my necklace returned. I can't lose that pendant, Sam. My parents gave it to me. It's always been one of my best memories and my inspiration each d—day as a children's doctor."

An unwelcome blush crept into her cheeks. Faltering words burst past her lips as a flurry of worry and fear hit in full force, "I'm determined to see this through."

"Alexandra, of course I'll help." His reassuring words were just what she needed to hear.

Sam's brown eyes were gentle and contemplative as he studied her. "And I want you to be assured that you're not alone in this. I'm on your side. I'll help you."

Alex looked down quickly, as tears pricked the back of her eyes. She was embarrassed about her messy emotions.

Being all alone was the only thing she knew.

Being all alone was the only way she controlled her life.

Being all alone was the only way she knew how to survive.

To have this man — someone whom she had hurt in the past — say that he was on her side and willing to help her was incredible.

She didn't deserve it.

Blinking quickly, she swallowed back emotion and lifted her head to look over at Sam.

Two things she never allowed herself to do anymore was to be vulnerable and to be out of control.

But now she had given in to her emotions. She would have to do better in the future.

Alex's voice came out wobbly as she replied, "Thank you, Sam. Your help means the world to me."

He shrugged uncomfortably at her words of thanks.

The silence between them grew and Alex shifted on her feet.

Her head turned at the creak of the front door of the coffee shop. More people continued to enter her friend's bookshop.

Looking back at Sam, she smiled slightly.

"Well, looks like the book club will be starting soon. We should probably go inside." A few women were entering Becca's coffee and book shop. "I see more people arriving."

He nodded quickly. "Yeah, looks like it. Let's go inside. Let's see what sort of answers we can find this evening."

As they walked towards the door, Sam asked, "How did it go with Zoe today? She came home very excited to begin carving a likeness of Milo."

She chuckled. "It was fun. Your daughter has a natural talent for whittling."

Sam grinned. "She loves it. It's good for her to learn new things."

She nodded. "I'm happy to teach her. She's a quick learner."

A thoughtful expression appeared on his face, his eyes studying her with a thoughtful intensity.

"Good. I'm glad." Opening the door to *Beans With Books,* he held it open while she walked inside.

A smile formed on her face, feeling the warmth down to her toes. Sam had always been a chivalrous man. It was one of those old-style gentlemanly actions she adored about this man.

As they stepped inside, they spotted about twenty-five people already sitting at the tables. Most were sitting together talking and sipping their coffee or tea.

Sam leaned down to whisper, "I must say, I never thought I'd see the day when I'd go willingly to a book club." Sam looked around. "However, I'll admit this place does look cozy."

She smiled to herself as he spoke.

Sam had always been an introvert. Being in a crowded room was something he'd always shied away from when they were teenagers, she recalled. Being here with all these people was most likely uncomfortable for him.

While she could understand his reserved nature, it was important they were here.

Alex turned to him. "It does feel cozy. Remember, we're here to try to ask questions from folks in the community here tonight."

"Yeah, I know." There was a kind of self-sacrifice to his tone.

The tightness around his lips eased into a smile that was almost apologetic.

Alex whispered, "Cheer up. Smile and be friendly. Grams used to tell me, "You'll catch more flies with honey than with vinegar."

Sam mumbled something about hoping it wouldn't take too long.

Out of the corner of her eye, Alex spotted another dear older lady walking her way. "Alex, dear, it's wonderful that you've joined us tonight." Mrs. O'Connor used a wooden cane to help steady her as she walked towards them.

"Thanks, Mrs. O'Connor. It's good to be here." She smiled easily and turned to Sam. "You remember Sam? He decided to join me here tonight."

A slow, secret smile hovered over the older woman's lips. "Of course, I remember. Sam, I'm glad you're here. Did you bring your daughter with you?"

Sam shook his head. "No. A teenager who lives nearby often looks after Zoe when I'm gone."

"Oh, well, good. It's lovely that you're both here for the book club. Come sit at our table. It's just me, my daughter Althea, and my granddaughter, Sarah," the grandmotherly lady replied with her usual sunny cheerfulness as she led them towards a window table.

"Althea and Sarah, do you remember Alex Stafford and Sam Chadsworth? I invited them to join us." Mrs. O'Connor sat beside Sarah while both Sam and Alex sat down across the table.

"Mom, I remember Alex and Sam from our school days here on the island. It's good to see both of you again." Althea nodded towards them, her fingers fumbling with the spoon next to her coffee mug.

"It's good to see you again too, Althea." Alex smiled at her. Mrs. O'Connor's daughter had always been quiet. Her granddaughter, Sarah, was much the same way. "And, Sarah, it's nice to see you again."

"Thanks, Alex. Hello, Sam," Sarah whispered.

The older woman turned to her granddaughter, handing Sarah her purse. "Could you get us each a hot cup of coffee, my dear?"

"Of course, Grandma." Sarah hurried away.

"I hope you two don't mind reading and talking about the newest romance mystery sensation. *Safeguarded Hideaway by Sabrina Bellini* is the novel we're talking about at the book club this week."

"The book title sounds interesting. It'll be great to listen to people talk about this book that's grabbed people's hearts. I look forward to reading the book, Mrs. O'Connor." Alex turned to Sam and back to the older lady, stirring uneasily in her chair. "To be honest, we've come here for another reason as well."

"Oh, why's that, my dear?"

Alex paused for a moment. "Well, we wanted to ask folks in the community a few questions about my missing necklace and if they remember details about the weeks leading up to my parents' deaths."

Sarah returned with a tray of coffees. After setting the tray on the table, she sat down beside her grandmother.

The older lady's eyes widened. "Sounds like you will be digging deep into unsolved mysteries. But I do remember Sarah mentioned something about your necklace being stolen?"

Alex nodded. "Yes. It happened after you left the party. Do you or Sarah recall seeing anyone who looked like they were eager to see my necklace that night?"

"I don't recall seeing anybody like that," Mrs. O'Connor replied. "Do you, Sarah?"

Sarah was silent for a few moments before she spoke, "I remember Lisa Cane and Slater Williams kept glancing over at you that night, Alex. I just don't know if it was because of your necklace or what the reason was."

"Thanks, Sarah." Alex turned to Sam.

He raised one eyebrow. "Looks like we'll need to have a talk with the two of them."

"Yes, that's a good idea." Alex chewed on her lower lip. Questions quickly sifted through her thoughts. Could it have been Lisa or Slater who stole her St. Michael's pendant? What reason would either of them have to take it from her?

Sam sipped his coffee, turning to study her.

Mrs. O'Connor turned to her, her voice gentle, "Alex, you told me you wanted to talk about your parents. What do you want to know, Alex?"

Alex took a sip of coffee trying to steady her nerves. "My sisters and I are trying to understand what happened the night of the accident. Do you remember anything that seemed a little off that occurred the week before their deaths?"

Setting down her mug, she looked up at the friend of her grandmother.

"I'm trying to think back to that time." Mrs. O'Connor entwined her fingers together deep in thought. "At the start of the week I remember visiting your dear grandmother. We talked about our families. Your grandmother did tell me that when John had stopped by to talk with her the day before, he seemed noticeably distracted or even worried about something. Your grandmother was frustrated that John wouldn't talk about it."

"Hmm. I wonder what dad could have been worried about back then. It doesn't make any sense." Alex sighed heavily.

Sam shrugged. "Maybe he had an argument with someone or got some bad news."

"Maybe that was it." Alex's brows knit together, wondering what could have gone wrong.

Mrs. O'Connor went on, "There was one other thing I recall about that week. My son, Sean, wrote an article in his newspaper column that caused people to remember a long-ago tale of the pink diamond. It was your great-grandfather Captain Henry Stafford who received it as a gift from a king, if I remember correctly."

Alex nodded. "It's true. Grams wrote about Henry Stafford receiving the tiara with the pink diamond in her diary."

"Well, my son — who was an investigative reporter — pieced together a little more of the story. After some digging, he learned that Henry Stafford's ship was wrecked when they crashed the hull against some jagged stones as they neared Sweet Beach Cove." The elderly woman went on. "Sean wrote that Henry Stafford and his small crew swam to shore that day. Henry had the tiara — but it was missing an important piece — the large pink diamond."

Alex's eyes widened at this news. "I didn't hear about that. I seem to be finding out more things about my great-grandfather all the time. I knew the pink diamond was missing, but not that it was lost in the shipwreck."

"That's what my son discovered and wrote in his newspaper column. Anyways, Alex, I'm happy to share what I remember anytime. I'm sorry I don't have more to tell you." Mrs. O'Connor released a weighty sigh.

"It's okay, Mrs. O'Connor, what you've told us is helpful." She turned to Sam who was in deep thought.

"Yes, thanks," Sam commented. "Now I have more questions than answers, however."

The older woman chuckled. "Knowing the two of you, you won't stop until you've found the answers you're looking for."

Alex turned to Sam and they both grinned. "That's true. You know us well."

"I do. And if you want to keep searching for answers, you should talk to more folks in the community who might remember. You could join a whole group of crafters at our weekly quilting bee at my new shop, *Yarn Around the Cove*." The older lady suggested with a twinkle in her grey eyes.

Dorothy O'Connor continued, "We meet on Thursday evenings. A few of us ladies stitch a few quilts a year for people in the community. This year we're making memory quilts, with a goal to do that for each of the founding families — those who were some of the first to settle here in Sweet Beach Cove."

"That's a really thoughtful idea. The families will appreciate it I'm sure." Alex sighed. "Which families will be receiving these quilts?"

"Families like the Cantrells, Harts, Bellangers, the Stafford family, and a few others. We like to tie in a little piece of history with each quilt. Maybe an old black and white photo or something similar, so it recognizes the historical connection of each family to Sweet Beach

Cove," Mrs. O'Connor explained happily. "It was Sarah's idea. And I'm excited to get started. You and Sam should come and join us. My quilting and yarn shop is only two blocks down from Becca's coffee shop."

"Thanks for the invitation. Maybe we will join you, Mrs. O'Connor." Alex sighed happily.

For the next couple of hours, the group talked eagerly about the novel they were reading.

When people started to get up to leave, Alex was hoping to talk with Lisa Cane and Slater Williams, but the couple hurried away before she could reach them.

Sam turned to her, speaking softly, "I see someone I want to talk with. Be back soon."

"Sure, of course." Alex nodded.

Her gaze swept the crowd of people.

Since Sam left, Alex decided she'd mingle.

Spotting Chesmu Sagamore and his stepsister, Dr. Mika Sagamore, Alex decided this would be as good a time as any to get answers to her questions.

CHAPTER TEN

lex

ALEX WALKED TOWARDS THEM. "Chesmu and Dr. Mika, it's good to see you again."

"Dr. Alex, good to see you too," Chesmu greeted her.

His stepsister's tone of voice was cool and distant, "Dr. Stafford."

There was a teenage girl standing next to Mika.

Alex looked at the beautiful teenager. "And who is this lovely young lady?"

"This is my daughter, Choluna," Mika replied, impatience in her voice.

Alex reached for her hand in greeting. "Choluna, I'm Alex Stafford. It's nice to meet you."

Choluna offered a shy smile. "It's nice to meet you too, Dr. Stafford."

The teenager had similar coloring and wide brown eyes like Mika. It was easy to spot the resemblance between mother and daughter.

"Are you in high school, Choluna?"

The young girl nodded. "Yes, I am. I am in my senior year."

"How exciting. Then it won't be long until you graduate." Alex smiled. "Good for you."

"Thanks, Dr. Stafford. I can't wait until I'm finally done with school." Choluna sighed.

Mika interrupted, "Yes, well, you'll still have more schooling after high school. Don't forget."

A look of tired sadness passed over Choluna's features.

She sensed it was a good time to change the subject.

Alex turned to Mika. "Dr. Sagamore, thank you for organizing those documents for me to pick up at your clinic the other day."

Mika simply nodded.

Alex wanted to ask her about the other night.

"Thank you both for coming to my welcome party the other night," Alex began.

"We were happy to join you and everyone else. It was a special evening," Chesmu said.

"Thanks, it was. That's why I was surprised when the evening ended with such a terrible jolt," Alex went on.

Chesmu lifted one eyebrow. "What do you mean?"

"A stranger dressed in black — wearing a black ski mask — ran up to me and ripped the necklace from my neck." Alex reached up one hand to her bare neck. "I remember you were both still at the party minutes before

I went out to the garden. Do you remember seeing anyone in the garden who looked suspicious?"

"I'm sorry Alex. I didn't realize there was a robbery." A deep crease formed between his brows. "To answer your question, no, I didn't notice anyone suspicious — or anyone who was dressed in black from head to toe for that matter."

Alex nodded. "How about you, Dr. Sagamore?"

There was a slight hesitation in Mika Sagamore's voice. "No. I don't remember seeing anyone who looked suspicious. However, I can understand why someone would be interested in stealing your necklace."

Mika shrugged and took another sip from her glass of red wine. "That rare pink diamond would be attractive to anyone. Not to mention that it's a duplicate — albeit, much smaller — of the large pink diamond that was on the tiara brought back to Sweet Beach Cove by your great-grandfather Captain Henry Stafford."

"H—how did you know about that?" Alex stuttered, surprised.

Her lilting laugh was edged with mockery. "Oh, come on, Alex. Everyone on the island knows the tale of your great-grandfather's tiara and the pink diamond. Most islanders remember that newspaper article Sean O'Connor wrote years ago. He wrote in great detail of the late Henry Stafford's gift from the king and that valuable pink diamond. I still remember the angry stir that article caused among the folks in Sweet Beach Cove." Mika regarded her with impassive coldness.

Disconcerted, Alex masked her inner turmoil with a

forced calmness before she replied, "I didn't realize you knew the story of the tiara and the pink diamond."

"Of course I know the tale. Everybody who's lived on the island long enough knows that story. Although we've yet to see the real diamond, so it's questionable if it's even real. However, there are probably some folks who would do almost anything to get that pink diamond into their hands." Mika scoffed.

A swift shadow of anger swept over Alex. "Including you?"

It was a bold question, but she needed to know the answer.

"If that's some sort of accusation, Alex, you can save it," Mika responded sharply, abandoning all pretense. "I've already been questioned by the police and I don't need to be interrogated by you too. But, just to be clear, once and for all, I did not steal your necklace. Why would I want anything of yours?"

Her body jerked at the venom in Mika's tone. The anger this woman held against Alex all these years, caused doubt to swell inside her heart. Was Mika telling the truth? And why was she so angry at her — what had she done?

This woman fit the profile of the robber. She was slender and slightly taller than Alex. Years ago Mika used to smoke cigarettes, but Alex didn't know if that was still the case.

Her motivation was easy to figure out — she'd never liked Alex. Competition or possibly revenge might be reasons for her to steal the necklace.

However, she decided she wouldn't question Mika any

more — at least for now. Forcing herself to remain silent, she bit down hard on her lower lip.

Alex didn't want to say something she'd regret.

Chesmu jumped into the middle of the heated conversation, "Mika, I'm sure Alex is simply troubled by the fact that someone stole a very sentimental and valuable family treasure. She's simply asking questions."

Mika turned to her stepbrother and nodded curtly.

Turning back to Alex, Mika quickly said, "Sorry.

Alex nodded. "It's fine."

A worried look crossed Mika's features and her feet shifted back and forth.

Chesmu raised a questioning eyebrow as he turned towards Mika. It was obvious the two of them shared some sort of secret code with each other.

Mika sighed and, turning to look at Alex, she quickly said, "It's a school night and I need to get my daughter home. See you later."

"Nice meeting you, Dr. Alex. See you later." Choluna waved a quick goodbye and followed her mom.

Alex waved at the two of them. "Bye. See you later."

Chesmu turned to Alex. "Dr. Alex, it was nice to run into you again. I hope to see you at next week's book club."

"I'd like that. I've started doing a few shifts at the local hospital, so I'll need to check my schedule to see if I can make it." Her smile widened.

"Sure, I understand." He hesitated before asking, "Do you think your sister Julianna would be interested in the book club? I remember you introduced us at your welcome home party. Julianna said she's a writer.

Perhaps she might like to talk about books by different authors."

Alex bit her lip to hold back a grin. It seemed her sister had an admirer.

"Chesmu, Jules will be glad you thought of her joining the book club. However, she lives too far away to join us," Alex explained.

The disappointed look on his face was priceless.

However, she didn't want him to feel too discouraged.

"Jules doesn't live on the island yet, but I think she's seriously thinking of moving back. My sister comes to Sweet Beach Cove about once every couple of months for a visit. I will let her know about the book club." The man's smile widened at her explanation.

"You will? Good. Thanks, Alex." It looked like he was about to say more, but stopped himself. "I should go find my stepsister and niece. It was great to see you, Alex."

"It was good to see you as well." Alex sent him a quick wave as he started to leave.

Turning her head, she glanced around the room. There were still a lot of folks who remained in the cafe, mingling with one another.

When she spotted Sam, she stopped.

He measured her with a cool appraising look.

Sam began walking her way, a glower hovering over his features.

"What did Chesmu want? Ever since your welcome party at Lizzie's inn, that man seems to have become your shadow," Sam ripped out the words impatiently.

Why did he seem annoyed with her?

She stiffened at Sam's unexpected anger.

For a moment she was too surprised to speak.

Finally, she managed a stiff reply, "He's not my shadow. We were simply talking. I told him about the robbery and he was concerned." Alex folded her arms across her chest.

Why was he being so snappish and surly with her all of a sudden?

Sam watched out the window as Chesmu walked down the sidewalk, disappearing from sight.

"I just don't like to see him hovering. And — what if he's the guy who took your necklace?"

Was Sam serious?

"Chesmu Sagamore take my necklace? Never. First, he's too tall and he has a bulky body build. He's not slender like the person who robbed me. Second, the man is quite open and honest. He's someone who loves to give back to his community. I really don't believe he's the guy who took my necklace," Alex stated with unwavering conviction.

Sam's eyes darkened with an intensity as he studied her.

His eyes drank her up and a probing query came from him. "Are you interested in dating Chesmu? Is that why you're protecting him?"

Her lips trembled with the need to smile.

"Sam, are you serious?" She stole a glance at his face.

The corners of his mouth twisted in exasperation — a tell-tale sign Sam was completely serious.

"I'm not protecting him. But if I didn't know better, I'd think you were jealous," Alex blurted, fighting to control her swirling emotions.

Sam gave her a black, layered look. A stoic silence descended between them.

He rubbed the back of his neck and clenched his jaw tighter.

His tone was velvet, yet edged with steel as he replied, "Maybe it's better if we re-focus our efforts on the task at hand. We need to continue asking questions to solve the mystery behind your parents' deaths."

Irritation welled up inside as he smoothly avoided answering her question.

Sam glanced around the cafe, before he suddenly stopped. "I see a familiar face. Mr. George Granger is an old-timer and a former ship captain. I'd like to find out what he remembers from years ago."

Without waiting for her response, Sam spun on his heel, walking to the corner table where a much older man sat drinking coffee.

Alex stared after him for a full minute. She was puzzled by his abrupt change in mood.

Her mind spun in bewilderment.

"I'm coming." Alex hurried after Sam, her thoughts swirling with confusion.

The old man was seated at his table alone. An old-style, wooden cane was slung over the back of one of the chairs.

Sam sat down at the table across from the old man. Alex sat next to him. Alex noticed Sam was rubbing his fingers on his chin.

Why was he so angry with her?

What happened to the level headed and even tempered Sam that she had talked with only yesterday?

One way or another, Alex decided she would get to the bottom of what was going on with Sam.

"Good evening, Captain Granger." Sam reached out his hand and the older man grinned in response.

His hair was a mixture of grey and white. A wealth of smile lines crinkled his skin near corners of his blue eyes.

If memory served, wasn't George the ship owner Sam used to work for as a teenager?

He'd always been a kind man and a fixture along the island docks. As Alex peered over at him, she guessed his age to be at least eighty years old.

"Samuel Chadsworth. Good to see you." An easy going smile lifted the corners of his mouth. "How have you been? And how's your daughter?"

"Good. We're both doing well. And you?" Sam's shoulders relaxed and an easy grin formed on his lips.

Sam had an easy way of talking with his old friend.

"Can't complain. Oh, I have aches and pains in my body, but I suppose that's all part of getting older. My mind is well, so I find enjoyment from reading and being part of this book club," Mr. Granger explained with a smile.

"That's good to hear." Sam turned to Alex and back to the older man. "This is Dr. Alex Stafford. Perhaps you remember the Stafford family?"

"I remember the seven Stafford youngsters — granddaughters of William and Elizabeth Stafford. I seem to recall you were often on the beach as children. But that was many years ago. Your grandmother had her hands full taking care of seven grandchildren after that terrible tragedy with your parents. Yet, when Elizabeth would pick up fresh fish from me, she was always happy." The older man's eyes had a faraway look in them, as memories swept over him. "Nice of you both to join me."

"Thanks," Alex replied, sitting across from the older man. Sam sat beside her.

"So, you must be the new children's doctor that I've heard moved back to the island."

"I am. It's good to be back, Mr. Granger." Alex smiled and turned to Sam.

"I'm glad. It'll be good to have you back doctoring the island's children. Well, that's a real good work you're doing." The crusty old man's wrinkle lines deepened around his lips as he smiled.

"Thanks." Alex hesitated and turned to Sam, who nodded at her to continue. "But I'm also asking folks who've lived on the island years ago, if they remember anything from around the time of my parents' boating accident."

"Ah." He chuckled and shook his head. "So, you're digging into that old mystery." The captain's bushy eyebrows shot up in surprise. "Well, I can't say I blame you. I always thought the police, at that time, closed the investigation into the case much too quickly. Old Sheriff Elias Hart — the father of our current Sheriff Jerry Hart — should've taken more time with that case."

Alex nodded. "I agree. I doubt we've been told everything that happened with my parents' accident."

"I agree." Sam lowered his voice, a reminder of the

fact that not everyone would appreciate their efforts to re-open this mystery. "That's why I've decided to work with Alex. Together we'll try to ask questions from folks who might remember. We'll see if we can find answers from people who still remember what happened years ago."

"That's good. What do you want to know?" Captain Granger's smile widened in approval.

Alex paused for a moment, then asked, "Years ago, during that last week my parents were alive, do you remember anybody along the wharf or docks who seemed out of place? Someone you didn't recognize or perhaps somebody who seemed nervous about something?"

"Well, that's a tall order. But I'll think about it — see if I can recall something." The old sea captain looked out the window for a long while, lost in memories of the past.

Alex's shoulders tensed as she waited for the older man to speak.

Turning her head, she glanced at Sam.

A muscle ticked along his jawline, betraying his deep frustration with her. She didn't understand what was going on with Sam or why he was so irritated with her.

But now they need to focus on finding answers.

She worried how they would get to the truth. Everything about their search seemed so hit and miss.

Alex had always been a person who needed to be in control of the world around her.

But, the truth was, there was no way she could be in control of this search for the missing pieces surrounding her parents' deaths.

She had to face reality. They could search for answers,

but the final outcome was something she would need to let go of.

Letting go of control, was akin to facing the impossible. At least for her.

Her brows drew together in misery, leaning closer to listen as the old sea captain began to speak.

"As I was thinking back to those good 'ol days, there were a few strange details I remember."

"That's really good. We're all ears." Sam leaned closer to listen.

The older man scratched his ear and began his tale, "Well, one day I was docking my fishing boat after a long day at sea. The orange-red glow of sunset was already flooding the harbor."

He paused, then explained, "That night, as I disembarked and began tying my fishing boat to the dock, I saw Susan and Bobby Sutton talking with each other. At that time, they'd been recently married. As they continued to talk, Susan became quite upset with Bobby. Finally, she finished her angry speech and turned on her heel, hurrying away. That's when Bobby got into his motorboat, and took off across the water."

Alex thought about that. "That's interesting. But, most likely it's nothing more than a spat between a man and a woman — which is fairly normal."

"Yeah, agreed," Sam agreed. "Anything else that you recall?"

The old sea captain rubbed the whiskers on his chin, before he whispered, "Yeah, one more thing. After I finished tying up my fishing boat, I started walking along the dock headed for home. When I turned a corner, I nearly bumped into Jerry Hart. At the time, Jerry was a police officer, not the sheriff. He was in the middle of a conversation with his mother-in-law, Mrs. Florrie Cantrell-Jones."

That seemed strange. Alex turned to Sam. His eyes widened in surprise.

"I overheard a few words, but it didn't make sense to me. Jerry told Florrie — *What we need most has sunk to the bottom. We've searched and can't find it. But we know someone who does know where it is.*" It was then that Jerry's mother-in-law replied, *"Do whatever it takes to find it, Jerry. I'll make sure to leave an extra bonus for you and Linda."*

Alex turned to Sam, tucking hair behind her ears. "I wonder what they could have meant by that?"

Sam asked, "What sunk to the bottom? Did they find some sort of treasure? And why would Florrie Cantrell-Jones tell Jerry that she'd pay him extra when he found it. What was so important?"

The old captain shrugged. "I'm not sure. I think that's why I remember their conversation from that night — because it all seemed so strange."

Alex nodded. "Thanks for letting us know. We're not sure what it could mean either. Looks like Sam and I will be busy searching for answers. But thanks for your help, Mr. Granger."

"Anytime, Alex and Sam."

THE SUN WAS BEGINNING to set as Alex walked with Sam outside to the sidewalk.

She turned to him, noticing that his expression was just as closed and unreadable as before.

Alex couldn't help being overwhelmed by all the questions that now plagued her.

Sam sighed with exasperation. "After talking with Captain Granger, it seems we have more questions than answers."

"I agree," Alex whispered, her thoughts whirling with questions. "Sam, what do you make of the conversation Mr. Granger overheard that night?"

Sam shook his head silently. "Honestly, I'm not sure. Bobby Sutton and Susan's argument seems to me like a normal spat every couple has. So, I don't think we should be concerned about that."

Alex nodded. "I agree. The real compelling conversation seems to have been the one between Jerry Hart and his mother-in-law."

He ran a hand through his hair. "Yeah. I have a lot of questions. Like, what did Jerry mean when he referred to what they needed most? Is it money or jewels, or what? Then, whatever that tangible item was — it sunk to the bottom. The bottom of what?"

Alex tucked a strand of blond hair behind one ear. "Was it money that sunk to the bottom of a bank account? Or does the word sunk imply that what they're looking for is in water? If that's the case, then it might be sunk to the bottom of the ocean."

"I don't have the answers." Sam shrugged his shoulders.

Impatience cloaked Alex's words as she replied, "It's frustrating to have all these questions, but no real answers. And it's especially frustrating to try to figure out how these puzzle pieces fit into the big question I keep coming back to: How were my parents involved in what these people were searching for — and did somebody plot to get rid of them?"

Awkwardly, he cleared his throat with a pensive shimmer in his dark eyes. "I wish I knew, Alexandra. These are all questions that trouble me as well."

Sam was getting ready to pull his bicycle out from the wooden bike rack when his phone rang.

Alex could hear the panic in Sam's voice. His face turned two shades whiter then before.

Sam spoke quickly, "Give Zoe her inhaler and help her stay calm. I'll be home as fast as possible." He ended the call and spoke in hurried tones, "I have to rush home. The babysitter said Zoe's having trouble breathing."

All of Alex's medical training rushed to the surface as Sam ended the phone call.

"Come with me in my car. We'll get there faster," Alex offered and ran quickly to her car parked nearby.

Sam ran to join her.

It didn't take them long to reach Sam's home.

Alex grabbed her large blue tote bag from the back seat of her car. It was the bag where she always kept emergency medical supplies.

Sam was already racing through the front door by the time Alex got the tote bag out of the car.

As she entered the house, she saw Sam seated on the sofa beside his daughter. He was helping her sit upright so the young girl could breathe easier.

An older teenager was standing to the side, looking nervously at Zoe. Alex realized this was the babysitter.

Sam was holding Zoe's asthma inhaler to her lips and the little girl was taking deep breaths from it.

Alex ran to where they were on the sofa.

She placed her stethoscope on Zoe's chest to get a better idea of the girl's breathing.

A crease formed between her brows as she heard the shortness of breath. "We'll get you breathing easy right away, Zoe. Just relax, okay?"

She turned to Sam. "Is this Zoe's rescue inhaler?"

Sam shook his head. His voice was raw and hoarse as he replied, "No, it isn't."

Alex reached into her tote bag and pulled out an inhaler with an orange label. "A few weeks ago, I took the liberty of keeping an extra rescue inhaler with Zoe's prescription in my tote bag."

Alex flipped the lid and gave it to Sam. Quickly, he placed the inhaler between Zoe's blue lips.

After a few deep breaths, Zoe seemed to be breathing easier again.

The wheezing lessened and the little girl's lips returned to a normal pink color once again.

Alex put the stethoscope on the little girl's chest once more. "I can see you are breathing easier already, Zoe. Good girl. You're doing well. Just relax and continue to breathe deeply. You're going to be alright."

From years of experience as a medical doctor, she spoke in calm, soothing tones. She found it helped all of her patients to calm down and it lessened their fears.

Alex turned to the babysitter. "Do you remember any

different smells or scents that Zoe might have come across this evening? It might have an effect on her asthma condition."

The blond haired girl took a minute to remember and then shook her head. "I don't think so. But someone rang the doorbell and left an envelope."

Sam frowned. "So, someone just showed up at the door and left a note?"

She cleared her throat and explained, "I didn't see anyone there. Whoever the stranger was, they left quickly. But they left a note for Sam."

Alex turned wide eyes to Sam, who frowned. "Where is this note?"

"It's on the countertop, near the other notes and papers," the babysitter explained.

"Thanks, Clarice, for letting us know what happened. I'm grateful to you for taking care of Zoe tonight. I'll let you know how she's doing." Sam handed her payment for babysitting his daughter.

Then, he grabbed the envelope with the note from the countertop. Opening it, his brows creased together as he read it.

When he looked over at Alexandra, she thought she detected a glimmer of fear in his eyes.

With a swift glance at Zoe, Alex saw she was fast asleep.

She walked closer to Sam and whispered, "your daughter is breathing normally again, Sam." Alex spoke in low tones so as not to wake Zoe from her sleep.

Sam released a long sigh of relief. "Thanks, Alex. I'm so relieved to hear that. You have no idea."

They both turned to look at his daughter. Milo lay on the floor beside Zoe, keeping watch.

"She's resting now. You should try to rest too. A short nap will do wonders for you. See you later, Sam." Alex waved and was about to leave his house, when Sam turned to her.

"Alex, wait. I'd like to talk to you outside." They walked out onto the front porch and Sam closed the door behind them.

Shifting her weight from one foot to the other, she waited for Sam to speak.

CHAPTER ELEVEN

PAIN SQUEEZED Sam's heart as he remembered what almost happened to his daughter.

A wave of thankfulness swept over him.

He had watched Dr. Alexandra Stafford quickly respond to give his daughter the medical care she needed. She was a dedicated and compassionate doctor.

He was in her debt.

Turning, he stared into her big blue eyes.

His heart thudded, full of the words he needed to say.

"I almost lost my daughter tonight. But I didn't because you were there. You saved her life, Alexandra." Sam's voice cracked with emotion. "I am deeply grateful to you for staying up all night at the hospital to help her.

The words, thank you, don't seem like they're enough, but from the bottom of my heart, thank you."

His hands trembled at his sides as pain swept over him.

"Sam, it's okay. And, you're welcome." Alex reached for his hand and held it with her own. "I am glad I was there to help. No thanks are necessary. It's my job to take action quickly whenever someone is in need of medical help."

"I know. You are a very good doctor, Alexandra," he admitted. His heart was taking him through a haze of feelings and desires that were new to him.

Nervously, she bit her lip. "Thanks, Sam. It means a lot to hear you say that. I'm grateful for your trust in me."

He swallowed and ran a hand through his dark hair.

Her words filled him with regret and guilt.

To his regret, he hadn't allowed himself to trust Alex again. His pain and heartache from their breakup years ago had stopped him from allowing her to get too close.

Something clicked in his mind and heart.

This woman had just saved the life of his daughter.

The undeniable truth was that he was beginning to trust her.

The thought barely crossed his mind before another followed.

Watching her talking with Chesmu Sagamore yesterday had ignited flames of jealousy.

In that moment, a terrifying realization washed over him.

He was very afraid he was beginning to fall in love with Alex all over again.

Now what was he going to do?

His voice shook a little as he said in low tones, "I also

wanted to apologize for being frustrated with you yesterday. I shouldn't have accused you of protecting Chesmu. You were simply being who you are — a good friend. I'm sorry for misjudging you, Alexandra."

She stared up at him baffled, a puzzled look on her face. "Thank you, Sam. I appreciate that. But I'm curious. What brought about this change of opinion towards me?"

Sam fought to control his swirling emotions. "I think I finally realized tonight — when you worked tirelessly to save my daughter's life — you are someone who is a good friend. And I hope I can return the favor and be as good a friend to you, as you've been to me."

A wide smile, like sunlight, raised her lips. Her blue eyes turned bright.

"Thanks, Sam. That means a lot." Alex smiled wide.

She noticed he carried the note in his hand. "Did you get bad news?"

He nodded. "It's another threat."

Alex inhaled quickly. "May I read it?"

Sam handed her the handwritten note.

Alex gripped the paper with shaky hands as she read out loud, *"Sam, stop helping Alex Stafford search for answers. You don't understand the can of worms you've opened... or the trouble that awaits you if you don't stop. This is your only warning."*

"Oh, Sam, I'm sorry. This is all my fault. Now you're being threatened because you're helping me. I think it's time you stop. I wouldn't be able to live with myself if something terrible happened to you or your daughter." Alex's hand shook as she handed the letter back to him.

Sam folded his arms in front of him and his eyes darkened.

He could feel new determination rising inside him. "Don't worry about me or Zoe. And I want you to know I won't stop helping you, Alexandra."

He lifted the letter up with his hand and shook it. "And this — this threat just means that whoever is trying to stop you is scared you'll find out the truth. And we will, I'm confident of that."

Alex replied in a shaky voice, "I don't know what to say. I'm grateful to you, Sam."

He smiled and ran a hand through his hair. "You're welcome. But you look tired, Alexandra. You should go home. Get some sleep."

"I'm on my way." Alex started to leave when she turned and hesitated. "Sam?"

"What is it?"

She bit her lip, then blurted out, "If you're serious about continuing our search, I think we should plan a time to look through Lizzie's backyard soon. I know the police were already there. But it's possible they over-looked something."

For a moment, his face clouded with uneasiness. Uneasiness crossed her face and he forced a smile in her direction.

"Of course. Tomorrow afternoon Zoe has a playdate at a friend's house. I could meet you at Lizzie's at four o'clock," Sam suggested.

"Yes, that will work. And Sam? Don't forget to pick up your bicycle that you left near Becca's coffee shop." Alex whispered a gentle reminder.

"Right. I'll do that. See you tomorrow, Alexandra."

"See you then, Sam." She waved as she hurried down the street, heading towards her home.

Sam's thoughts were busy trying to find answers as Alex left.

Someone out there had not only threatened Alex, but now they had threatened him too.

Fear ran up his spine, its spidery tentacles wrapping around his lungs.

❧

ALEX BRUSHED through her thick blond hair, letting it fall in shiny waves just past her shoulders.

Icy fear twisted around her heart as she remembered the new threat looming over her.

Setting the brush on top of her wooden dresser, she reached for the small plastic bag.

Inside she had placed the stranger's handwritten note.

Quickly, she stuffed the plastic bag into the pocket of her jeans.

Only a short time ago, she'd gotten off the phone with Detective Sullivan. The detective promised to meet her and Sam at Lizzie's place that afternoon.

The detective said he needed to see that note.

She wondered if the detective would find anything from something as simple as a handwritten note.

Alex agreed to bring it along.

Finally, she set her hair brush down.

Spotting the photo, she stopped.

Reaching out, she fingered the old picture of herself and her late twin sister Anne.

The two of them had been five years old at the time.

Memories swirled in her mind of that day long ago. Her parents had taken their daughters onto dad's boat for the afternoon.

It had been a sunny Saturday.

Dad was steering his old, thirty foot, river houseboat along the calm, blue waters of Vineyard Sound.

Annie had insisted they go to the top deck of the houseboat. They climbed the ladder and sat down on the two lounge chairs.

When their dad had originally bought the river houseboat, he had custom made layers of railing all around the top deck, to protect anybody who would venture up.

They were quite safe to enjoy the sun and the view here.

It was when they had finally settled in comfortably, that their mom called from the deck below.

"Girls, did you put on your sun hats?" Anne Stafford had always been a stickler that their family kept their bodies and skin healthy.

Alex had hurried to reach for the two hats. She tossed one to her sister and quickly pushed the other hat onto her own head.

"We're putting the sun hats on now, Mommy." Young Anne called down to their mom.

Less than a minute later, they heard steps coming up the ladder to the top deck.

Their mom's smiling face appeared. "Oh, you two. Alright, I can see you put the hats on. Good. You two look lovely." She reached down to grab something.

Only a second later, she pulled up a camera and, with a grin, said, "Smile, girls."

Their blue eyes grew wide in surprise. Leaning close together, the twins giggled.

Right at that moment was when her mother snapped the camera.

She remembered that day with vivid clarity.

Alex loved this picture of her and her twin sister.

Tracing her finger over Anne's face once more, she sighed. A familiar ache surged once again in her heart.

Alex missed her twin and her parents so much.

This was the reason why she needed to keep searching for answers.

And the reason she must reclaim her lost necklace.

Did the person who stole it, simply want it because they needed the money?

Quickly, she straightened her blue t-shirt and hurried downstairs to the front door.

The sound of hammering met her ears. Turning, she saw Jason measuring the space and Dylan and Troy pounding nails into some wood boards.

They were beginning to make a large countertop for the front reception desk and work area. It seemed like the details were progressing faster than she expected.

She stood still with her hand on the doorknob watching the men work for a moment.

Looking around, she saw the big wall had been removed. Only the two much-needed load bearing pillars remained.

The room was more spacious and somehow seemed brighter.

She could already see in her mind's eye, the children

and their parents in this waiting room as they came to visit her for their medical checkups.

It was something she looked forward to.

She couldn't help the wide smile that flooded her as she set off to Lizzie's inn.

ᏞᎬ

ALEX HURRIED to the rear door of *The Vineyard Inn.*

Slipping inside, she spotted Lizzie busy talking about the weekly menu to her new cook.

It wasn't long before Lizzie turned and saw her.

"Alex, how nice to see you. What are you doing here?" Lizzie walked over to her.

"Just wanted to let you know I'm here to do a more thorough search of your garden and your bushes. I didn't want you to be alarmed when you looked out your window and saw people in your backyard," Alex explained.

"Right. You called about looking around in the backyard. Sorry, I forgot. Of course, search wherever you need to." Lizzie grinned. "Are things going alright for you?"

"Yes. We didn't get many helpful answers at the book club, but Sam has agreed to come with me to Mrs. O'Connor's quilting club sometime soon. Maybe we'll find more answers there."

A knot of anxiety formed in her stomach. "We'll see."

"Well, someone in this community must know something, Alex. Don't give up," Lizzie encouraged. "Now go. You mustn't keep Sam waiting."

At her sister's less than subtle wink, Alex rolled her eyes. "I'm going."

Alex hurried down the back steps and into the garden area.

The red roses and purple wildflowers shimmered with drops of rain from the showers they had during the last two nights.

Heavy dew rested on crisp green grass.

Everything smelled so fresh and new from the recent rainfall.

She walked over to where the tall lilac bushes grew at the back of the garden area.

Walking around to the other side of the bushes, she spotted Sam at the far end.

He was on his knees, pulling back the plants to see if there was anything her attacker had left behind from the night of the welcome party.

"Have you found anything yet, Sam?" Alex crouched on her haunches beside him.

He pulled back from where he'd been digging in the bushes.

Sam turned, his face brightening at the sight of her.

"Not yet, I'm afraid." His gaze narrowed slightly. "But I won't accept the fact that the robber got away with stealing your pendant. There must be a way we can find out the identity of the robber."

Alex exhaled a long sigh of relief.

After receiving that threatening note last night, it felt good to have someone who was on her side.

His eyes traveled over her face, his searching gaze intense. "Are you doing okay?"

Their eyes locked and their breathing came into unison. Her heart jolted and her pulse pounded at his bold assessment of her.

Protective concern was in the warmth of his voice.

Her heart thumped uncomfortably and a knot rose in her throat. She looked down, gripping the gloves in her hands.

He was so disturbing to her in every way.

Sam reached over and gently pushed back a stray tendril of hair that covered her eyes.

"Alexandra, are you alright?" At his low whisper, she looked up and her heart lurched madly.

For some reason she couldn't explain, a longing rose inside for him to hold her close.

Heat rose from her neck to her cheeks from the intensity of his gaze.

His concern touched an empty place in her heart. Alex found that she was captured by him.

Quickly, she caught herself.

Sam had told her once before that he regretted kissing her. She couldn't let herself be swayed by her own intense emotions.

Instead, she forced herself to switch the direction of her thoughts to the matter at hand.

She cleared her throat, pretending not to be affected by him. "I'm alright, Sam.

Anxiety curled in her belly as she remembered the note from last night.

"I didn't sleep that well, thinking of the threat from last night."

His expression darkened with an unreadable emotion.

"I was expecting pushback from all the questions we are asking folks on the island. But for that person to attack both you and me and my family? No. I won't stand for it. That's going too far."

Warmth flooded her.

His protectiveness kindled feelings that she had no right to.

Sam continued, "I think that note was written by the same person who feels threatened by our search for answers."

She caught herself glancing uneasily over her shoulder.

Alex's voice drifted to a hushed whisper, "I think you're right. I just wish we knew who it was."

She shivered visibly. Panic rioted inside her.

"Come here." Sam reached over and slipped one arm around her shoulders as they sat on the grass in front of the tall lilac bush.

"Thank you, Sam." Alex settled close to him with her head on his shoulder, enjoying his care for her.

It had been years since she had a man who cared about her.

In fact, it had been since she had dated Sam years ago that there had been a man in her life whom she trusted enough to be vulnerable.

For these past almost thirty years she had dated different men, but never let them get too close.

Ever since the day she'd been attacked as a teenager, her wounded heart didn't allow her to trust men.

But somehow – here today — Sam was one man she was starting to feel safe with.

It was sadly ironic that the one man with whom she

could let down her guard — was the same man who she had hurt years ago.

❦

SAM'S HEART hammered in his chest.

Memories sifted through his mind.

He remembered holding her close the first time they kissed.

She had wound her arms around his back and he'd buried his hands in her blond hair.

Their kiss had been all he'd ever dreamed of and more.

For so long, holding Alexandra in his arms was all he had ever wanted.

Her head fit perfectly in the hollow between his shoulder and neck. The heady scent of lavender encircled her. Stray tendrils of silky, blond hair teased his cheek.

At this moment, he yearned to kiss her again.

To taste the strawberry sweetness of her lips.

However, Sam's heart still had holes. He didn't know what would happen if he offered his heart to her.

Would she reject him again?

That's why he held himself back from pursuing their relationship.

But he couldn't sit idly by and not protect her.

Just the thought of Alexandra being hurt tore at his insides.

Someone had threatened her.

Icy fear twisted around his heart.

Without conscious thought, he pulled her closer to his side.

He would do everything in his power to see that she was safe.

Sam thought about the reason they were here today. They needed to search for if there were any clues to who stole her necklace.

Her body shivered a little.

"Alexandra, tell me what's on your mind. Are you worried about the note?"

"A little, I guess." She quickly pulled her body away from him. With shaky fingers she tucked a wisp of hair behind one ear. "I just wish we could find answers to our questions, fast."

"I understand. I want that too," he whispered.

Sam found himself studying her beautiful profile.

In some ways Alexandra Stafford was a mystery to him.

She was a woman who had achieved great things. She'd spent so much of her time caring for sick children. Now she was taking steps to set up a children's medical clinic in Sweet Beach Cove.

She offered so much help and healing to others — but with her personal life he sensed she often withdrew emotionally.

Sam didn't understand her.

Her question interrupted his musings.

"So what do we need to do to move our search along faster?"

He couldn't help grinning at Alexandra's question.

She had always been a doer.

Whenever this woman set her mind on something, she always focused on reaching a solution as quickly as possible.

"Alexandra, it takes a few days to collect evidence. Then, after that, it can take a few weeks to get the evidence analyzed by the police. Hopefully, it won't take very long. But it might be a few weeks yet until we have the answers we need."

Alex nodded. "You're right. I guess I just want to find out who this person is, so I can get my necklace back."

"That's understandable. We'll get there soon. Patience." Sam looked over at her. He grinned at the look of frustration on her face.

"I know, I know." Reaching into her pocket, Alex pulled out a pair of gloves she brought with her. "So, I should stop complaining and start to help you search instead, right?"

Sam quirked an eyebrow.

A slow smile lifted the corners of his lips. "I guess so."

Alex smiled as she quickly slipped on her gloves.

Soon they were both pulling back the branches of the thick lilac bushes.

They continued to work their way down towards the end of the row of trees along Lizzie's backyard.

They were nearly to the end when Alex saw something that shimmering in the sunlight.

Reaching a gloved hand into the bush, she pulled out a gold, rectangular shaped object.

Turning to Sam, she said excitedly, "Look, Sam. I found something."

He turned from his crouched position beside her.

"What is it?" His eyes widened at the object.

Alexandra shook her head. "I'm not sure."

"It looks like the outer layer is gold."

"Yeah. And there's a lid that pops open." Alexandra opened it up. "It looks like a cigarette lighter."

"Hmm… a lighter." Alex turned it over in her hand. "Looks like there's an engraving on the other side."

"What sort of engraving?" Sam leaned over to have a closer look. "There is a picture of an ocean in front of a sandy waterfront near a beach house. To the right side I see an old-style captain's ship. That's certainly a unique design."

Alex nodded. "I wonder who it belongs to?"

Sam raised an eyebrow. "My guess? I think it's the same person who stole your necklace."

"I'll take a photo. That way we'll be reminded of what we found here today." Alex pulled the smartphone from her pocket and snapped a picture of both the front and back side of the gold lighter.

Sam was amazed that Alexandra could remain calm when they found details that might be evidence against her attacker.

"Maybe that's not all the thief left behind." Sam leaned over and reached an arm into the bushes. "Since we found a lighter in these bushes, it stands to reason that we might discover a few cigarette butts too."

"Of course. Why didn't I think of that?" Alexandra commented.

Hurriedly, Sam searched under the layers of dirt along the bottom of the lilac bushes.

After a few minutes, he found something, hidden under a layer of dirt.

Pulling his hand back, he removed dirt from two white used cigarettes. "Here they are."

Suddenly, a tall figure stepped around the corner of the end of the row of trees.

Detective Jonas Sullivan.

What was he doing here?

"Did you find something?" The detective's low voice shattered the silence.

CHAPTER TWELVE

lex

ALEX TURNED and focused on the detective.

"Detective Sullivan, I'm glad you're here." She stood to her feet. Turning to Sam, she said, "I asked the detective to meet us here."

"Of course. Good to see you, detective." Sam nodded. His expression was one of pained tolerance.

She turned to the detective and opened her gloved hand. "To answer your question, yes, we did find a couple of items. This gold lighter is one of them. And Sam found some used cigarettes hidden under the dirt."

"Hmm. That is interesting." The detective quickly pulled on his gloves and picked up the lighter and cigarette butts.

Placing the items in a plastic bag, he drew his lips in thoughtfully. "I'll have our forensics team look into it and see if they can find any DNA samples. I'm not convinced they'll find much of anything that might reveal the identity of the perpetrator, especially since the items were left outside in the rain. But we'll see."

"I understand. I look forward to hearing back if they find anything." A crease of worry formed between Alex's brows.

"I'll let you know." Detective Sullivan slipped the plastic bags into a small nylon bag he carried with him.

Turning to Alex, he asked, "So you called earlier today. Something about a threatening note?"

Alex nodded quickly. "Yes. A note was left at Sam's house.

"You were careful not to leave fingerprints when you picked it up?"

"Yes, I was. Hopefully you'll be able to get the robber's fingerprints." Alex took a deep breath. She really didn't like to think about that terrible night.

"It's possible. Did you bring the note with you?" The detective held out his hand.

Alex dug into her pocket and pulled out the plastic bag. She handed it over to him.

Detective Sullivan held up the note to get a closer look.

He read out loud. "Sam, you should stop helping Alex Stafford search for answers. You don't understand the can of worms you've opened… or the trouble that awaits you if you don't stop. This is your only warning."

A muscle twitched along his jawline. "It looks like now you've both been threatened."

"That's about it. But whoever wrote this note can threaten all they like. I won't stop asking questions until I have the answers I need." Alex's jaw clenched, her eyes slightly narrowed.

The detective chuckled softly and shook his head. "I'm not surprised, Alex. All you Stafford girls have always been forces of nature."

Alex shrugged. "I can't help it. That's how I feel."

"I know you do." Detective Sullivan's voice suddenly turned softer, "Just promise me you'll be careful, Alex. And you too, Sam. I don't like the looks of this. We really don't know how far the person who wrote this note is willing to go to sabotage either of you. They might intend to harm you both or even take your lives."

Alex sucked in a breath. Her stomach churned with anxiety and frustration.

Turning her head, she couldn't help but notice Sam's lips formed a thin line at the detective's warning.

Silence loomed between all three of them like a heavy mist.

"I'll do my best to be safe, Detective." That was the only promise she could make.

"Good. Then I have just one more question." Jonas Sullivan cleared his throat and hesitated. "Do you know of anyone who might have any reason – at all — to harm you?"

Biting her lip, she replied in a shaky voice, "I really don't know."

She could think of some people who didn't like her — but angry enough to harm her?

It didn't seem possible.

"A few ideas come to mind," Sam's low voice interrupted her thoughts.

"Who do you think would have an agenda against Alex, Sam?" Detective Sullivan took out his smartphone and started writing some notes.

Sam glanced at her, and his expression darkened with an unreadable emotion.

"I can think of three people in the Sweet Beach Cove community who might have an agenda to steal Alex's necklace. Perhaps as a way of getting back at her." Sam's lips thinned with anger. His low voice held a steely quality.

Alex turned to Detective Sullivan, and she fought to control swirling emotions.

"Tell me." The detective continued to write notes before looking over at Sam expectantly.

Sam drew a deep breath. "First, there is Lisa Cane. Alex has known Lisa since middle grade school. I recall some things Lisa used to say. Whenever she talked of Alex, she seemed jealous that Alex came from a family that was well off while Lisa's family struggled to make ends meet."

"So you think it's possible Lisa Cane could have taken the necklace hoping to sell it?"

Sam nodded curtly. "That's my guess."

"Hmm. Who are the other two people?"

Alex swallowed. Who was he going to mention next?

"Slater Williams," Sam continued with resolve. "Slater dated Alex during her sophomore year and took her to the homecoming dance. He was angry when Alex broke up with him right after that. It's possible he might still hold a grudge."

"You think Slater took the necklace to get Alex to notice him again or to get back at her?" The detective continued to write notes.

"It seems possible." Sam studiously avoided looking at her.

"The last person that comes to mind is Dr. Mika Sagamore." Sam sighed in exasperation. "Mika never did like Alex. There was no reason for the dislike that made sense to any of us. During our growing up years, Mika would speak harshly about Alex. She always competed with Alex in sports or grades to try to prove she was better than Alex."

"Hmm. That is interesting." The detective studied both Sam and Alex intently for a moment. "You think Mika might have stolen the necklace to win one last round against her nemesis?"

Sam shrugged. "Maybe."

She sighed, pressing her lips together. It was annoying that Sam knew her so well. Alex had forgotten all those times she'd told him about the people that frustrated her years ago.

"You agree with this, Alex?" Detective Sullivan watched her, staring at her intently.

"I guess. I did ask Mika the other night if she took my necklace. She denied it. But perhaps she's not telling the truth." Her brows drew together in an agonized expression. "Yet, at the same time, I hope none of the people Sam mentioned took it. It's very difficult for me to believe that people I've known for years might be the very ones who took something precious to me."

"I understand." The detective wrote down more notes.

"But, in my experience as a detective, there are a good many crimes that are committed against people by folks who know them well."

"That's awful." Alex managed a shaky smile.

"It is." Detective Sullivan sighed before continuing, "We will get these items analyzed by our forensics team. And I will talk to the three people you mentioned. However, I must tell you we might not find conclusive evidence that points to the identity of the robber."

Alex nodded. "I understand. Thank you, Detective Sullivan, for doing your best."

"Glad to do it." Detective nodded at Sam and her in unison. "I'll be in touch."

As the detective walked away, Alex turned to Sam.

"I didn't realize you remembered the names of people who caused problems in my life years ago." Her voice trembled slightly.

A quiver surged through her veins at the intensity of his gaze.

"There's a lot that I remember, Alexandra." The huskiness in his voice held layers of pain.

His words aroused old fears and uncertainties.

A heavy weight of regret fell on her shoulders. "I know. I'm sorry, Sam. We should talk about what happened between us years ago."

Hurriedly, he interrupted, "We will talk sometime. But let's save that conversation for later, alright?"

She nodded, her voice drifting to a hushed whisper, "Sure. I can wait."

"Thanks." He rubbed one hand on the back of his neck.

"For now, we should figure out our next steps. Now that we've given the detective those items to analyze, we should probably make a plan to question those people. We need answers now."

"Good idea," Alex readily agreed. "Since I already talked with Mika, maybe we should ask Lisa Cane next. The restaurant where she works is near the beach. We could meet there on Saturday evening."

"Alright." Sam nodded and looked at his watch. "However, for now, I've got to get going. It's time to pick up my daughter."

They started walking towards Lizzie's house. "Of course. See you later, Sam."

Alex sighed as she watched him walk to his car.

She was grateful Sam was willing to go with her to get answers from Lisa Cane.

It seemed all the personal questions she wanted to ask Sam would need to wait for another day.

TWO WEEKS WENT by before it worked out for Sam and Alex to make the short drive to the west end of the island.

When Alex's doorbell rang, it was late Saturday afternoon.

She took one last look in the mirror.

Her blonde hair had been brushed back into a low ponytail. She wore a blue t-shirt that matched her eyes. Her black capri pants were perfect for a sunny day.

Hurrying down the stairs, she opened the front door.

Sam stood there, a slow smile forming when he saw her. His gaze roved and lazily appraised her.

As usual, he looked very handsome with his large brown eyes framed by wavy brown hair.

His white t-shirt was a sharp contrast to his tanned muscular arms. Probably from all those warm summer days spent outside with his daughter.

"You look beautiful, as always, Alexandra. Shall we get going?" He asked.

"I just need to grab my shoes. Come on in, Sam." Alex hurried over to the closet where she kept her shoe rack and pulled out her leather sandals.

"Your house looks so different now. The construction crew looks like they are almost finished with the renovations. It looks great," Sam commented as Alex slipped on her leather sandals.

Alex nodded and smiled. "Yes, I'm happy the renovations are almost done. Now that there is a large countertop with drawers and cabinets, it's beginning to look like a real children's medical clinic."

"It does. The new wood flooring is a nice touch too," Sam commented.

"Yeah. I thought so too. The room looks much larger now. This house now has a fresh design and a calm atmosphere which is what I was hoping for. All that's left now is for the construction crew to finish renovating the two bathrooms, and I also need to get my business approved by the board of selectmen." Alex tucked a stray tendril of hair behind one ear.

Sam turned to her. "You'll get approved, Alexandra.

Who would say no to something that is so helpful for folks on the island, like a children's medical clinic?"

She shrugged. "I hope you're right."

Sam walked to the door and opened it with a flourish. "Shall we get going?"

"Sounds good." Alex followed Sam to his car. "Where is your daughter today?"

Sam replied, "Her grandmother is looking after Zoe. She's happy to have a sleepover with Grams. They both love their time together. I'll pick her up tomorrow."

Soon they were driving along the narrow, winding, hilly road that led from Sweet Beach Cove to Aquinnah.

They passed through the town of Chilmark. It was neat to see the wild foliage growing along the sides of the road. Some of the greenery included grape vines.

She remembered, during her childhood years, that usually those vines didn't produce grapes. However, she wondered if someone would tend to the vines – if there wouldn't be grapes growing soon along the side of the road.

"I love being surrounded by nature. It's like a little bit of heaven," she sighed in a whisper.

SAM SMILED AT HER WORDS.

He agreed. He felt the same thing.

However, for him, it was simply being by Alex's side that was a little bit like heaven.

He was glad it worked for Alexandra to finally have the day off today. She had been working more shifts at the hospital lately and they'd had to rearrange their schedules a few times.

Sam turned to Alex, admiring the ray of sunshine shimmering on her blond hair. "I was thinking, since the weather is nice, we could park at Moshup Trail and walk along the beach."

"I'd love that."

The sun cast its bright light along the sandy beach and the nearby blue water as they arrived. The familiar sight of the trail and the beach beyond brought back memories.

Sam remembered when they used to take their bicycles and go to a few of the beaches on the island.

Together they had explored the sandy shores that were part of the up-island towns.

The two of them had laughed and played in the water together.

Did Alexandra remember how it had been between the two of them, years ago?

For Sam, their time together in their childhood were some of his best memories.

Back then he'd been desperate for a little bit of happiness.

Heaven knew he needed it. Especially since his childhood had been a mess.

Harry Chadsworth — Sam's father — left when he was ten years old and his little brother Caleb was only seven.

Without warning, their family's world had turned upside down.

Their family had been broken up — seemingly beyond repair.

His younger brother began to cling to Sam.

His mom became depressed and leaned on him for everything from that day onwards.

Cecilia Chadsworth's life had changed from married to single, without any warning.

She had gone from being active and happy to being discouraged and hopeless.

Alex turned to him. "How is your mother doing? Is she still working at the library?"

"Yeah. She loves her work. My mom is doing a lot better than she was years ago. My brother, Caleb, and his wife, Shelley, visit her from time to time. And she's always happy to see Zoe," Sam replied.

He didn't tell Alexandra that after he had sold his first software, he'd used a big portion of the money to pay off the mortgage on his mom's home or that he still helped his mother by sending money every month. Ever since his dad left them years ago, Sam had felt it his duty to help with the bills.

Sam was glad to do what he could to bring peace of mind to his mother.

"Good, I'm glad to hear your mom is well." Alex nodded and turned to look over at the blue water.

Sam walked beside her, following her gaze.

"The blue water is beautiful and calm today. It feels so peaceful. That is something that has been sorely lacking in my life ever since the night of the welcome party." Alex sighed and turned to him.

A crease of worry formed between her brows.

Sam sighed heavily. "Yeah, that was a terrible ending to a beautiful evening. I'm sorry about the stolen necklace, Alexandra. I wish I knew who was responsible. Did you hear back from Detective Sullivan about the lighter and used cigarettes we found in Lizzie's backyard?"

Alex nodded and sighed. "Yeah, he called me yesterday. He said they didn't find fingerprints on either one. However, one guy on the forensics team said the image engraved on the gold lighter looks familiar. He thought it looked similar to an old photo taken of Captain Henry Stafford's ship."

Sam turned to her in surprise. "Hmm. It's strange that your great grandfather's ship would be imprinted on that lighter. Who does the lighter belong to? And I can't help but be curious about the reason behind the engraving?"

Alex nodded. "I've been asking myself the same questions. But we'll keep searching. At some point, we'll discover more answers to our questions."

Sam continued, "I can't help but wonder why these people are so desperate to stop you?"

Alex shrugged. "I don't know. Somebody is likely hiding something. But I can tell you, my sisters and I are determined to uncover what happened to our parents years ago. Nor will I give up until I find out who stole my necklace. I must get it back."

"I understand. And I'll do whatever I can to help you. I just worry about your safety, Alexandra." Sam rubbed the back of his neck.

"I understand that, Sam. And I appreciate your concern." Alex sighed heavily. "I'm really looking forward to the day when these mysteries are finally solved."

"Yeah, that will be a relief, that's for sure." Seeing her brows creased in worry, he bumped her shoulder, offering a gentle smile. "But, let's talk about something more exciting — like your medical clinic. When do you plan on having your grand opening?"

Alex grinned. "You're right, Sam. That is a much happier subject. I would like to have my grand opening the week of my birthday. So that will be in two weeks. At the start of September."

"That's not far away. You'll have everything ready to go?"

"As far as the renovations go, Jason Harper has assured me that they'll have the work done before that date. By that time, it will only be a matter of cleaning up the place. I already have the medical equipment bought and waiting in storage. I'll be able to move it to the clinic by the opening date."

Sam asked, "Have you chosen a name for your medical clinic?"

"I'm still thinking about that. I'm not sure at this point." Her face was noncommittal, a faraway expression in her large, blue eyes.

Sam lightly grasped her hand in his and stopped.

Alex turned to him, a puzzled expression on her upturned face.

His pulse quickened at her nearness.

Sam studied her, his dark eyes intense. "Alexandra, you continue to amaze me."

Her brows squeezed together in confusion. "What do you mean?"

"I mean, despite continued attacks and threats swarming around you, you've continued to stay committed to take action towards goals that are close to your heart. You are truly an inspiration," Sam spoke softly and looked over at her.

As their eyes met, he felt a shock run through him.

Alexandra stared wordlessly at him, her large blue eyes wide. "I ah — I don't know what to say, except — thanks, Sam."

All he could think of, was that Alexandra really had no idea that the type of commitment to a cause and a determination to see things through — was rare. At least, that had been his experience among the women he knew.

Her cheeks burned with a dark pink stain.

Sam was convinced she had no idea how adorable she looked.

"Welcome," he mumbled a response — still deep in thought.

His blood soared with unbidden memories.

He looked past Alex to the shoreline — where the sandy beach met the blue waters.

She shifted on her feet.

He sensed she was uncomfortable with his praise. Perhaps she needed a reminder of happier memories they shared.

"Remember when we used to walk together along the beach?" Sam asked, hoping to bring a smile to her face.

A glow appeared in her big blue eyes. "I do. I loved how we chased through the water on those hot sunny days. I miss that."

"Who says they need to end?" A wide smile crossed his features.

Without a word, Alex stopped and pulled off her sandals.

He grinned.

She used to take off her shoes whenever they would come to the beach.

"You're right. I've missed this. Feeling the sand squishing between my toes is one of the best feelings in the world."

Sam chuckled. "I remember watching you as you used to run through the sand. You would dip your toes in the water along the shoreline." Alex turned to him, her blue eyes bright and smile wide.

"And I remember you were always hesitant to follow me into the water." Her eyes shone with a familiar gleam. "I bet you can't catch me."

Suddenly, she turned on her heel, and ran across the sand and into the rolling blue waves.

She continued walking in the water until she was up to her waist.

"Oh yeah?" Sam chuckled and hurriedly shucked off his tennis shoes and socks.

Running to the water, he grinned as Alexandra scooted deeper into the water.

Without warning, he dove under the water.

He swam until he was beside her.

All of a sudden, Sam burst up out of the water.

Alexandra gasped. "Sam, how did you —?"

"Surprised you, didn't I? I've learned a few tricks since we used to spend time together on the beach." He gently grabbed her arms.

Grinning, he whispered, "I've caught you now."

"Oh no you don't." Alexandra squirmed, trying to escape his grip.

With strong arms, Sam pulled her close until she was snug against his chest.

"Do you cry uncle?" He teased, looking down. Her big, blue eyes sparkled, mesmerizing him with their beauty.

She grimaced. "No way!"

Sam laughed out loud. "Then I'll need to see what I can do to help you see things my way."

He began to tickle her. He remembered how ticklish she was years ago.

Alexandra burst into a long fit of giggles. "Alright, alright. Uncle!"

He chuckled. Pulling her back into his arms, he looked into her beautiful face.

Sam could feel her uneven breathing as he held her close.

Leaning his cheek against the top of her damp hair, he sighed.

He whispered, his voice low and hoarse, "Alexandra, it's been much too long since I held you in my arms."

She swallowed. "It has. I've missed this."

"I have too. I adore spending time with you, Alexandra. It's so good to hear your contagious laughter once more." Sam glimpsed a softening around her eyes at his words.

Biting her lip, she hurriedly looked away.

Sam noticed she was trying to control her emotions.

Alex's voice broke slightly, "I hardly remember how to enjoy myself anymore. Laughing feels strange to my own ears. I guess it's been too long."

"That makes me sad," Sam whispered. "I can't help but believe something must have happened in the past to steal the laughter from your life." His dark eyes studied hers solemnly.

She swallowed. The truth of his words battering her shattered emotions like a sledgehammer. "If you ever want to talk about it, I'm here. I hope you know you can share anything with me, Alexandra."

With gentle fingers, he pushed back a tendril of damp blond hair.

Her blue eyes misted as she stared up at him.

"Maybe," her low whisper — a half promise.

He moved his hands to cradle each side of her lovely face.

"You can trust me, Alexandra."

His gaze moved from her wide blue eyes, downwards to her soft pink lips.

Sam was captivated.

Without thinking, his mouth came coaxingly down on hers. He kissed her hungrily — like a man starving for his last meal.

He moved his lips over hers, devouring its softness.

For Sam, it seemed as if he couldn't get enough of her sweet kisses.

ALEX SLOWLY PUT her arms around his neck, returning Sam's kisses with reckless abandon.

She was shocked at her own eager response to the touch of his lips on hers.

Shivers of delight flooded her at his touch.

Blood pounded in her brain, leapt from her heart, and made her knees tremble.

Sam's strong arms pulled her close to his heart, holding her snugly.

She relaxed, sinking into his cushioning embrace.

When was the last time she had felt safe enough to relax and enjoy herself with any man?

A flash of wild grief ripped through her over all she'd lost throughout the years.

Alex swallowed hard and blinked back tears. She buried her face against his throat, finding comfort there.

Most of her life so far had been filled with loss and loneliness.

It had been far too long since she had felt the tender strength of a man's arms around her.

It had been far too long since she'd felt safe with any man.

Now she was with Sam again — it felt like coming home.

Her clamped lips imprisoned a sob.

"Alexandra, are you alright?" Sam's warm breath whispered against the top of her head.

With a shaky voice, she whispered, "I'm okay, Sam. My emotions are raw — what with all that's been going on since I moved back to the island."

"I can understand that." Sam studied her, his dark eyes filled with compassion.

"But I will tell you that I feel like the part of me that went missing years ago — is starting to return again. You did that for me, Sam."

"I'm glad." Sam kissed her cheek. "Because I long for

the two of us to begin again, Alexandra. You and me together — just like the old days. What do you say?"

Her heart thumped erratically.

The soulful look in Sam's eyes was nearly her undoing.

Quickly, she looked down.

Her feet shifted nervously.

"Yes, Sam. We could try again," her voice cracked a little. "I'll admit I'm not very good at relationships. But I'm willing to try."

She tried her best to clamp down on her raw emotions.

He had no idea how she longed to be close to him — but fear haunted her at the same time.

He hinted that something had changed in her.

Sam referred to it as something that happened to steal the laughter from her life.

He was right — something terrible had happened to her.

Still, after all these years, she hadn't told him about being attacked by that stranger just before their junior year of high school.

It was the big secret that she'd held back from telling Sam.

For so many years, she had worried — fearful he'd discover the truth.

Alex was convinced – as soon as she told Sam the truth about the stranger's attack years ago — his good opinion of her would change.

He would see her as a soiled and ruined woman.

He would see her as a woman with whom he could no longer be friends.

He would see her as a woman too broken and no longer worthy of love.

Could she take the risk and tell him the truth of what happened years ago?

Fear squeezed her heart, coiling tighter, forcing her to catch her breath.

No. She couldn't tell him.

Not yet.

She would wait.

Alex looked up once again, stealing a glance at Sam's face.

He was so very good-looking and she reacted so strongly to him.

His dark eyes riveted her to the spot — studying her.

Something intense flared through his entrancement.

Her wildly beating heart was the only sound audible.

His warm eyes sparkled and shimmered with joy. If she didn't know better, Alex could almost believe it was appreciation she saw in his eyes — but most likely that was her imagination.

She couldn't help but be drawn by the intensity in his dark eyes. A glow of warmth flooded Alex.

Yes, there would be a better time to tell Sam all about her past — she decided.

Alex swallowed, knowing she was beginning to fall for him. Was it wise? She might only have her heart broken in the end.

"I'm glad, Alexandra. This will be a new beginning for us." Sam grinned and gently pulled her close.

His kiss was as light and tender as a summer breeze before he released her.

She smiled up at him.

As they walked out of the water, Alex couldn't help but dread the day when the approval and appreciation he had for her now would no longer shine in Sam's eyes.

It would be the same day that Sam would realize that she wasn't worthy of his acceptance and love.

A heavy thud — like a piece of lead — seemed to drop to the bottom of her belly at that thought.

Her legs trembled and her feet stumbled a little as they continued walking on the beach.

CHAPTER THIRTEEN

lex

"I THINK SHE FINALLY SPOTTED US," Alex whispered to Sam as Lisa Cane began walking towards their table.

Only a few hours after their fun on the beach, they sat at a table at one of the new cafes on this part of the island.

The *Comfy Cove Cafe* lived up to its name as one of the most comfortable restaurants to relax and enjoy a meal along the island cove.

From their corner table, they enjoyed the view of the historic Gay Head lighthouse in the distance.

Originally built in the year seventeen hundred and ninety-nine, it was the first lighthouse constructed on Martha's Vineyard.

The goal for building the lighthouse, at the time, was to help safe passage for ships as they sailed through the hazards of Vineyard Sound between the Gay Head clay cliffs and the Elizabeth Islands.

It was inspiring to see the lighthouse still standing strong after all these years.

In a way, the lighthouse reminded Alex that some things that shone a light on a person's path were meant to stay faithful and strong — even through the storms.

Perhaps her relationship with Sam was like that.

Could the two of them make it through the storms they faced now and were still to come?

"So, you decided to check out the new cafe." Her wandering thoughts were interrupted as Lisa arrived at their table.

Her black hair was tied back in a low ponytail and she wore an apron around her slender waist.

Lisa Cane had been her friend since grade school. Sure, there had been many times they'd argued, but they had always made up and were friends again.

Seeing Lisa's easy-going smile caused Alex to doubt the wisdom of her and Sam's idea to ask her friend questions.

"The cafe looks great, Lisa. Do you enjoy working here?"

Lisa shrugged her shoulders carelessly. "The extra money helps pay the bills."

Lisa glanced back and forth between the two of them, her eyes finally landing on Alex. "So, what can I get for you?"

"I'll have a coffee and a plate of your homemade fries." Alex looked over at Sam. "We can share the fries if you like?"

Sam grinned. "Sure. And make that, two coffees."

Lisa's pen was busy writing their order. "I'll be right back."

"Wait just a moment, please, Lisa." The words rushed out and Lisa turned to her. "If you could spare a few minutes, we'd like to talk to you."

A crease formed between Lisa's brows. "What is this about?"

"Sam and I want to ask you about what or who you spoke with on the night of the welcome party at my sister Lizzie's house," Alex explained.

"Why?"

Alex released a heavy sigh. "My necklace was stolen that night. I've been asking around — from folks who were at the party — if they saw anything unusual."

The crease between Lisa's brows deepened. "I've already answered the detective's questions a couple weeks ago."

"I know. But it would really help us out if you could spare us a few minutes too. Please?" Alex coaxed her friend.

"Oh, alright." Lisa looked around the cafe and nodded quickly. "I'll need to ask my boss if I can take a break. Be back soon."

"Sure. Thanks." Alex watched her walk away and turned back to Sam. "I have to admit, I feel weird asking Lisa all these questions. I mean, she's been my friend ever since grade school. I really don't think she would have anything to do with taking my necklace."

Sam shook his head. "Maybe not. But remember how

Lisa used to be jealous of your family's influence and money?"

Alex nodded. "I remember. But look at her now — many years have gone by since then. She's older now and more mature. I think she's changed. I don't believe Lisa had anything to do with my missing necklace."

"You might be right, Alexandra. But let's ask Lisa a few questions anyway, alright?" Sam persisted.

"Sure, we can do that. It just feels weird to have these suspicions about a friend I've known for years." Alex sighed. She had always been a very loyal person. It seemed terrible somehow to be mistrustful of her friend.

"I understand." Sam smiled. "And I admire your loyalty, Alexandra. That's a very good quality."

"Thanks, Sam." Alex turned to see Lisa walking their way.

She shifted her chair closer to the window, so Lisa could take the seat beside her.

Lisa handed them their coffees and fries before she sat down.

Turning to Alex, she asked, "I managed to get my fifteen-minute break. You said you had questions. So, what do you want to know?"

Alex shifted on the chair beside her and tucked a strand of blond hair behind one ear. "We wanted to ask what you remember about the night of the welcome party. Who did you talk to that night? And did you notice anybody who looked like their actions were out of character or perhaps someone who seemed suspicious in any way?"

Lisa toyed with the mug of hot coffee in her hand and set it on the table.

Her friend stirred restlessly.

Clearing her throat, Lisa spoke, her voice cool and detached, "Well, I came to the party with Slater Williams. We've been friends for a long time, so sometimes we attend events together."

"Of course. Go on." Alex nodded.

Lisa glanced at Sam before explaining further, "Anyways, I talked with most of the people I knew from the Sweet Beach Cove community that night. Like Ida Cantrell, her son, Ted, and his wife, Lola. I also talked with Florrie Cantrell-Jones. And, of course, Sheriff Hart, his wife, Linda, and their two sons, Ryan and Dylan. And I talked with Bobby and Susan Sutton. There were others. I can't remember everybody."

"And you stopped to talk with me." Alex grinned.

Lisa smiled. "Of course, you were the guest of honor that night, Alex. Oh, I also had a chat with Lizzie and her husband, Jonathan. And later, I spoke with Dr. Grace Waverly, Dr. Mika Sagamore, and her stepbrother Chesmu. I think that's all the people I remember from that evening."

Sam's low voice jumped into the conversation, "Since that party was to welcome Alexandra back to the island, I wanted to ask if you had conversations with people on the topic of Alex or her necklace?"

Lisa chewed on her lower lip, seemingly deep in thought.

Alex looked over at Sam, who was studying Lisa's face carefully. A crease of worry appeared on her friend's face.

"Just tell me, Lisa, it's alright. If it's criticism, I'm strong enough to handle it." Alex turned to her friend, trying to encourage her to speak.

Her dark eyes darted from Sam to Alex. She stirred uneasily in the chair before she spoke.

Awkwardly, Lisa cleared her throat. "Well, I do remember conversations with a few people that night. Ryan Hart, Mika Sagamore, and Slater Williams talked a little about Alex."

"Do you remember what they said?" Sam asked.

Something flickered far back in her eyes and she hesitated. "Well, I'll tell you, but you might not like it."

Alex swallowed hard, squaring her shoulders.

She nodded. "Go ahead, I can take it."

With a shaky voice, Lisa continued, "When I talked with Ryan, he went on and on about how annoyed he was with you, Alex. He said your search into the deaths of your parents, years ago, was causing problems for his father, the sheriff. Ryan said he wished Alex would go back to the big city where she came from."

Alex nodded. "That's no surprise. Ryan told me much the same thing that evening."

Sam nodded in agreement. "He did. Lisa, then you talked with Dr. Sagamore. What did Mika tell you?"

Lisa's expression stilled and grew serious. "Well, Mika was the one who told me there wasn't much she liked about Alex. But there was one thing that Alex had that she wouldn't mind having as her own: Alexandra's St. Michael's pendant with the pink diamond."

At Lisa's low whisper, Alex's blue eyes widened.

"Hmm, that's a new twist." Alex turned towards Sam.

"It is," Sam replied, his tone cooly disapproving. He rubbed his chin thoughtfully and was quiet for a few moments. "Did Mika say anything else?"

Alex turned to Lisa, watching the play of emotions on her friend's face.

Lisa fidgeted with the teaspoon near her mug for a moment before she answered, "Then Mika told me, 'Alex doesn't deserve a priceless heirloom like that necklace. If anyone deserves that family treasure — and didn't get what was owed her — that person is me.'"

Alex's body stiffened in surprise.

With her blue eyes wide, Alex turned to look at Sam and stared at him wordlessly.

She couldn't help but wonder what he would say to that shocking bit of news. In Alex's mind, it was starting to look like the guilty person in this robbery was Dr. Mika Sagamore.

However, in his usual casual way, Sam didn't respond to Alex's questioning look. Instead, he turned to Lisa asking for more information.

"Well, that is a surprise. We're eager to hear more," Sam spoke in even tones, encouraging Lisa to keep talking.

"Sorry, but I must disappoint you. Mika didn't say anything else." Lisa shrugged and explained, "However, as we walked away from our chat with Dr. Sagamore, Slater Williams said something that puzzled me."

"What's that?" Alex coaxed.

Lisa hurried to explain, "Slater turned to me and said he agreed with Dr. Sagamore. When I asked him why, he told me, 'Alex has always had the advantages in life — I think it's made her spoiled. I personally experienced her spoiled 'rich princess' nature, when after the homecoming dance of our sophomore year, Alex said she no longer wanted to date me. I agree with Mika when she said Alex doesn't deserve such a priceless heirloom, like that necklace."

Stunned, Alex took a sip of her coffee. Her hand shook, the mug, almost spilling the hot liquid.

Looking over at Sam, she saw the concern in his dark eyes.

Alex forced a smile. "Well, that is surprising coming from Slater. I guess this is a day full of surprises."

Sam jumped in, "Lisa, did Slater tell you anything else?"

Lisa shook her head. "No, that's all."

"Did you have conversations with anyone else about Alex or her necklace?" Sam persisted.

"No, that was it. I told you two a lot more than I said to that police detective who talked with me a few weeks ago," Lisa added.

Alex turned to Lisa. "Just one more thing, were you with someone later that evening when everyone started to leave the party?"

Lisa folded her arms across her chest.

Her tone was cool as she replied, "Alex, I think what you're really asking me is — do I have an alibi? Can I prove that someone was with me and that I didn't steal your necklace?"

Alex shrugged. "I guess that's what I'm asking."

"Yes, I have an alibi." Lisa turned her head to look at Sam and then at Alex, her anger evident. "Slater was with me the whole time — even late into the evening. You can ask him yourself."

"We will. Thanks for talking with us, Lisa." Alex forced a smile.

Sam added, "Yes, thanks for helping us out. Looks like we'll be continuing our search."

"Well, I could have told you that from the beginning." Lisa tossed her head and eyed each of them with cold triumph. "I need to get back to work. See you both later."

Abruptly, Lisa stood to her feet and walked from them.

Alex turned to Sam. "Well, I guess that answers our questions about whether Lisa took my necklace."

There was a pensive shimmer in the shadow of Sam's eyes. "Apparently Lisa has an alibi in Slater. We'll need to have a talk with him."

Alex bit her lip, deep in thought. "Yes. But it's strange that the more we talk to people, the more unanswered questions we seem to have."

"It is. There must be a piece of the puzzle we're missing." Sam sighed.

"I wish I knew what that was." Alex sighed.

Both of them were deep in thought as Sam drove her back to her place.

Sam parked the car and hurried over to her side to open the door.

Ever the gentleman, he helped her out of the car and together they walked to the front porch of the old stone cottage.

"Sam, thanks for today. Despite the fact that we didn't get the answers we were looking for, I really had a good time today with you," Alex whispered as they stood in the doorway.

"I did too." Sam folded both of her hands in his, squeezing gently. "In fact, this is the best day I've had in years. And it's all because of you, Alexandra."

"Thanks, Sam." A heady sensation flooded her with his words.

Sam leaned closer. His low whisper tickled her ears, "Come sailing with me on Friday. I want us to spend time with you on the open waters."

Alex pulled back a ways her eyes widening. "I didn't know you had a sailboat, Sam."

"When I sold the second software I created, that's when I decided it was time to get a seaworthy vessel. It's been just the escape I've needed." Sam grinned. "What do you say to sailing on Friday?"

"Sure, Sam. That sounds like fun." Her words seemed to trip over one another as she replied.

Tension from nervousness filled her.

It was a strange feeling to be beginning a relationship with Sam again.

Are you sure you want to do this? He's going to find out all your secrets. A little voice inside her head asked, trying to fill her with doubt.

Alex looked up at him, a hesitant smile on her lips.

His hands reached up to her shoulders, his dark eyes tenderly melted into hers.

A sense that she was safe with Sam filled her once more.

She hardly had time to think before Sam pulled her

close. Leaning down, he claimed her lips with a kiss as tender and light as a summer breeze.

Alex relaxed against him, drinking in the sweetness of his kiss.

After Sam left, the questions continued to force themselves into her mind.

It had been years since she'd had a relationship with a man. Ever since the day she refused Sam's proposal, she hadn't had a real relationship.

She dated men, but limited it to only one or two dates.

Alex always believed she was unable to give herself completely to any man.

Would this new beginning with Sam last the test of time?

A FEW DAYS LATER, Alex was back at *Beans With Books* for the weekly book club.

"Alex, I wanted to show you a photo of my new granddaughter, Lavinia. My daughter named her baby after her great-grandmother." Becca opened up some photos on her smartphone.

She smiled at the excitement in Becca's voice.

"That's very exciting. I'm very happy for you, Becca. Now I can officially call you Grandma." Alex chuckled, teasing her best friend.

"Well, that's one label I'm thrilled to claim as my own." Becca grinned as she slipped her phone in her pocket.

Becca stood behind the coffee bar. She was making Alex a hot latte. The book club had just finished for the evening at *Beans With Books*. People were mingling, the low hum of chatter surrounded them.

"Good. That's how it should be." Alex grinned, happy for her friend that they were welcoming the next generation of their family.

Alex couldn't help but feel a tug of longing in her heart. She still longed for a family of her own.

Even though Alex could accept she was probably too old to give birth to children, still, there was a yearning in her heart for the acceptance, and love that came when a person belonged to a family.

Becca reached over and handed her the frothy mug and asked, "Will you have time to come to the baby shower this Saturday?"

"I plan to be there, Becca," Alex replied as she took the hot latte from her friend.

"Good. It'll be fun to have the baby shower at Mrs. O'Conner's quilt and yarn shop. You'll have a chance to look at the quilts the women have been working on. They've put a lot of thought and work behind the crafts for our annual Sweet Beach Cove Quilt and Craft Day," her friend commented. "And you'll get to see the Stafford family quilt."

"There was a quilt made for our family?" Alex quirked up one eyebrow in surprise.

"Yes, but I shouldn't say too much. You'll just have to wait and see when you come to our community's annual Quilt and Craft Day. The quilts will be on display at that event." Her friend had always been good at hooking her and making her curious. "Let's talk about your sisters. I see the two of them over there, speaking with handsome men." Becca grinned.

Alex released a disappointed sigh. It looked like Becca wasn't going to reveal any secrets about the quilt.

She followed her friend's gaze and spotted her two sisters.

It was a surprise when both Jane and Jules arrived on the island for a couple days. On a whim, Lizzie, Jane, and Jules had decided to come with Alex to the book club tonight.

"Julianna is talking with Chesmu Sagamore. I think he's interested in her. He was asking about Jules last time I spoke with him. I wonder if this might be the beginning of a relationship between them?"

"Could be. Maybe that would be an incentive for Jules to move back to the island." Becca grinned.

Alex nodded, smiling. "Yeah, I think so too. And I see Jane talking with Ward Hampton. Back in her college days, Jane dated Ward for a while. But they broke it off, I'm not sure what happened. Then Jane dated another man, who treated her terribly. She's been gun-shy about dating men for years."

"I'm sorry Jane went through that. It's difficult to want to try again after you've gone through pain and heartache. You would understand that, Alex." Becca commented.

"I do understand."

At that moment, Mrs. O'Conner, Sarah, and Lizzie walked over to them.

Soon, Sam joined them, eager to chat with them.

"I couldn't help but overhear you talking about pain and heartache, Becca," Mrs. O'Conner commented. "You must be referring to the romance novel we talked about tonight. It was so awful to read about the physical and mental abuse the heroine Sabrina endured at the hands of her husband. I'm glad she ran away."

Alex didn't set the older woman straight — that they had been talking about her sisters' love lives. It would be safer with the new people who had now joined their chat, if they talked about the book instead.

"I'm glad the heroine got away safely," Lizzie spoke up. "But I'm not surprised the hero — the man the heroine dated years ago — was shocked when she showed up at his front door."

Sarah jumped into the conversation, "But I think it's so romantic that the hero takes her into his home and gives her shelter and protection."

"Still, he's not realizing all the secrets she's been hiding from him for years," Mrs. O'Connor commented. "Those secrets end up being uncovered near the end of the story. It's the secrets that cause the romance to be derailed for a short time."

Alex sucked in a quick breath as she recognized her own life in the heroine of the story.

Her eyes misted as the trauma of her past flooded into her thoughts.

A wave of anxiety swept through Alex as her eyes met Sam's dark eyes.

Sam's look of compassion was nearly her undoing.

Alex swallowed back emotion.

Her voice broke a little as she spoke, "A person doesn't really know what they would do until they live through the trauma of abuse. It can haunt you and warp how you see men — and how you see yourself. You can lose your confidence. Often your perspective changes – of people and situations around you."

Sam stared at her, a look of puzzled confusion on his face.

Heat rose to her cheeks at the intensity of his dark eyes that seemed to bore holes into her.

Did he realize she was speaking from a terrible past experience?

Her mind fluttered away in anxiety.

Fear rioted inside her.

What would Sam think of her when he found out her terrible secret? The swirling thoughts gnawed away at her confidence.

Her heart thudded.

How would Sam respond? Now that they had decided to be in a relationship. What would he say when she told him the truth?

Sarah's soft voice interrupted her silent thoughts, "But, at the end of this romance, both the hero and heroine fall in love. Despite obstacles, they get together at the end. I feel like the story has a very satisfying ending."

Alex swallowed.

She didn't think that would be her and Sam's story — especially after she revealed the truth of what happened to her years ago.

lex

"GRAMS' old stone cottage looks amazing. It's like a night and day difference in this room since the day we first walked through it weeks ago," Lizzie commented as the three sisters walked through the newly renovated main part of the house.

Alex grinned, pleased that her sisters approved. "Jason Harper and his workers still have a few more details to finish up, but other than that it's ready to go."

"It looks great. The renovations have been done beautifully. I love this large reception and sitting area. Do you have chairs and coffee tables arriving soon?" Jane asked. Her organized mind was what made her sister an in-demand wedding planner.

"Yes, I am expecting the new furniture for the clinic to

arrive soon." Alex ran a hand over the new kitchenette area in the break room.

"And what did the board of selectman say about your new medical clinic?" Lizzie asked. "I remember it took me a couple of times before I was approved."

"Well, I don't need to worry about that anymore. The board finally approved me this week. So, I'm happy to say, almost everything is good to go." Alex smiled wide.

She couldn't help but be pleased that all the details were starting to come together.

"That's great news, Alex." Lizzie grinned widely. "Sis, we're proud of you. And I have a feeling Mom and Dad would be too."

A little sigh escaped Alex as she remembered her parents.

They had been so supportive of her longing to be a doctor. But they died before seeing her reach her goal.

"Thank you, Lizzie. I've thought a lot about Mom and Dad especially since moving back to the island. I hope they would have supported me with this new project." Alex sighed.

Jane gave her a sidelong glance of disbelief. "Can you doubt it? Of course, they would support you with starting this medical clinic. And so would our sister Anne, I might add."

A wave of contentment flooded Alex at Jane's words.

"Both Gramps and Grams would be proud of you, Alex," Lizzie added. "You know our beloved grandmother longed for you to come back to the island to start a medical clinic for children."

"She did and I'm grateful. Thanks for the encouragement, Lizzie and Jane. I needed to hear that today." Her smile widened. "With all that's going on in my life, I sure wish I could glean from Grams' wisdom right about now. It would be good to have her perspective."

A thoughtful expression flooded Lizzie's features.

"I know that look, Lizzie? What do you have planned?" Alex asked, remembering that familiar contemplative gleam.

Lizzie shrugged. "Since we're in Grams' old house and thinking of our grandmother's wisdom, this might be a good time to read the next chapter from her journal."

"I'd love that, Lizzie," Jane commented.

Alex nodded. "That's a great idea. I'll grab some folding chairs and we can sit down."

Hurrying over to the storage closet, Alex brought out soft chairs and set them by the large picture window.

As they settled into the chairs, Lizzie reached into her purse and pulled out their grandmother's tattered leather journal.

"Let's read the next entry." Lizzie turned to the spot she had bookmarked.

I saw Jean Bellanger today at our community farmer's market. She shared with me how her son, Matty, had appreciated John's friendship.

"My son and your son were like two peas in a pod, Elizabeth. Where one went, so the other would follow." I couldn't help but smile. It was true. John had often talked about Matty and the fun he had with his friend.

Jean had a soft smile as she remembered her son.

Then she said, "You know, Matty used to tell me he wrote down all the interesting things he did with his friends in his journal. He started writing in it when he was only ten years old. He didn't stop writing down his thoughts until the day he died."

I told her, "That's a touching keepsake to have of your son, Jean."

"It is. I just wish I could make sense of some of the things he wrote there about his friends and families we know on the island." Jean sighed.

Lizzie paused and looked over at Jane and Alex. "I wonder what Matty wrote in his journal about the people we know?"

"I'm curious too." Jane turned to her. "Alex, maybe you should meet with old Mrs. Bellanger. She might let you read Matty's journal. You might find something that would help in our search into our parents' deaths."

Alex was thinking the same thing. However, time was an issue.

"Jane, it's a good idea, but I don't have the time right now. I might need to leave Matty's journal for you to look into. You can talk with Mrs. Bellanger. I believe she'd be happy to talk with you about her son."

Jane sighed. "I supposed I could do that. However, I have a similar problem as you — the issue of finding the time."

Alex grinned. "You'll find a way, Jane. Because I know you're as eager as I am to learn more about what happened to our parents."

"As are all of us sisters." Lizzie nodded. "Well, let's keep reading. Grams has more to say in this entry."

Later on that day, I also ran into Florrie Cantrell-Jones. I was picking up fish from Captain Granger and met her there.

I said hello to Florrie, but she was quite rude and angry. It seems she is still quite upset that my son, John, broke off his relationship with her daughter Clementine.

I remember when my son used to go to that old carriage house on the Cantrell-Jones property to pick up Florrie's daughter when they were dating.

John used to go out of his way to make Clemmie happy but, in the end, he decided that she wasn't the girl for him.

Florrie still insists that John broke Clemmie's heart and that's why, only two years after the break up, her daughter died. Rumors are that the doctor said the reason she died was heart failure — that Clementine had trouble with her heart since childhood.

But Florrie doesn't see it that way. She would rather put blame for Clemmie's death on my son, John, for breaking off his relationship with her.

Not only that, but Florrie told me again and again that it was my family's fault that her daughter died.

I'm stunned that she would place the blame on us. I wonder if Florrie will ever realize that it's not John's fault that Clemmie died?

But I'm not hopeful that I'll see that change anytime soon. If her past history is any indication, Florrie is an outspoken woman who will harbor a grudge longer than a coon's lifetime.

Alex gasped out loud. "How come we didn't hear about that from our parents? I didn't realize that our father dated Clementine Cantrell-Jones or that Florrie blamed our dad for her death."

"It's a surprise to me too." Jane shook her head and a crease formed between her brows.

Lizzie cleared her throat. "Looks like we're not done with surprises yet."

Alex's thoughts were busy with trying to remember. "You know, a few weeks ago Sam and I talked with old Captain Granger. He recalled years ago, he was returning from a fishing trip when he ran into Florrie and her son-in-law Jerry Hart, who is now the sheriff. Captain Granger overheard a little bit of their conversation, but it didn't make sense to him."

"What did he overhear?" Jane's eyebrows lifted in curiosity.

Alex recalled the words of the old ship's captain. "Jerry told Florrie — *What we need most has sunk to the bottom. We've searched and can't find it. But we know someone who does know where it is.*" Then Jerry's mother-in-law replied, "*Do whatever it takes to find it, Jerry. I'll make sure to leave an extra bonus for you and Linda.*"

"That doesn't make sense," Jane said, a puzzled expression crossed her face.

"I agree," Lizzie added.

Alex nodded. "Sam and I couldn't understand it either. Hopefully we'll find a way to get to the bottom of that mystery."

"Yeah, I hope so." Lizzie sighed heavily. "Well, let's keep reading the last portion of Grams' journal entry."

Alex leaned closer to listen as Lizzie began to read out loud.

The other day William and I were having a talk about his father, Captain Henry Stafford. He began to share more details that he remembered about his dad's life.

My husband once again surprised me.

William said, 'I haven't told you everything about my father, Elizabeth. I guess I was too ashamed. Most people see him as a hero. He's a great ship's captain and he did save the life of a princess. But there is a darker side to him.'

I asked my husband, 'You've surprised me again, William. Tell me.'

He went on to tell me news that shocked me, 'My father and mother were happily married, but, sadly, my dad strayed from his vows and had an affair. My mother told me the story after my father passed away.'

To say I was shocked is an understatement. I asked, "That must have been very difficult for your mother. What happened?"

My husband explained, "It was a year after my sister, Charlotte, died. My mother said he changed after his daughter passed away. He seemed lost somehow. Before Captain Henry Stafford died, he confessed to my mother what happened.

My dad was talking with one of the Wampanoag tribes about a new shipment, and a young woman caught his eye. Her name was Watameetoo. Anyway, my father ended up having an affair with her. And when my father returned to the tribe a year later, Watameetoo held a baby in her arms. She told my dad that the girl was his daughter. She had named her baby girl Aponi.'

I asked William what happened to Watameetoo and her daughter. He said, 'My father felt guilty and gave her a big sum of money to help care for the child. But he never went back to the tribe again. However, Aponi did have a daughter named Katari. I don't know what happened to that family. That's my family's scandalous history, Elizabeth.'

I told my husband thanks for sharing that story. I could tell it was hard on him.

After I learned about Watameetoo and her daughter Aponi, I decided to do some searching on my own. I finally found people *within the Wampanoag tribe who had the answers to my questions.*

It turns out that Katari married a man named Squanto Sagamore. Squanto brought a young son into their marriage. His name is Chesmu. A couple years later Mika was born.

To say I'm surprised by this news, is an understatement. Turns out we are related to more people on the island than we realized.

Alex stared at Lizzie, blank, amazed, and very shaken.

"Grams was right. This is a shock to all of us," her voice shook. "I can't believe us sisters are related by blood to Mika Sagamore. We aren't related to Chesmu, but we are relatives to Mika. That explains a lot."

"What do you mean, Alex?" Lizzie stammered in bewilderment.

Jane nodded. "Yes, please tell us."

She stirred uneasily in the chair. "Knowing this explains why Mika Sagamore has been angry with me ever since grade school. Her mother must have told Mika that she was related to the Stafford family. And it's possible that Mika is angry that she was never acknowledged by our family as a relative."

Lizzie commented, "Maybe that's the reason. Or perhaps her mother, Katari, felt like she was rejected and never received attention or her share in the Stafford family inheritance. And maybe Mika felt the sting of rejection too. But is there a way we can right this wrong?"

"Good question. Since Mika and her mother are our relatives, we should do something. But I don't know what?" Jane added.

Alex rubbed her forehead, her thoughts swirling at this

bit of news. "Well, first I need to try to have a conversation with Mika. She doesn't seem to like talking to me. I need an opportunity to talk with her."

"I hope you can have that talk, Alex. It would go a long way towards bringing restoration between our families." Lizzie chewed on her lower lip, deep in thought.

"I'll try. That's the most I can promise." Alex swallowed hard, managing a feeble answer.

Together they sat in silence, each of them deep in thought.

All of a sudden, the ringing of the doorbell echoed in the empty room.

"I wonder who that could be? I'm not expecting anyone." Alex hurried over to open the door.

Alex's eyebrows lifted slightly when she saw Dr. Grace Waverly standing on her front porch.

"Hello, Dr. Waverly." Alex waved her arm to show her inside the house.

"Hello, Alex. And call me Grace, my dear. Now that I'm retired, I'd feel better at hearing my name." The older woman stepped inside the large room.

"Grace, it is then. Come on in." Alex smiled warmly.

"Oh my, Alex, this room looks lovely. It's perfect for a medical clinic."

Alex grinned. "Thanks, Grace. It means a lot to hear you say that — especially coming from you."

"You remember my sisters, Lizzie and Jane?"

Grace nodded. "Of course. How nice to see you ladies again. Sorry, I didn't mean to interrupt your visit."

Alex shook her head. "You didn't really interrupt. We were just catching up on each other's lives."

"Alright, that's good." Grace held a magazine of some sort in her hand. A crease of worry formed between the older woman's brows as she looked downwards.

"Is something wrong?" Alex probed. She knew her old mentor well. The usually calm woman had been rattled by something.

"Yes, there is." The older woman's face clouded with uneasiness. "I just received my copy of *Island Stories.* I've subscribed to the magazine for years."

"Of course. Was there an interesting story in this month's issue?" Alex asked, curious about what could be worrying the dear woman.

Grace sighed. "Not so much interesting as it is troubling."

Her sisters came to stand beside her, ready to hear what she had to say.

"I don't want to be the bearer of bad tidings, but in this month's issue of Island Stories, there was a most insulting article written about you, Alex." Grace sighed heavily. "As soon as I read it, I came right over, thinking you would want to see it for yourself."

Alex frowned. "Could I see it?"

"Of course." Grace handed her the magazine.

Jane commented, "Alex, please read it out loud. We'd all like to hear what this writer has to say."

Alex nodded. "Sure. This is what it says."

In the past few weeks, we have welcomed a new member back to the island. Doctor Alex Stafford.

The middle-aged children's doctor moved back to the island from the big city of Boston.

Much like her older sister, Lizzie Stafford Wentworth, Dr.

Stafford returned home to claim her inheritance from her late grandmother, Elizabeth Stafford.

An old, stone cottage.

Alex has settled into the house and has begun renovations. Her plan? To renovate that old heap of stones into a children's medical clinic.

Even though plans are in the works for this new medical clinic, I wonder if the families in the Sweet Beach Cove community are aware of recent developments?

Dr. Stafford was given a welcome home party at her sister Lizzie's home — The Vineyard Inn. However, by the end of the evening, Alex Stafford had already stirred up a hornet's nest with her talk of searching for answers to the boating accident that took her parents' lives years ago.

Then, to make the evening more dramatic, there was a robbery.

Someone stole Alex Stafford's necklace. A gold St. Michael's pendant with a rare pink diamond.

That necklace is very valuable, so it's no surprise that someone would try to steal it.

However, it makes this writer question if the robbery of Dr. Stafford's pendant wasn't all planned to gain attention — by the owner of the necklace herself?

Since Dr. Stafford is trying to set up her medical clinic, perhaps she faked the robbery. Perhaps her real intention is to bring in more patients.

This writer believes that there might be something questionable going on with Dr. Stafford and her medical clinic.

Perhaps those of us in the Sweet Beach Cove community need to keep a close watch on what's going on with our new children's doctor. And perhaps we need to ask ourselves seriously if we really want to expose our vulnerable children to Dr. Alex Stafford and her new medical clinic?

"Oh, Alex, what an awful article." Lizzie gasped. "Who wrote this rubbish?"

A suffocating sensation tightened in Alex's throat as she looked at the author's name under the headline.

Her eyes widened. "I should have guessed. "It was written by Slater Williams. He's never like me much."

"Isn't he the guy you dated and then broke up with?" Jane asked.

Alex nodded. "Yeah. Maybe this is his way of getting revenge."

Dr. Waverly sighed heavily. "I told you, Alex, this article was insulting and underhanded. I am worried that people in our community will begin to mistrust you — and refuse to bring their children to you when they need medical help."

"I'm worried about that too, Alex," Lizzie agreed.

Jane added, "I don't know how Slater can get away with this nonsense. He's ruining your reputation, Alex."

Alex sighed heavily. "I think it's time I had a talk with Slater Williams."

"That's a good idea. Hopefully, Slater will write a retraction in the next magazine issue of Island Stories." Lizzie's mouth thinned with displeasure.

"I hope so, for your sake," Jane muttered softly, looking over at Alex.

Dr. Grace Waverly chimed in, "Maybe he will write a retraction, but I wouldn't count on it. It's a popular magazine that has a history of writing questionable stories about islanders whose opinions they don't agree with."

Grace walked to the front door and Alex followed. "I need to be going, my dear. But don't be disheartened by this article. You do have support from islanders like myself, your family, and friends. I'm looking forward to the day you open your medical clinic, Alex."

"It means a lot to hear you say that. Thanks, Grace." Alex pulled the older woman into a quick hug before she left.

As Alex closed the door, Lizzie turned to her.

"So, after the unexpected surprises today, how are you feeling?" Lizzie walked over and slipped on her shoes.

"I'm still reeling from the news written in Grams' journal. And now this latest attack — Slater's article — definitely feels like he's trying to ruin my reputation. But I'll have to push through somehow. Hopefully, I won't lose patients over this." Alex managed a tremulous smile as her eyes met Lizzie's.

"Yes, you will. You'll come through this Alex. We're here to cheer you on and support you however we can." Lizzie replied.

Jane added with a grin, "Alex, you also have Sam Chadsworth in your corner. By the way, how are things going between the two of you?"

She managed a small, tentative smile. "Sam's been helping me to search for answers to who stole my necklace. So far, we don't have any real leads, but we'll keep searching. Tomorrow, Sam is taking me sailing. I'm sure it'll be fun."

"Oh, that will be fun. It reminds me of those times when dad and mom took us out on the water in their houseboat. Those are wonderful memories." Jane sighed, her smile dreamy. "I'm happy for you, Alex."

"We both are." Lizzie hugged her and Jane followed suit. "We'll see you later, Sis."

"Sounds good." Alex closed the door after her sisters left, her thoughts swirling with memories of Sam.

His gentle words. His warm embrace. His sweet kisses.

She felt blood coursing through her veins like an awakened river.

Even though she told herself over and over again, not to get too excited over her relationship with Sam, her heart wouldn't listen.

Her heart swelled with a feeling she had thought long since dead.

She was starting to fall in love with him.

The admission was dredged from a place beyond logic and reason.

Her thoughts tumbled over one another with fearful clarity.

She was scared to fall in love with any man.

Yet she had to remind herself this was Sam. Her childhood friend. The same man who was gentle, kind, and was now going the extra mile to help her find her necklace.

She could admit that her fears were beginning to lessen when she was close to him — and her trust in him was growing.

Alex couldn't help but wonder where tomorrow's day sailing together would take them in their relationship.

CHAPTER FIFTEEN

S am

"WHAT DO you think of sailing so far?" Sam turned to Alexandra from where he stood behind the wheel of his fifty-foot Bermuda Sloop sailboat.

His father — before he left their family — had taught him and his brother to sail. That's where he developed a love for it.

It was going to be a great day — most of all because he was spending time with the woman he loved.

He was happy she had agreed to join him today. His daughter, Zoe, was over at a friend's house for a playdate this afternoon. To top it off, it was a beautiful, sunny day.

She turned to him, a slight breeze lifting a silky tendril of blond hair away from her face.

She looked beautiful.

Her royal blue t-shirt drew attention to her rosy cheeks and large, blue eyes. The white shorts contrasted nicely with her long, tanned legs.

Alexandra looked like she belonged here.

Not only on his sailboat. But also, in his life. *Forever.*

But would he be able to convince this beautiful, independent woman they were meant to be together?

She continued to hold some of herself back from him. What was she afraid of — was it him? How could he make her feel safe enough to share with him her heart?

His mind and heart were conflicted with old fears and uncertainties. This woman refused his love years ago, what would it take to convince her to accept his love this time?

Her words interrupted his swirling thoughts.

"I'm enjoying this very much, Sam. Thanks for asking me to go sailing with you today." The warmth of her smile echoed in Alexandra's voice. "I must say, I've missed this."

"I'm glad you joined me, Alexandra. So, you've missed sailing?"

She nodded. "To answer your question, yes, I miss being out on the water. My parents had a houseboat we would take out for day trips on the weekends. We would bring the food we needed with us and spend the whole day on the water."

He smiled. "What did you enjoy most about being on the water?"

"It's an incredible feeling, almost like, navigating into a whole new world. To see the broad expanse of the skyline as it touches the blue water. In many ways, when you're floating across the wide blue ocean, it feels like you're an explorer discovering a whole new world."

Sam grinned. "I couldn't agree more — especially since I get to share the day with you."

His eyes swept her with appreciation.

A rush of pink stained her cheeks under the heat of his gaze.

Every time her gaze met his, his heart turned over in response.

He needed her next to him.

"Do you want to take the wheel?" He couldn't resist asking.

Her eyes widened and she stammered, "My father taught me about steering the houseboat, but only a little. I've never been at the helm of a sailboat before, Sam."

"No problem. Come over here. I'll teach you." Sam watched as she walked towards him, a hesitant smile on her face.

He motioned for her to step in front of him and take control of the wheel.

"You'll need to refresh my memory." Alex grinned as she placed her hands on the wheel.

She stood behind the helm with one hand tentatively on the wheel.

His heart jolted and his pulse pounded at her nearness.

Sam stepped close until he stood tall behind her slender body. As he leaned close, his cheek brushed her silky, blond hair.

The scent of wildflowers filled his nostrils, and he breathed deeply of her essence.

This woman, whom he had loved for so long, was back in his arms.

He knew this day would stay in his memory forever.

❧

"Use both hands so you have a steady grip. I'll show you," Sam's low whisper tickled her ear and the warmth of his breath fanned her cheek.

Alex shivered with awareness of him.

He stepped close behind her and placed his hands on hers.

She settled back, enjoying the feel of his arms around her.

Warm tingles spread from her hands up her arms at his touch. His chest rubbed against her back as he showed her how to steer the tiller to stay on course.

Muscled arms brushed against hers on both sides and she felt snuggled in a safe cocoon.

"There are a few boating rules to remember. When two sailboats are approaching each other and the wind is on the same side of each boat, the boat that is windward - in the direction of the wind - must give the right of way to the vessel that is leeward."

"Another important guideline to remember is that if you get too close to another boat, whichever boat has the other boat on its starboard side - right hand side - must yield the right of way." Sam's instructions were helpful and she only hoped she'd remember everything he taught her.

"Ah, yes, it's coming back to me. I feel like such a

newbie." Alex gripped the wheel tighter and steered the boat away from a boat they passed on their starboard side.

"You always were quick at figuring things out, Alexandra."

"I have a fairly good teacher." Alex turned to him with a wide grin.

Sam's face was close to hers, and a whisper of his warm breath caressed her cheek as he spoke.

He was so close she could easily lean back into his arms. Scents of sand and sea rose off his skin and Alex inhaled deeply.

Lifting up her eyes, she was lost in the intensity of his gaze — two dark pools that reflected her own desire — pools she could drown in.

Those two dark orbs lowered from her eyes to hover over her lips. He started to lean down. Butterflies began to form in her belly as she anticipated another kiss with the same man she'd been dreaming so much about lately.

Without warning, a couple of Herring Gull birds screeched loudly in the sky above, startling them both.

Abruptly, they stepped back from each other.

Alex glanced at him with an uncertain smile on her face, before quickly turning to look forward.

With her gaze straight ahead, she started babbling again, "Sailing is so wonderful. It's a place to breathe and feel safe." Rubbing her arms, she let out a long sigh.

Don't dwell on that almost kiss. And don't show your disappointment to Sam. Just let it go.

Alex swallowed quickly and looked over the quiet waters that surrounded them, letting a rare moment of calm wash over her. They had slowed down a little and the waterway ahead was clear of boats for the moment.

Turning to look back at Sam, she noticed his brows puckered in worry.

"Why the serious face?" Alex asked.

Sam sighed. "You said you felt safe when you're on the water. I think that's one of things I worry about most is your safety, Alexandra."

"Thanks, Sam, for your concern for me. To be honest, it's been years since I felt truly safe," Alex admitted the truth. "But since moving back to the island and experiencing these threats against me, my fears have returned."

She walked over to the side of the sailboat and leaned against the railing.

Sam shook his head. "I admit, that's a big worry of mine too. Have there been any more threats against you recently?"

Alex nodded and bit her lip, quiet as emotions of worry and fear warred inside her.

"Tell me what happened," Sam urged.

Alex moved restlessly before she spoke, "Yesterday, Dr. Waverly stopped by my house. She brought with her an article from the popular island magazine *Island Stories.*"

Sam turned to her from his watch at the helm of the boat. "What did it say?"

"It was basically an article that demeaned my reputation. The author was condemning the fact that I was looking into the mystery of my parents' deaths and said I was stirring up a hornet's nest on the island. The writer then went on to hint that it's possible I planned for someone to steal my necklace, to gain attention. I was angry and stunned to say the least."

Sam's expression was clouded with displeasure. He replied in a low voice, taught with anger, "That's just plain wrong. I'm sorry, Alexandra. The only reason I can think of for anyone to attack you like that, is if someone is intent on character assassination. Who wrote the article?"

"Slater Williams." She looked at Sam, not surprised to see his eyes widen with new understanding.

"Why am I not surprised?" He spat out the words, rancor sharpening his low voice. "Slater must still feel angry with you for jilting him years ago. He's decided to do what he can to ruin you. Sounds like we need to have that talk with him."

"We do, Sam. The sooner the better," Alex agreed, sighing heavily. "But let's talk about happier things for today. We're out sailing on a beautiful sunny day after all."

"You're right. Let's enjoy this beautiful day without cloudy thoughts."

She detected a thawing of his angry tone.

Sam turned to her. "Tell me what it was like in your family before your parents passed away. I would love to know you better."

Alex smiled, her thoughts drifting back to the familiar heartwarming memories.

"I have a lot of good childhood memories." She began, "I remember going to the beach as a family. And we would often picnic there on warm summer days. Dad would play with us in the water. He's the one who taught all of us girls to swim well. He was a marine biologist, after all, and spent most of his life on the water."

Sam grinned. "Of course. That makes sense. I'm sure your dad was an excellent swimmer."

"He was. Mom used to tell us girls, 'Your dad is as comfortable in the water as he is on land.'" Alex smiled at the memory. "In other words, each of us know how to swim well. We have less fear of the water than some folks."

"That's a good thing. Go on, I want to hear more." Sam smiled.

She remembered a few other things about her childhood. "I told you we would often take the houseboat and make a day trip on the weekends. Me and my twin sister, Anne, would climb up onto the deck to enjoy the sun and watch the clouds go by."

"Wait — what? You have a twin sister?" Sam turned to her, his eyes wide with surprise.

She was caught off guard by his surprise. Then she remembered. She hadn't told Sam anything about her twin.

Alex stammered a little, "I *had* a twin sister. Anne died when she was six years old."

"I'm sorry for your loss, Alexandra." Compassion filled his features as he looked her way.

"Thanks. It was a long time ago." Her emotions were all shook up. She swallowed hard. "S—sorry, I never told you, Sam."

"I'm confused, Alexandra. Why didn't you?" Under his steady scrutiny, she couldn't think.

They had been friends since grade school. There had been many times that she could have told him the truth. But she'd been too afraid.

Memories that haunted her for years suddenly

returned and she blurted, "I—I think it's because I've been abandoned too many times and lost too many people I loved. I've found it hard to trust people with my secrets."

He looked over at her with a flicker of compassion. "I think I understand. It's alright. I guess it means we still have a little further to go before we truly trust each other."

Alex offered him a weak smile. "I suppose."

"Don't worry, Alexandra. We'll get there." He winked at her with a small smile. "Now, why don't you tell me the rest of the story. You were saying you and your twin sister climbed onto the deck to watch the clouds?"

She smiled, sighing in relief. "Yeah, we enjoyed that. Anne and I would wear our sun hats and sip on sweet iced tea, feeling the heat of the sun on our skin. We'd tell stories and spend the afternoon giggling together."

"You two were very close."

"She was my best friend." Alex nodded. She smiled and continued with her story, "I remember, one time, when we were on the houseboat sunning ourselves on the deck, my mom climbed the ladder and took a photo of the two of us giggling with our sun hats on our heads. I still keep that photo on my bedroom dresser. Next to the necklace, it's my most treasured memory."

Sam regarded her with somber curiosity. "I'm glad you have something to remember her by, Alexandra."

Alex sighed heavily. "Thanks, Sam. I am too. Anne and I were so close, sometimes I was sure we could hear each other's thoughts."

Sam's keen probing eyes held an inscrutable expression. "So, what happened? How did your twin sister die?"

Tears glistened in her eyes as she remembered. "We

had decided to go swimming. The water wasn't as warm as usual, but still, we had fun. But when we came back Anne developed the sniffles. The next day she developed a cough. A week later she was very sick with pneumonia. That's how my beloved twin sister died."

"I'm so sorry for your loss, Alexandra."

The compassion in Sam's voice caused tears to well up in her eyes.

"You don't understand, Sam. It's my fault she died. If I wouldn't have insisted, we go swimming that day, Anne would still be alive."

Tears slowly found their way down her cheeks.

Sam waved his arm for her to come closer to him.

She walked towards him. It was comforting to feel his arms around her. He held her close to his heart.

"No, you're not responsible that your sister died. Anne decided to go swimming with you. It's a terrible tragedy that your sister got sick and died, but it's not your fault, Alexandra," Sam whispered, his dark eyes riveted on hers.

She swallowed hard and bit back more tears. She really wanted to believe him, but for too long she had lived with guilt and remorse. "As she lay dying, I made Anne a promise that I would become a doctor and help sick children get well."

Sam looked at her with compassion and new understanding brightened his eyes.

He spoke softly, "Now it's all starting to make sense. Your passion for doing well in school and for completing your medical schooling. When I went to see you in your first year of medical college, you were very focused on your goals."

Alex nodded slowly. Her heart ached with an inner pain as she remembered refusing Sam's proposal back then.

For a while Sam grew quiet and withdrawn.

Then he spoke, his low voice thick with emotion, "I must ask. Did you refuse my proposal, because you thought I would interfere with your dreams?"

She nodded. "Well, that was partly the reason. And I'm truly sorry for hurting you years ago, Sam."

"It's true that my heart was broken, because I truly loved you, Alexandra. I didn't date another woman for years after you." Sam turned, deep emotion in his voice.

"I'm so sorry, Sam." Alex didn't know what to say.

Sam turned to her, kissing the top of her head. "But I'm okay. I accept your apology and I forgive you. As you can see, I survived." He paused as if deep in thought, before he added, "Thank you for sharing your heart. Maybe, someday soon, you'll be willing to tell me the other reason you refused my proposal years ago?"

Alex stuttered her words, feeling deep agony of emotion. At least it seemed like Sam was giving her a little time to tell him all of it. "I will Sam. Sometime soon I'll tell you everything."

"Good. That's all I ask." With one hand he gently moved a tendril of blond hair away from her face. "Thank you for trusting me enough to share your heart, Alexandra. I feel like I know you better now than I ever did before."

She sent him a nervous smile. "I'm glad we talked. If we're to be in a relationship, it's important to be honest with one another."

"Good. I'm happy you see it that way," Sam replied. "Because I need to tell you, I am falling in love with you again, Alexandra."

Her heart accelerated at his words. Nervously, she bit her lip. She wasn't ready to admit to love yet. "I don't know what to say —."

"Shh. You don't have to say anything. And you might not feel that way about me — at least not yet. But I hope you will soon, Alexandra," Sam whispered, as his dark eyes stared intensely into hers.

Sam looked over the clear blue water for a moment. "Since there are no ships in sight, the water is clear and it's smooth sailing, I think it's time."

"Time for what?"

Alex hardly had time to ask the question, before Sam leaned closer.

"For this," He whispered softly, before his mouth slowly descended to meet hers.

Alex kissed him back, lingering, savoring every moment. She could admit she had been dreaming about kissing Sam all day long.

He pulled her close to his heart and his lips coaxingly caressed hers. Slipping her arms around his neck, she returned his kiss with reckless abandon.

Alex quivered and her knees went weak from the passion of his kisses. She clung to him, drinking in the sweetness of his kiss.

For Alex, it felt like she could feel Sam's love for her in every kiss, in every caress.

She blinked back tears that pricked the back of her eyelids.

Amazed that this man truly did love her.

Alex's heart rolled over in response. This had been a truly remarkable day.

❧

ALEX WAS STILL SMILING as she stepped into her home a few hours later.

For a few minutes, she leaned her head against the wooden door, as her mind burned with the memories of Sam's caring heart, his kisses and his words of love.

He was truly the best of men.

She sighed deeply as she looked around her home.

The house renovations looked wonderful.

But it looked like Jason Harper and his workers had finished for the day.

She hadn't checked her phone messages all day. She didn't want to think about work or renovations or anything else.

But she saw the voicemail on her phone.

Jason had called and left a message. "Alex, we finished the last of the renovations this afternoon. But if you find any last minute touch ups you'd like us to come back for, just let me know. Thanks."

She would look around the house and check the work that had been done, but not tonight.

Tonight, she would relax and think about the beautiful memories from today.

Climbing up the stairs to her bedroom, she couldn't keep her lips from forming a smile.

However, as she walked into her bedroom, that smile quickly changed from happiness to distress.

Her bedroom smelled like that familiar scent of stale smoke.

She looked around.

Someone had moved things around in her room.

The teddy bear, usually in the middle of the set of pillows, was now far on the other side of the bed.

She walked over to her dresser and began opening the drawers.

Someone had been digging around in her neatly ordered drawers. She could tell, because usually her socks and shirts were folded neat and tidy — but now everything was messed up.

Someone who wasn't welcome in her home had combed through her private space.

Fear and panic flooded her.

Who had been in her room? And who had touched her things?

With wide eyes, Alex searched her room, icy fear twisting around her heart. That awful smoke smell seemed to permeate everything in her bedroom.

The smell was strangely familiar.

Without warning, a vivid vision — a haunted memory, returned.

Terrified, she bit her attacker's arm and pushed him away.

He yelled in pain, quickly yanking his arm away from her neck. Once more she pushed against him with all her might.

She could hear his feet stumble against the wood floor.

As he fell, her fingers grabbed something and pulled it off his arm.

His watch.

She saw a long, deep scratch of blood as she yanked the black watch from his arm.

Alex turned to look over at her attacker. His face was hidden by a black ski mask.

All she could see were hate-filled brown eyes.

All of a sudden, memories returned.

It was as if the trauma that had been blocked in her mind was suddenly unblocked and she remembered what happened years ago.

The scent of that horrible man was exactly like this cigarette smell.

But not only that, she remembered that black watch.

She remembered what happened — finally.

She didn't lose the watch as she ran back to grandmother's house, as she thought at first.

No, now she remembered that she had stuffed the bloodied watch into a large rip that was on her old teddy bear. She had stuffed the watch deep inside and then added more stuffing to the back of the teddy bear.

It was like she was hoping to completely wipe away the evidence of her shame.

Today, that traumatic memory finally was unblocked.

It was the attacker from years ago.

She knew it was true.

Her attacker was back.

Dread and fear flooded her mind and heart.

Sitting on her bed, with shaky hands, Alex grabbed her teddy bear.

Turning him over, with one finger she traced the long line of stitches on the back of his soft fur.

She remembered Grams had stitched up the back of her teddy bear a week after the attack.

But now it was time to reopen the wound again.

Finding scissors, she gently cut through the stitches until it was wide open.

Slipping on plastic gloves, she reached a shaky hand inside the teddy bear.

She dug around inside until she finally felt something.

Pulling it out, Alex stared at the black watch.

Here, at last, was the evidence she needed.

Maybe.

Would the detective be able to find DNA samples of skin or blood or something from this watch?

lex

"WHY DID you write this article, Slater?" Alex sat beside Sam at Slater's dining room table.

Earlier that morning, Alex had called Detective Sullivan telling him that someone had been in her house.

She asked if someone from the police could search her bedroom for fingerprints. As she spoke about her memory being unblocked, she explained to the detective there was an item she needed to give him which might lead to her attacker from years ago.

Alex told the detective she would bring the item by later that morning.

She was grateful Sam had been willing to come with her — she was determined to get answers from the man who was writing lies in that popular magazine to ruin her good name.

Slater shrugged then replied, "It was a story. I've been hired to write stories for the magazine, *Island Stories*. That's what I do."

Sam interjected, "Slater, don't you think the words in your article were closer to an attack on Alex's character than simply a story?"

"No, I don't see it that way. My words might have called into question some of Alex's actions, but I did not directly accuse her of anything. I let the readers think for themselves." Slater crossed his arms over his chest, glancing between them with a smugness Alex found annoying.

Firmly, Alex spoke, "Let me refresh your memory, Slater. You wrote, *"However, it makes this writer question if the robbery of Dr. Stafford's pendant wasn't all planned to gain attention — by the owner of the necklace herself?*

Since Dr. Stafford is trying to set up her medical clinic, perhaps she faked the robbery. Perhaps, her real intention is to bring in more patients."

Alex persisted, "The way I read this article, it sounds like you're blaming me for setting up the robbery of my own necklace."

"Well, it might be true, I don't know," Slater suggested. "Maybe you did it to get the attention you need because you're starting up your medical clinic."

Alex gasped. "You honestly believe I would do all that, somehow plan for someone to steal my necklace, to gain attention?"

"Maybe. Alex, you strike me as someone who feels like

they deserve extra attention. I wonder, is it because you grew up with all the advantages in life? Perhaps your spoiled 'rich princess' nature — revealed when you dumped me after the homecoming dance of our sophomore year — is finally coming to the surface, showing your true colors." Slater leaned back on his chair and folded his arms across his chest, a smug expression on his face.

Sam jumped in, his low voice cold and lashing, "Slater, did you write this article to take revenge on Alexandra for dumping you years ago?"

Slater's brows puckered in worry and he ran a shaky hand through his hair.

Alex could tell he was nervous and anxious. Hopefully, now, the truth will come out.

"I—I wasn't getting revenge, exactly. I was just slanting the story in a way that suited me. All authors do that with articles they write," Slater's voice shook as he replied.

Sam commented, "That's some slant — especially when your words will likely ruin Alexandra's reputation."

"I would like a retraction written by you in an article in next month's magazine," Alex demanded.

"I'm afraid that has to be approved by the editor. Talk to him." Slater swallowed convulsively, before he stood to his feet. "But, right now, I've had enough of this interrogation. I think both of you have asked enough questions. It's time for you to leave."

Alex and Sam both stood to their feet and walked towards the door.

Alex turned to face Slater, who followed them.

"One more thing, Slater." Alex felt her temper flare

even more. She reached into her pocket and pulled out the plastic bag with the black watch. "Because you've criticized me publicly and proven you've basically hated me for years, I have another question for you. Does this watch look familiar?"

Slater stammered, "I—I don't think so." He leaned down to get a closer look. "No, definitely not."

Alex she wasn't sure if she could believe him.

"Your words aren't good enough for me to believe you. Prove it."

"What? Just how would I do that, Alex?" Slater sputtered, bristling with indignation.

If he was her attacker from years ago — she needed to know now. She remembered the long and deep wound that she managed to give her attacker when she yanked off his watch.

"Roll up both of your sleeves and I'll know if this watch belongs to you," Alex directed.

"What? You're nuts, woman." Slater's voice was inflamed and belligerent.

"Do it. Now," Alex commanded.

"Alright." He rolled up the shirt sleeves for both of his arms. "There. Are you happy?"

Alex took a closer look. There were no scratches or a long scar or anything.

Slater wasn't her attacker.

Alex sighed heavily.

"Thanks for showing me your arms." Alex turned to Sam. "We can go now. We have all we need."

They stepped out the door and began to walk towards the car.

"And don't come back," Slater called after them before slamming the door.

Alex drove away with Sam in the passenger seat. "I don't understand what that last question was all about. Why did you ask Slater to roll up his sleeves?"

Alex sighed heavily. She knew he would want to know all the details.

"I'll tell you, Sam. But first, I need to stop at the police station. I promised the detective I would drop something off. After that we can have that talk." Alex bit her lip and stared straight ahead.

She was dreading this conversation with Sam.

"Of course," Sam replied.

Alex parked her car in front of the police station. It didn't take her long to drop off the black watch. She asked that the watch be given to Detective Sullivan as soon as possible.

She had already called earlier that day and explained to the detective about the memories that had returned. So, he was expecting to see the watch soon.

As she got back in the car beside Sam, she drove towards Sam's home.

Alex's body tensed as she prepared to tell Sam her dark secrets.

***

THEY GOT comfortable on two of the soft, backyard chairs in Sam's backyard.

Alex decided she would talk with Sam — get the story

out — then she would leave to go to Becca's daughter's baby shower.

She could feel the start of a tension headache. That wasn't surprising as it had already been a day filled with tense emotions.

However, she had promised Sam an explanation.

This terrible secret needed to finally be out in the open.

Sam turned to Alex. "Zoe's at a playdate a few houses down. She'll be sad she missed seeing you. But I wanted to tell you, my daughter has really enjoyed learning from you how to whittle. It's rare that I've seen her so keen to learn something new."

"Good. I'm glad." Alex grinned. "Zoe is a wonderfully smart girl. She is willing to follow directions and is a fast learner. I'm happy to teach her something new."

Sam relaxed and sipped his sweet iced tea. He had filled up two cool glasses of their favorite drink and brought them outside to the small table between them.

Alex took a long sip of the cool drink, hoping it would give her the strength she needed for this talk.

"I'm glad we had that talk with Slater," Sam said. "I think it made him nervous that we were taking him to task about his article. But he needed to be confronted about the fact that his story was ruining your good name."

"I agree." Alex sighed heavily. "He needs to be reminded that there are real people who have to suffer from the fall-out of his critical words."

"Are you going to request that retraction from the magazine editor of Island Stories?" Sam asked.

Alex nodded. "I am. But I seriously doubt the editor

will agree to my request that Slater write a retraction in next month's issue. I'll try, but I don't have much hope it'll do any good."

"Alex, at least you got your chance to have your say. That's important." Sam was always so encouraging and supportive. It was one of the things she liked most about him.

She nodded in agreement.

But her thoughts swirled with doubts and fears.

After she told Sam about her terrible secret — most likely he would not be supportive of her at all.

She believed that after Sam listened to her story, he would change his mind about their relationship.

But she couldn't blame him.

If he chose to end their dating relationship, it would only confirm all the doubts and fears she harbored deep inside.

She couldn't wait any longer. It was time.

"Sam, I think it's time I told you the rest of my story. It does relate to the black watch, and I'll explain that," Alex's voice was shaky as she began to speak.

Sam nodded, turning to face her.

She looked down for a moment, her fingers fidgeting with the bottom of her t-shirt.

Then she turned to him, wearing a tremulous smile. "Do you remember that summer back when we were about to enter our junior year?"

Sam grinned. "I do. That summer we spent so much time together. It's always been one of my fondest memories."

Alex's smile dimmed. "It was one of mine too."

Awkwardly, she cleared her throat. "It was during the first few weeks at the start of our junior year of high school that something happened to me."

"Go on." A crease began to form between his brows.

She hardly heard Sam, as the memories circled her. "I used to go jogging in the evenings as a teenager. It helped to clear my head. I had found a road that was very quiet with hardly any traffic in the evenings. It was about a mile from Grams' beach house."

Alex's belly clenched in tight knots as she told her story. "One evening, a few weeks after school began, I went jogging on that road. It was quiet as usual. However, as I began to run farther, I sensed there was someone following me."

Sam's face clouded with uneasiness.

She swallowed hard before continuing, "I turned to look behind me and, sure enough, I saw a large, tall man running behind me. He wore a blue baseball cap and a black jogging suit. It was starting to get dark outside. He was still far behind me, so I couldn't make out his face."

"But it scared me. I started looking around trying to decide what to do. I thought this would be my opportunity to try and lose him. Rain was starting to pour down and made it difficult to see ahead." Her fingers tensed in her lap, but she kept going.

"I noticed a field with a lot of trees to my right. I turned off the road into the field, running faster than before. I hoped to escape. But the pouring rain made the ground soft and muddy. I tried to escape, but was always slowed by the muddy, uneven ground." Alex shuddered.

"The stranger followed me into the field and began to

catch up with me. Then, suddenly, I tripped and fell to the ground. As I tried to get back on my feet, the man grabbed me and hit me on the back of my head with something hard. I blacked out."

A gasp escaped Sam's lips.

But Alex forced herself to keep talking, "When I finally woke up, I was lying down in a dimly lit, tiny room with broken wooden boards for walls. My hands and feet were tied and the man had put a gag over my mouth. But the stale smell of cigarette smoke was so strong all around me that I almost gagged."

"Oh my, Alexandra." Sam barely got out the words.

Alex continued in a shaky voice. "When the stranger came back, he violated me. I won't go into the awful details, but I was in pain, helpless, and terrified." A sob escaped Alex, and, hurriedly, she swallowed back any more tears.

"When my attacker left, I was determined to find some way out of there. Then I found a nail in the wood along the wall. I rubbed the ropes on my hands against the nail. It took some time, but by the time the man returned, my hands were free. When he approached me again, I fought him and was finally able to escape." Alex stopped for a moment. "But during the struggle to get free, I yanked the attacker's black watch off of his wrist. I saw blood running down his arm. I think by grabbing his watch I left a deep scar along the stranger's arm."

Alex's body trembled slightly as she went on, "I escaped and ran back to my grandmother's beach house. My grandmother took care of me. It took Grams' four days to convince me to see Dr. Waverly. I was scared for anybody to see me looking like I did — all cuts and bruises. I didn't want to answer the questions that I knew would come."

With a shaky hand, Alex tucked a strand of blond hair behind one ear. Her voice shook as she told the rest of her story. "Dr. Waverly took care of the bruises and put bandages on the cuts and scratches on my body."

Alex shuddered as memories that haunted her for years, returned. "Both women kept silent about what happened. I didn't want anyone else to find out about the attack. The mean girls at school had already called me a flirt because I dated Slater and then later started dating you. I didn't want to give them a reason to continue their name-calling."

"Unexpectedly, one morning a few weeks later, I started feeling nausea and noticed blood on my panties." With a trembling voice, she hurried, "My grandmother rushed me to the hospital. A different doctor did emergency surgery on me. Later, I was told I had a ectopic pregnancy — which meant a tiny baby had started to form in one of my Fallopian tubes. They removed the tube and then told me that my other Fallopian tube was also damaged. That's when I was told I would never be able to have children."

"Oh Alexandra, I'm sorry. I can't imagine the trauma you suffered." Sam whispered softly, shaking his head at hearing her story.

"Thanks Sam. It was a terrible time." Alex swallowed back emotion, "When I finally returned to school, I wore heavy makeup to cover the bruises and cuts on my face and I wore a long-sleeved shirt so no one would see what happened."

Alex turned to look at Sam, afraid of his response.

A muscle flicked angrily in his jaw and a dark expression covered his face.

Sam's words erupted in a low growl, "Whoever this man was — I would like nothing more than to beat him senseless for what he did to you. Attacking an innocent girl. There's no excuse for that sort of behavior."

A momentary smile curved the corners of her mouth at Sam's protectiveness.

She wasn't surprised. Sam had always been a gentleman. He wasn't the kind of man who would ever be physically or verbally abusive to a woman.

Most likely that was why, out of all the men she knew, she trusted him the most.

Sam ran a shaky hand through his hair.

Turning to her, he whispered, "Did the attacker say anything to you? Did he know who you were?" He tilted his brow, his questioning eyes meeting hers.

Alex said, "Yes. I couldn't see his face because he wore a black ski mask. But the stranger kept going on and on about how his mother and grandmother would be so happy for him. He said they would now finally be proud of him. He seemed proud that, finally, a girl from the island's well-known Stafford family would be his."

"Sounds like this man knew your family well." A crease of worry formed deep grooves on his forehead. "I'm glad you brought that black watch to the detective. Maybe they'll find some sort of evidence in the forensics lab."

Alex nodded. "I hope so."

"What made you bring the black watch to the police now after all these years?"

She sighed. "Well, I didn't tell you what happened. After I came home from our time sail boating, I could smell that scent of stale smoke in my bedroom. That smell had always terrified me, but I couldn't understand it."

Alex paused. "But, at that moment, it was like suddenly all my memories of that horrible event were unblocked. I know that probably sounds strange."

"No, that's not strange at all. That's a very real, scientifically proven fact, that a person who has experienced trauma can have their memories from decades ago unblocked in a moment." Sam's calm, reassuring voice was a comfort to Alex somehow.

"That's comforting to hear that." Alex sighed, before she continued, "Well, that night I remembered all the details from the attack. Then I remembered the black watch. And I could recall stuffing the black watch into the big hole I had in the back of my teddy bear. I guess doing that was my teenage reaction — a way of hiding what happened to me."

"I understand your reason for wanting to hide that horrifying moment from the world — and even from yourself." Sam shook his head, an even deeper crease forming between his brows.

Alex couldn't really tell if he was worried, angry, or disgusted at hearing her story.

"I was devastated to learn that the result of that terrible man's attack had been pregnancy." Alex voice came out sounding hoarse, "And later to learn that I would never be able to have children — something I always longed for — was a crushing blow."

"I'm so sorry, Alexandra." Sam ran a shaky hand through his hair, moisture in his eyes as he stared at her. "I don't know what to say."

Alex swallowed back tears that threatened to spill down her cheeks. "I understand, Sam."

Silence stretched between them like a rubber band being pulled and expanded to its limit.

Alex felt the nauseating sinking of despair at Sam's continued silence.

Her throat ached with defeat.

A raw and primitive grief overwhelmed her.

There was no way Sam would want to continue to be in a relationship with her now.

Now that Sam had heard her story of shame, he would no longer want to be associated with a woman like her.

He had a beautiful, innocent daughter to protect after all.

Alex was convinced that her past — the shame, embarrassment, and humiliation of what she lived through — would only drag him downwards.

His good name would be tarnished — because of her.

His peaceful life would become worse — because of her.

It was possible his very life would be threatened — because of her.

There was no way she could let that happen.

She wouldn't.

All of a sudden, Alex stood to her feet.

"Sam, I need to be going. I-I promised Becca I'd be

there at the baby shower," Alex stammered as the words rushed out of her mouth. "But I want to say thanks for listening to the sordid story of my past."

She winced and looked over at him.

Sam stood to his feet and followed her — surprised and shaken.

"Alex, I want to say— "Sam began to speak, but Alex interrupted.

She couldn't handle his rejection right now. They could talk about it later.

"No, Sam. You don't need to say anything, I understand." Alex rushed on, "I realize I just shocked you with this horrid tale. Don't worry, I'll give you all the space you need."

He took in a quick, sharp breath.

He stared at her, wordlessly.

She hurriedly kissed him on the cheek. "Thanks, Sam, for everything. I'll see you later."

Alex hurried to her car, tears rolling down her cheeks.

She had done it.

She'd told him her awful, shameful secret.

His face seemed to show the anger and disgust he felt at hearing the details of her past.

She couldn't blame him. She felt the same way.

Driving away she could hardly see, blinded by tears.

Rejection, abandonment, and fear all stabbed at her heart like a thousand tiny knives — solidifying the knowledge that she had been right all along: *she was no longer worthy of being truly loved.*

CHAPTER SEVENTEEN

lex

ALEX FORCED a smile as she sat among the women and a few men at Becca's daughter Amanda's baby shower.

They were seated in Mrs. O'Connor's Quilt and Craft shop, *Yarn Around The Cove.*

All kinds of quilts hung on the walls, each with different designs and colors. Beautiful knitted and crocheted socks and sweaters were also on display.

The shelves were stocked to the brim with all sorts of wool and craft accessories and tools.

In the far corner was a very large common room area where, today, many people had gathered for the baby shower.

She remembered Mrs. O'Connor telling her the room

could hold up to three hundred people at a time. It was a perfect space to hold galleries or art and craft shows.

Nervously, her fingers fidgeted with the bottom of her shirt. Her emotions were still reeling from her recent talk with Sam.

But she'd done her best to wipe away evidence of tears before joining the people at the baby shower.

She hoped no one would be able to tell her emotions were fraying at the edges.

Alex's gaze swept over the familiar faces.

Dr. Grace Waverly had come to the shower, beside her was Mrs. Vickle who ran the book club. Ida Cantrell sat next to her daughter Nellie, her daughter-in-law, Lola, and her granddaughter, Ava.

Mika Sagamore had joined them today with her daughter, Choluna.

Lizzie and her daughter, Annie, sat on Alex's left hand side and Mrs. O'Connor sat on the other. The older widow was happily telling her all the goings-on in the new shop.

Everyone had gone through the usual baby shower games and now the happy, first-time mother was unwrapping some of her last presents.

Becca walked towards her, holding the tiny baby girl in her arms.

"Alex, it's your turn to hold this little one." Becca didn't give Alex a chance to say anything, but immediately handed over the cute, little pink bundle.

Alex held the baby girl, admiring the soft skin and the small, curly blond hair. "She's beautiful, Becca."

"Isn't she?" Becca was glowing with pride. "This is my

first grandchild and I intend to enjoy many memories with her. I'm so happy."

Alex handed the baby back to the proud, new grandmother. "You'll make the best grandma, Becca. She's blessed to have you."

"Thanks, Alex." The baby let out a small cry. "Oh, she might be hungry. I should get this little one back to her mama."

Alex grinned as her friend walked away. Becca was in her element, loving her new duties as grandmother.

Lizzie leaned over and whispered, "You're looking a little pale today. Is everything alright with you?"

Her sister was far too perceptive.

Putting on her stoic face, she replied, "I'm fine, Lizzie. Don't worry about me."

"If you say so." Lizzie reached over and squeezed her hand. "I wanted to ask you what we should do with what we learned recently in Grams' journal."

Alex turned to her sister and whispered, "Are you talking about the fact that Mika and her daughter are our relatives?"

Lizzie nodded and looked over in Mika Sagamore's direction.

"I was thinking about that — and the quilt and craft festival came to mind," Alex whispered, a strange inner excitement warming her as she thought of the idea.

"I see we're thinking the same thing. Mika and her daughter are relatives, after all." Lizzie nodded, smiling. "You'll talk to her?"

Alex nodded.

As soon as all the gifts were unwrapped, the official

party was over. Mika and her daughter were busy saying their goodbyes to Amanda and Becca.

Alex walked towards Mika, just as she was leaving. "Hello, Mika and Choluna. I'm glad to see you both here."

"Yes, well, Becca invited us to join them today," Mika said in her usual cool tone of voice.

Alex smiled warmly. "I'm glad she did. I understand, from Becca, you were the doctor who delivered Amanda's beautiful little girl. I can certainly understand why the family would want you here to celebrate with them."

Mika seemed to soften a little at her words. "Yes, well, delivering babies is part of my job. I'm glad the little girl and mom are both healthy and doing well."

"I am too. I know you're eager to leave, but I wanted to catch you before you left, Mika. I wanted to invite you and your daughter to come to Mrs. O'Connors annual Quilt and Craft Show next weekend." Alex smiled at Mika, whose eyes widened.

She stammered her words, "W-why do you want me to come?"

Mika stared at her, confusion and distrust written all over her face.

"Well, let's just say my sisters and I have something we would like to give you and your daughter. Mika, if your mother wanted to come to the event also, that would be wonderful." Alex smiled warmly, looking at the woman who had seemed to distrust and dislike her most of her life.

Would she agree?

Mika asked, still hesitant, "You're serious?"

"Totally serious. I think it'll be a happy surprise. Will you come?" Alex coaxed.

Mika sighed. "I suppose. I'm not usually one who likes surprises, but now I am curious. We'll be there."

"Thanks, Mika. See you both later." Alex smiled as the two women left. She was glad that they had agreed to come to the event. It was the one bright spot on an otherwise trying day.

Soon Alex was driving home, her thoughts busy.

Entering her house, she decided this would be her chance to finally relax.

As she walked up the stairs to her bedroom, she was unexpectedly surrounded by the familiar, stale smell of cigarette smoke.

Alex gripped her purse tightly and pulled out the pepper spray. She kept it on hand in case of trouble.

Slowly, she took small steps towards her bedroom.

Silence filled the old stone house.

She couldn't hear footsteps or any other sounds.

Was someone in her room?

As she approached, the smell of smoke only got stronger.

Stepping into her bedroom, she looked around quickly, holding the pepper spray in one hand.

But she couldn't see anybody.

However, as her gaze swept the room, Alex could see that her personal belongings had been moved around yet again.

Turning to look at her dresser, she stopped suddenly.

Her eyes widened and she gasped.

The photo of her twin sister, Anne, was gone!

Hurrying over to her dresser she took a closer look.

In the same spot where the photo frame used to be was a piece of paper.

With shaky fingers, she gripped the note tightly.

Alex swallowed as she began to read.

As you can see, I took one more precious item of yours.

If you want both the photo and necklace back, meet me at the old, brown carriage house on Granger Lane.

Be there tonight when the church bells ring at seven o'clock.

Come alone.

A COLD KNOT formed in her belly as Alex approached the old, run-down carriage house.

Fear gripped her, coiling like a snake around her belly and moving upwards to her throat.

The building looked vaguely familiar from the nightmares that haunted her of that terrible night.

On that dark night years ago, she'd only seen the hazy outline of the building.

Memories gripped her.

She stood motionless in the silence.

Hurriedly, she swallowed back bile.

Anxiety gripped her throat.

It was difficult to believe she was back here.

Returning here — to this painful place — was the last thing she had ever wanted.

A voice inside her whispered: *Run away. Don't step inside this horrible place. You don't know what's waiting for you on the other side of that door.*

In the short hours since Alex first read the note, she had agonized about what to do.

But she had prepared anyway. She touched the fanny pack tucked under her sweatshirt. Inside were important items like pepper spray, a small first aid kit, an emergency asthma rescue inhaler, and a couple of protein bars.

In the end, she came to a decision.

She must have her necklace and the photo back.

They meant too much to her.

They were priceless treasures.

She refused to let her attacker hold on to what was hers.

Turning her head, Alex thought she heard footsteps. But she couldn't see anyone.

Turning back, she stopped in front of the scraped wooden doors.

That threatening note had told her to come alone.

But she wouldn't have wanted to bring anyone.

Especially anyone she cared about.

Like Sam or his daughter, Zoe.

Alex refused to let someone she loved to be hurt or worse, by this madman.

Without warning, the church bells rang in the distance.

She gasped.

Icy fear twisted around her heart.

It was seven o'clock.

Holding her breath, she knocked on the door.

Who would be on the other side?

All of a sudden, the door opened and, before she could say anything, a hand grabbed her and pulled her inside.

The scent of stale smoke filled her nostrils.

One second later, a black cloth was yanked over her head.

She couldn't see anything.

"W—what are you doing?"

"Making sure you stay," a low voice replied.

Alex breathed in shallow, quick gasps.

He pulled on her arm and led her up a flight of stairs.

She tripped, trying to feel her way forward without the use of her eyes.

When they arrived on a flat, wooden floor, she was shoved forward until he finally stopped her.

"Sit down," he commanded, his low voice loud and gruff.

With rough hands, he pushed down on her shoulders, forcing her onto the hard surface below.

Suddenly, she could feel ropes being tied around her legs and wrists.

"Why are you tying me up? I thought I came here today because you were going to give me what's mine."

At his raspy chuckle, anxiety spurted through her.

"Not until I know you deserve to receive it. My grandmother always told me, 'special gifts must receive special attention.' And so, it must be with you," his voice rasped.

She couldn't understand what he meant. Was this man deranged?

"Who are you? And what do you want from me?" Old fears and uncertainties taunted Alex.

What did this crazed man plan to do to her?

Mixed emotions of anger and fear warred inside her as she sat motionless and tied up — unable to see — with the black cloth over her head.

"You want to know who I am? I'll tell you in a minute. But first, I want to ask if you remember why today is important?"

"I don't remember." Alex couldn't imagine what he was referring to.

"Today is the same date that I finally had you in my lair twenty-eight years ago." His raspy voice laughed in a mocking sort of way. "I'm disappointed you don't remember me, Alexandra. I remember so much about you."

All of a sudden, she remembered. On the night she'd been kidnapped and attacked, the Sweet Beach Cove church bells started ringing at seven o'clock that evening.

She remembered the bells ringing just before this man hit her on the head and she blacked out. Today's date in September was the exact day everything happened twenty-eight years ago.

"That's why you wanted me here today." With this new insight, Alex questioned the sanity of this madman's calculated and ruthless way of thinking.

"It is. I needed to see you again face to face." His voice was cold and lashing. "Your beauty and the Stafford family name has always attracted me to you, Alex. But there is also a meanness about you. I have the scar on my arm to prove it."

Without warning, the black cloth was yanked off her head.

Alex looked over at him, her eyes widened in shock as she stared at the man in front of her.

Dylan Hart.

"It's you." She gasped loudly.

But how could that be? The man years ago was over-weight and he seemed taller. He must have lost weight over the years.

"It's me. I caught you years ago and now I've caught you again. I knew you'd be surprised. I'm far too clever-by-half," he gloated, basking in the knowledge of his power.

Alex could feel the blood drain from her face.

"You have been working with Jason Harper's construction crew. You've been in my house from the beginning." Her stomach churned with anger, anxiety, and shock at the realization.

Alex was horrified that this cruel and awful man had been in her house every day for the past few weeks.

The same man that attacked her years ago — she'd crossed paths with every day for weeks on end.

"I can tell you're putting all the pieces together," Dylan replied with a smug look on his face. "Yes, I kidnapped you years ago. And yes, I stole your necklace and your precious photo."

Alex swallowed back bile that threatened to choke her. "How did you get inside my house and steal the photo of my twin sister?"

Dylan sent her a mocking laugh. "That was easy. I used your house key that Jason Harper gave me when we began the renovations."

Her body stiffened in shock.

This madman had easy access to her house — he'd been nearby ever since she moved back to the island.

She wanted to throw something in her anger.

But her hands were tied, literally.

Dylan went on, "And don't forget, I stole what belonged to you because I needed to pay you back for stealing my black watch years ago. Look at what you did to me."

Dylan shoved his left arm in front of her face and Alex stared at the large, jagged scar on his arm.

"I see the scar." A cold knot formed in her stomach.

Did this man honestly think that her stealing his watch and leaving a scar was as horrible as what he did to her?

"Good. Now you see vividly all the problems you've caused me. But now that you're back here, I'll need to think about what to do with you." Dylan turned his back and reached into his pocket for a cigarette.

Alex turned to look around the room.

The carriage house was very old and dingy inside. He had brought her upstairs to the balcony which overlooked the downstairs main room.

Her eyes widened when she looked over to see one of the side doors open slightly.

There were two doors. One that went directly down stairs and the other looked like a storage closet.

Zoe peaked her head around the door that was the storage closet.

Her jaw dropped open.

Alex mouthed to the little girl. *Stay silent.*

Mouthing again silently to the little girl, she asked. *What are you doing here?*

Zoe moved her lips. *I followed you on my bicycle. I was supposed to come to your house today.*

Alex gasped. She'd forgotten that Zoe was to come to her house again today.

She turned her head and noticed Dylan was beginning to turn his head towards her.

Alex mouthed to Zoe. *Hide.*

She moved her head, motioning to the little girl to hide behind the door.

Her heart beat accelerated. She couldn't let his man hurt this precious little girl.

Alex loved Sam's daughter as if she were her own.

There must be a way to protect Zoe from harm.

That familiar, awful smell of smoke filled the room. Alex worried that it would cause problems for Zoe's breathing.

The little girl's asthma was easily triggered by smells.

The doctor in her was on high alert.

Alex knew she needed to figure out a way to keep Dylan talking. She needed to give her nemesis a reason to walk away for a few minutes.

Calmly, Alex said, "While you are deciding what to do with me, I have a question."

"What?" Dylan's cold, dark eyes stared at her. A cold knot formed in her stomach.

"You say you have my necklace and photo, but I don't see them anywhere," she began. "Maybe you're not telling me the truth."

A sudden anger lit Dylan's dark eyes. "How dare you say I'm not telling the truth. I'll guess I need to prove it to you."

Dylan hurried to the side door,

She could hear his footsteps going down the stairs.

Alex whispered, "Zoe. Come here."

The little girl stuck her head out from her place behind the door.

Alex motioned for her to come to where she was tied up.

When the little girl arrived by her side, Alex whispered. "I can see your face is pale. Are you having trouble breathing?"

"Yes." Zoe nodded her head.

Alex hurriedly whispered back, "My hands are tied. Can you unzip the fanny pack around my waist? Find the rescue inhaler for your asthma. Then I want you to go hide again. Use the inhaler and take deep breaths like I taught you."

"Okay." Zoe unzipped the fanny pack and found the rescue inhaler. She pulled it out and zipped it back up, pulling the bottom of Alex's shirt down to hide the fanny pack.

"Now go, breathe in the inhaler. When you're feeling better, hurry back home. Tell your dad what happened, okay?" Alex whispered to her.

Zoe nodded.

Dylan's footsteps could be heard coming back up the stairs.

"Okay, go now, quickly, before that man returns and sees you." Alex whispered to Zoe.

The little girl ran, returning to her hiding place in the alcove behind the door once more.

Alex sighed in relief as no sooner had Zoe hid behind the closet door, then Dylan walked into the room.

"Look what I have in my hands, Alex. And you doubted

me." Triumphantly, Dylan held the necklace and photo in his hands.

"Alright, so you do have them. When will you return the necklace and photo to me, Dylan?" Alex asked.

Dylan thought for a moment.

He paced in front of her, smoking his cigarette and puffing out smoke circles.

"I'm not sure." He tapped his chin, then turned to her. "Maybe I want you to meet my grandmother first — so I can prove to her that I finally caught a Stafford girl."

Alex eyebrows lifted in surprise.

This man was delusional if he thought he had caught her.

But she needed him to keep talking.

She wanted to see if he would reveal more secrets and reasons for his actions.

"Who is your grandmother?" Alex hadn't paid too much attention to who was related to who on the island.

Dylan started to pace again. He turned his back to Alex and walked to the other side of the room.

Alex turned to the closet door and saw Zoe peeking between the crack in the door. She mouthed. *Now's your chance. Run home.*

Zoe hurried out the closet door and through the other door that went down the stairs.

Dylan turned around. "Did you hear that sound?"

Alex panicked, thinking Dylan would find out Zoe had been here. Hurriedly, she replied, "I heard a bird making a racket outside."

He paused, thinking. "Maybe that's all it was. Now where was I? Ah, my grandmother. Yes, Florrie Cantrell-

Jones is my grandmother," Dylan said. "She's a powerful lady that controls the purse strings in my family."

A deep crease formed between Dylan's brows. "The old lady has always been hard to please. Grandmother, for some reason, always wanted what the Stafford family had. She wanted your family's pristine reputation and connections, your waterfront properties, and your wealth."

Alex remembered reading about Florrie Cantrell-Jones in Grams' journal.

"My grandmother wrote in her journal that my father dated your Aunt Clementine from this old carriage house years ago," Alex added.

Dylan nodded. "My grandmother is still angry at your dad for breaking her heart. She believes your dad caused her death."

Alex shook her head. "Well, I think that's ridiculous. Do you think that's why your grandmother seems focused on taking revenge against the Stafford family?"

"Yep. Once the old lady has a person in her crosshairs — there's no way of getting out of it. I am living proof of that." Dylan went on, "For instance, my grandmother will only give me my inheritance if I make her proud of me. I've been in her crosshairs for years. So now I'm forced to do everything I can to please her."

Suddenly, Dylan's tone of voice seemed to switch to that of a lost little boy.

He paced the room, as if deep in thought, and used his fingers as if ticking items off a list. "I have some of the items my grandmother always wanted. I have the Stafford girl. I have the small, pink diamond. Now maybe I'll get the money from my inheritance."

Alex shook her head, bewildered at what she was hearing. Was Dylan delusional or confused?

"Alex, did I show you the logo I created for my family? It has your family's beach house alongside your great-grandfather Captain Henry Stafford's ship. Grandmother always wanted both, so I created our new family logo. I designed it myself. See?" Dylan showed her a large gold circle with the engraving.

"Why would you use our family's beach house and my great-grandfather's ship for your family's logo, Dylan?"

It didn't make sense to her at all.

"Because whatever grandmother wants, she usually gets. That meant, I needed to make a logo that included the beach house and Captain Stafford's ship." He giggled like a little boy.

Questions flew around in Alex's mind.

Why would Florrie Cantrell-Jones want the Stafford beach house and her great-grandfather's ship? Was it revenge? According to Grams' journal, Florrie still held her dad — and the Stafford family — responsible for the death of her daughter.

As she looked again at the engraving Dylan held in his hands, all of a sudden, she remembered. "I recognize that engraving. Sam and I found a gold lighter with that same engraving in Lizzie's backyard."

"Yes, I made a mistake and dropped my gold lighter when I stole your necklace. But it worked out in the end. I got the necklace and I got Alex Stafford too," Dylan crowed, with smug delight.

"I needed to steal your necklace. It had the small pink diamond on it, you see. I needed to prove to my grandmother I could take something from the Stafford family that would be valuable to the Cantrell family."

Alex couldn't help but think something was seriously wrong with Dylan. The way the man was talking it sounded like he was coming unhinged in his mind.

But perhaps if Dylan kept talking, he would share more secrets.

Dylan continued to walk around the room, smoking his cigarette, and blowing smoke circles into the air.

She asked, "Why did you need to prove to your grandmother you could get something valuable from the Stafford family, Dylan?"

He paused to catch his breath, his expression one of a lost and rejected little boy.

"My grandmother and both my father and mother don't believe I can do anything well. They think I'm good for nothing. They think I'm not as good as my brother, Ryan." Dylan's voice drifted into a hushed whisper, "Throughout my childhood all I heard was, 'Dylan, why can't you be more like your twin brother?' I was never good enough for my family."

Alex remembered the insults and put downs spoken by Dylan's father and brother. She had witnessed his family's terrible treatment of Dylan at her welcome party and later at the police station.

It seemed to Alex, this man was desperate to prove he was good enough, worthy enough to be accepted and to belong.

Dylan hesitated. "My father and brother don't think I'm very smart. But what they don't know is that I've overheard some of their conversations when they thought no one was listening."

He grinned gleefully.

Alex noticed Dylan was walking dangerously close to the edge of the balcony. Looking over to the lower level, she estimated it was at least sixteen feet from the balcony to the ground floor.

"My brother, Ryan, is hiding some big secrets that if anyone knew, he would get fired from the police force. And my father, the sheriff, has big secrets too. My brother is protecting dad, so dad won't tell on him. My father knows details about the boating accident that killed your parents. It wasn't an accident at all — just ask my dad's good friend, Bobby Sutton."

Alex sucked in a breath at this new piece of information.

Before she could ask questions, Dylan continued on his tirade.

His hands were shaking as he paced back and forth.

"Anyway, I needed to show my father, my brother, and my grandmother that I am good enough. Now, I have proved that I can do things as well – or better – than my brother. I showed them all that I am good enough for our family — that I do belong." His lips thinned with anger as he spoke. "I took the necklace and your photo — and now I have you."

Dylan turned, his dark eyes glowering at her.

"And now I've finally decided what I'm going to do with you. I'm going to keep you here with me, Dr. Alex Stafford. Someone else can run your medical clinic, I need you with me more than those children need you."

"No, I refuse to be kept here," Alex choked out the words.

In a resolute tone of voice, Dylan continued as if she hadn't spoken,

"I'll need to keep you upstairs, in the secure room I have over there, of course — but only for a little while, until you adjust to living here with me." His voice was firm, final.

Alex replied in a rush of words, "There's no way I'm staying here with —"

Without warning, the door to the stairs opened.

Alex sucked in a quick breath and her eyes widened.

Sam walked into the room. Detective Sullivan and Police Officer Miles Carter followed close behind.

"Dylan, we've heard enough. We heard your confession. You're under arrest for multiple charges, including kidnapping, assault..." Detective Sullivan suddenly stopped.

His mouth dropped open.

Everybody in the room's eyes widened in shock. Each one horrified by what happened next.

Dylan, thrown off balance by the entrance of the police officers, took one step backwards and fell from the balcony to the ground floor below.

Alex gasped and her eyes flew open in shock.

The heavy thud of a body hitting the floor below echoed off the walls of the carriage house.

Was Dylan badly hurt — or worse?

CHAPTER EIGHTEEN

lex

AN AGONIZED EXPRESSION hovered over Sam's face as he ran towards her.

The detective and police officer ran down the stairs to check on Dylan and see if he was badly hurt.

Alex tried to stand up, but the ropes around her ankles restricted her movement.

"Hold on, Alexandra. I'll get these ropes off of you." Sam hurried to cut away the ropes on her ankles and wrists.

"Thank God you're alright, Alexandra." Pulling her into a tender embrace he held her tightly. "When Zoe came home and told me what happened to you and where you were — I panicked. I feared for your life. I thought I'd lost you forever."

Alex was too surprised by Sam to do much more than slip her arms around him.

Her heart pounded an erratic rhythm as she felt the electricity of touch.

It felt so good to be back in Sam's arms again.

She relaxed into his comforting embrace.

Tears pricked the back of her eyelids at Sam's protectiveness over her.

Alex appreciated that about him.

Even if she wasn't worthy of his love, she hoped he would still remain a friend.

He pulled back, staring deep into her eyes.

"As you can see, I'm alright, Sam," she replied in a wobbly voice. "How did you know where to find me?"

"My daughter drew a picture of what she remembered of the bad man's face. Both Detective Sullivan and I recognized Dylan Hart's features." Sam frowned. "It was the detective who remembered where he lived."

Alex nodded.

Today, more than ever, she was grateful for the little girl's talent as an artist.

A crease of worry formed between his brows. "Want to tell me what happened?"

"After I got back from the baby shower, I found the photo of my twin sister missing. In its place was a note telling me to come to this old carriage house at seven o'clock tonight if I wanted to get both my necklace and photo back." Alex chewed on her lower lip as she remembered.

"Why didn't you tell me, Alexandra?" Sam's dark eyes probed hers.

Alex awkwardly cleared her throat. "A couple of reasons. The note said I was to come alone. But also, after our talk, I thought we'd agreed I was to give you some space."

Sam insisted, "And I remember you were the one who wanted to give me space. But the last thing I wanted was to have distance between us, Alexandra."

Had she been wrong about him?

Maybe she needed to make things crystal clear.

"I—I thought after I told you about what happened to me as a teenager, you wouldn't want to have anything to do with me anymore. I guess I thought my shameful past would ruin your good name if you continued a relationship with me, Sam," Alex stammered as she explained.

The voice in her head was quick to condemn her. *Here it comes, you asked for it. Now Sam will spell it out clearly that you are right. He'll tell you he doesn't want to be seen with you.*

Sam's dark eyes grew big and round. "Alexandra, are you serious?"

She stole a look at him, her body tense like a high strung violin. Her belly quivered, waiting for the hammer of rejection to come down hard on her.

"I can see that you are." Sam placed two hands gently on each side of her face, lifting it up so he stared into her eyes. "Oh sweetheart, I think you've had far too much trauma in your life. All the hardships have made it difficult for you to believe you can trust any man again."

A stray tear gently rolled down her cheek.

How did this man have the ability to see deep inside her soul? It was like he knew her fears, worries, and insecurities.

"But what I told you is all true," Alex replied, her voice shaky.

She needed to make it clear so there were no doubts — to make sure he clearly understood about her horrible past.

He wiped away her stray tear with his thumb. "I know it's true. And I want you to know your past won't ruin me or my good name. I want you in my life, Alexandra. It doesn't matter to me about your past. We all have wounds or mistakes or regrets. The fact that you suffered through that horrible attack years ago – and survived today's kidnapping — only proves that Dylan Hart is a terrible person, not you. None of that reflects badly on you. I only see you as a brave, compassionate, and strong woman, Alexandra."

"Oh Sam." She sighed in relief at his words. "Do you really mean that?" Her voice wavered with thick emotion.

Her heart desperately wanted his words to be true.

Alex could hardly believe what she was hearing.

His words were like a healing balm to a heart tormented by years of rejection, unworthiness, and shame.

Sam kissed her forehead and whispered, "I meant every word, Alexandra. You are not those terrible things others have said about you over the years."

Her breath caught in her throat and a long sigh escaped her lips.

For so many years she had lived an isolated life — rarely dating any man. Fear had controlled her every waking moment.

In an effort to rid herself of the tormenting thoughts,

she set her mind and hands to working as hard as she could as a medical doctor.

All these years — the past twenty-eight years — she had mentally tortured herself. She had believed she wasn't good enough or worthy enough to be truly loved.

For all those years, she had been unable to be vulnerable with any man.

Fear, rejection, insecurity, and shame had kept her locked in a cell of her own making.

But today, with Sam's words, she could feel hope rising inside of her.

"To me, you are a woman who is confident, intelligent, kind, and beautiful. If anything, I love you now more than ever," he whispered.

Alex's heart swelled with a feeling she had thought long since dead.

This man — the one man she was convinced was lost to her forever — still loved her, even after he heard the terrible truth.

Shock-like electricity bolts flooded the length of her body at the depth of his feelings for her.

Her heart turned over in response to Sam's words of love.

"Sam, I'm surprised and relieved at your words. I never expected to hear you tell me you loved me — especially after learning the terrible truth of my past." Alex swallowed, her mind floundering as she looked up at him.

"Sweetheart, you are all that's beautiful, pure, and lovely — the past is wiped clean. That's how I see you, truly." Sam pulled her close, kissing both cheeks.

"Oh Sam. I love you so much." Alex sighed, relishing the way he made her feel so cared for and loved.

His eyes riveted on her face, then moved downwards to focus on her lips.

This man had unlocked her heart and soul.

The smoldering flame in his eyes was his way to ask permission, something which she was happy to give.

Slipping her arms around his neck, she whispered, "Kiss me, Sam."

"Gladly." Sam's lips pressed against hers, then gently covered her mouth.

Alex felt his lips touch her like a whisper.

Her legs weakened and her heart quivered at the sweet tenderness of his kiss.

She kissed him back, lingering, savoring every moment.

Just as she was enjoying Sam's kisses, they both heard a loud thudding coming from the ground floor of the carriage house.

Startled, Alex stepped back. "What was that noise?"

Sam turned, looking towards the door. "I don't know. But maybe we should go downstairs to see what's going on. We will definitely finish this later, I promise."

Heat stained Alex's cheeks and she started toward the stairs.

Sam followed close behind.

Soon they reached the door to the main floor of the house.

Alex's eyes widened at the sight.

Paramedics were carrying Dylan's body on a stretcher through the open door.

Detective Sullivan followed close behind.

He stopped when he saw them.

"Alex and Sam, good. I'm glad you're still here." The detective walked together with them outside. "I have something here I think you'll be happy to have returned, Alex."

He reached into his pocket and pulled out her necklace and a broken photo frame.

He placed them into her waiting hands.

"The photo frame and glass are broken. For some reason, Dylan had items in his hand that belong to you when he fell." The detective said, shaking his head.

"Dylan wanted to prove to me that he had my things. How is he?" Alex's voice shook as all the memories came flooding back.

"According to the paramedics, when Dylan fell from the balcony, the height of the fall wounded his head and they believe there are breaks in one arm and leg and possibly fractured ribs. They gave him a sedative. The paramedics said they don't know if he will live," Detective Sullivan explained.

She felt guilty at the relief that flooded her. "Thanks for letting me know."

The detective explained, "But if he does wake up, he'll be arrested. Remember, we've heard Dylan's confession."

Sam spoke. "Good. At least Alexandra will be safe from Dylan."

Detective Sullivan nodded. "Yes, Alex, you won't have to worry about him anymore."

Alex nodded, grateful for that at least. "Thanks for all you've done, Detective."

The detective nodded, his eyes pensive. "Sorry we couldn't find who was behind those threats before Dylan showed his true colors. I'm just glad you're alright."

With that, the detective walked away to his waiting car.

Alex turned to Sam. "I'm relieved that Dylan will no longer be able to threaten me. In a strange way, I feel sorry for him. All the years of being rejected by his family has made him mentally destructive and unstable."

"Well, be that as it may, I'm just glad you're finally free of being terrorized by him." Sam drew a deep shaky breath. "And from now on I plan to be by your side to protect you and to cheer you on."

"Thanks, Sam." Alex grinned. "I'm going to need it, especially with the grand opening of my medical clinic this week."

He grinned. "I'll be here to help you, with whatever you need, Alexandra."

Somehow, she knew that about this man.

Sam had shown her over and over again his good character.

He was a man she could trust.

He was a man with whom she could be vulnerable.

He was a man who would stay by her side through thick and thin.

THE SUN SHONE bright in the sky on the day of the Grand Opening of the children's medical clinic.

Dr. Alexandra Stafford's blue eyes grew wide at the

sight of many groups of people walking towards her new place of business.

With nervous fingers, she touched the St. Michael's pendant that once again hung around her neck. Gratefulness bubbled up on the inside that finally the heirlooms she cherished most had been returned.

The street in front of her place was crowded with cars. It seemed people were coming from every direction.

"Alex, congratulations. This is a big day for you. We're so excited to celebrate with you." Lizzie and Jonathan hurried towards her, grabbing her in a big hug.

Following close behind Lizzie were her three adult children who each gave their aunt a big hug.

"Aunt Alex, I think what you've done here is amazing," Annie said, looking at the newly refurbished building.

Alex's smile widened. "Thank you, Annie. And thank you for the beautiful new website you created and for setting up the social media for me. I think all the work you've done is a big reason why so many people from the community have come to the grand opening today."

"Aww… thanks, Aunt Alex. I was happy to help out." Annie grinned.

Alex looked up in surprise to see the rest of her sisters walking towards her.

"All of you showed up?" Alex placed one hand on her heart. "I'm touched. Thank you for coming."

"Of course, we're here, Alex. We wouldn't miss your big day for the world." Charlie grinned. "Lizzie gave us the family discount at her inn, so that's a bonus too."

Lizzie smiled at that.

Jane added, "Alex, each of us caught a flight to the

island to celebrate this day with you. You put a lot of hard work into getting this done." Her sister leaned close to whisper, "Lizzie mentioned that after all this time you came face to face with your attacker from years ago. How are you doing, truly?"

"I'm shaken, but good. I made it through, thank God. Now I can focus on my medical practice." Alex offered a wobbly smile.

"Good. And don't forget now you'll have time to focus on Sam too." Jane winked.

"Yeah. He truly is a wonderful man. I thought he would give up on me after he heard about my past, but he stuck by me. I'm truly blessed."

"You have a good man, Alex. I'm happy for you," Jane replied.

"Thanks." Alex whispered in her sister's ear, "But what about your love life, Jane? I hear Ward Hampton has returned to the island. If you move back here, maybe you two will finally have a second chance."

Jane shifted on her feet, a pensive shimmer in the shadow of her blue eyes. "I don't know, Alex. I think I'm scared of getting into a new relationship with a guy. What if I can't trust him? What if my heart is broken again?"

"I understand, Jane. It's how I felt for years. But, at some point, you should consider opening your heart to love," Alex added. "Ward has always seemed like a steady and honorable guy."

"I believe he is too. It's my own fears holding me back. Somehow, I'll I hope I'll get this part of my life figured out," Jane muttered uneasily.

Alex smiled warmly and slipped her arms around her

sister. "Somehow, I'm confident you will, Jane. And I hope you move back to the island soon. I want more of my sisters nearby."

Jane nodded. "I'm seriously thinking about it. Well, I should move along, there's more folks who want to talk with you, Alex."

As soon as Jane left, her younger sisters, Jules, Katie, and Torrie, grabbed Alex, each smothering her in hugs.

Each of them congratulated Alex on the opening of her new medical clinic and then walked over to talk with Lizzie.

Alex looked at the crowd of people and spotted the TV reporters and another reporter from the *Island Stories* magazine.

The editor of the magazine had refused her request for a retraction of Slater's slanderous story about her. However, folks from the community still showed up to celebrate the Grand Opening of her medical clinic today.

She was surprised and thankful.

Grace Waverly walked towards her. "Congratulations on your grand opening, Alex. I've looked forward to this day. Your medical clinic will be a huge success, I can feel it."

"Thanks, Grace. If it's a success, it'll be in large part to your mentorship and support." Alex grinned at the older woman. "You've already given me a big boost with the new patients you brought my way."

"Glad to do it, Alex. I believe in you. You're a great doctor," Grace added.

"Thanks, Grace." Alex turned suddenly, hearing a large commotion in the crowd. "Oh, it looks like the Mayor of

Sweet Beach Cove has arrived to help with the ribbon cutting."

"I'll talk to you later, Alex." Dr. Grace Waverly walked over to where the rest of the crowd was beginning to gather.

Alex grinned as Sam and Zoe walked towards her.

"You look beautiful, Alex. Look at all these people. The grand opening for your medical clinic is a success." Sam's gentle smile calmed her anxiety over this busy day.

"Dr. Alex, we came to help you celebrate today," Zoe said with a happy smile.

"Thank you, Zoe." Alex's heart bubbled over with the little girl's enthusiasm. "I'm so happy you're here with me. We'll talk later, alright?"

"Sure." The little girl grabbed her dad's hand.

Before leaving, Sam leaned close to whisper, "I'm proud of you, my love. We'll be waiting to talk with you later."

"Alright, Sam. Thanks so much." Happiness flooded her at seeing Sam and Zoe again. She would definitely talk with him after the event was over.

Soon Alex had folks from the city council walking her way.

Mayor Olive Parker approached and said, "This is an exciting day for you and for Sweet Beach Cove, Dr. Stafford."

"It is an exciting day. Thanks for coming and for agreeing to say a few words to the people in our community here today, Mayor Parker."

"Happy to be here." Mayor Parker smiled. "Well, it

looks like the crowd is waiting. Should we begin the ribbon cutting ceremony?"

"Sounds good."

Alex followed the mayor as she stepped onto the porch stairs of the house and stood behind the podium.

"Good morning, everyone. Welcome to the Grand Opening of the Sweet Beach Cove's new children's medical clinic." Mayor Parker spoke and the crowd cheered. "This is an exciting day for all of us. It's the first medical clinic focusing on children's health and well being in our community. Dr. Stafford, why don't you say a few words and tell us what inspired you to open up this medical clinic in our community."

Alex walked over to the microphone, a shaky smile on her lips. "Thank you, Mayor Parker. And thank you, everybody, for coming to the grand opening today."

She waited for the applause to quiet down, before she continued, "I want to begin by thanking all the people who helped me get this clinic started. I want to thank Jason Harper and his crew for working many hours on all the renovations. I also want to thank the board of selectmen for the approval of my business license and for giving me the opportunity to serve this fine community."

Alex looked out at the crowd and, seeing the women she recently hired, she went on, "I also want to thank my new receptionist, Clara Waters and my nurses, Nurse Morales and Nurse Steward, for agreeing to join me at the medical clinic. And, finally, I want to thank the many other family and friends who have supported and cheered me on."

She paused a moment before continuing, "This children's medical clinic has been a dream of mine ever since I was a child. It started when my twin sister, Anne Stafford, died when she was six years old. I promised Anne, someday I would grow up and help to heal sick children. My beloved grandmother, who passed away a year ago, bequeathed me this house in her will. Grams wanted this house to be used as a medical clinic. I'm happy to say, today is the beginning of seeing her dream fulfilled."

The mayor stepped to the microphone and asked Alex, "I'm sure your grandmother and sister would be thrilled by what you've done here, Dr. Stafford. Before we cut the ribbon, what name have you given this medical clinic?"

Alex swallowed back emotion before speaking into the microphone, "I'm proud to present to you all, the *Anne Stafford Memorial Children's Medical Clinic.*"

She couldn't help but look over at Sam at the words. He nodded, with a big smile on his lips of happiness and pride.

Alex turned and Mayor Parker spoke again, "There you have it, folks. Here's the ribbon that surrounds the new medical clinic. Dr. Stafford, we'd be pleased if you would cut the ribbon to officially open the doors of the *Anne Stafford Memorial Children's Medical Clinic.*"

Alex stepped down the stairs towards the large red ribbon with Mayor Parker by her side.

Holding the scissors in her hand, Alex cut the ribbon and said, "The doors are officially open."

Alex was wrapped in a cocoon of happiness as the crowd cheered.

Tears moistened her eyes at the support she received from the Sweet Beach Cove community.

She could hardly believe that, after all these years, her dream of a children's medical clinic was finally coming true.

But it looked like that wasn't the only dream that was coming true.

Sam said he loved her.

Perhaps her other dream would finally come true — that of being part of a family.

Happiness bubbled over and her smile grew wide.

For the first time since she was a little girl, there were no shadows across her heart.

CHAPTER NINETEEN

lex

"I'M happy to welcome everyone to our annual Sweet Beach Cove Quilt and Craft Day." Mrs. O'Connor took her place behind the podium, speaking to the crowd that arrived at the large gallery room in her shop, *Yarn Around The Cove.*

Mrs. O'Connor cleared her throat and continued speaking, "For today's event, we will showcase memory quilts that were hand stitched by folks in our community. These memory quilts tell a short story of some of the first families to settle on Sweet Beach Cove, back in the late eighteen hundreds and early nineteen hundreds."

Alex clapped along with the rest of the folks gathered there. Sam and Zoe stood next to her on one side and on her other side stood Lizzie, Jonathan, and her other sisters.

She turned her head to look behind her and spotted Chesmu Sagamore and Dr. Mika Sagamore. Next to Mika was Choluna and an older woman who looked similar enough to Mika to be her mother.

"This year, we were able to finish three of the quilts, with many more to come for the annual quilting show next year," Mrs. O'Connor explained.

"We'll begin with the quilt stitched for the descendants of Ansel and Abigail Bellanger. Mrs. Jean Bellanger, widow of the late Matthew Bellanger, has graciously come today to receive her quilt." Sarah O'Connor and Althea O'Conner took the white sheet off the quilt and everyone clapped at its unveiling.

The artwork for this quilt was a ship design along with an antique sewing machine.

Jean Bellanger spoke into the microphone, "This is a perfect memory quilt of my late husband's great-grand-parents. Ansel worked on the ships and Abigail was a seamstress for many ladies on the island. Thank you so much, Dorothy and all you ladies who stitched this quilt." Mrs. O'Connor folded the quilt and handed it to old Mrs. Bellanger.

"Next we have a quilt stitched for the Cantrell family." Mrs. O'Connor began.

Alex looked around the room and spotted old Mrs. Ida Cantrell, Ava Cantrell-Worth, and Lola Cantrell.

However, she didn't see Florrie Cantrell-Jones or her daughter Linda Hart anywhere. Most likely they were at the hospital with Dylan Hart.

Dorothy O'Connor continued to say, "This quilt was made for the descendants of Ike and Clara Cantrell. You'll notice the design on this quilt is also a large ship, as Ike Cantrell was often at sea. But the other part of the design is a house on several acres of land. This is because the Cantrell family has become known on the island for their annual Cantrell Family Fall Festival. Mrs. Ida Cantrell, widow of the late Eli Cantrell, has graciously joined us today to receive her quilt."

Applause again filled the room as Ida Cantrell walked to receive her quilt.

"I'm pleased that folks on the island took the time to stitch these quilts for the first settlers in this community. I'm happy to accept this gift on behalf of the Cantrell family. Thank you, Mrs. O'Connor." The older lady took the quilt and walked back to where she sat with her family.

"Last, we have a quilt stitched for the Stafford family." Mrs. O'Connor went on to explain. "This quilt was made for the descendants of Captain Henry Stafford and his wife Mary. You'll notice the design on this quilt is a large ship as Captain Stafford was a well known sea captain."

The older lady continued, "The other part of the design is a beach house on the waterfront. This is because the Stafford family has owned that waterfront property for over a hundred years now. Dr. Alex Stafford, great-granddaughter of Captain Henry and Mary Stafford, has kindly joined us today to receive their family's quilt."

Folks around them clapped as Alex walked up onto the stage.

Nervously, Alex took her place behind the podium and

began to speak, "Thank you, Mrs. O'Connor. The quilt is beautiful and my sisters and I are grateful for this gift."

She swallowed, "However, since our beloved grand-mother passed away last year, we have been reading her journal, and my sisters and I have made a surprising discovery. We learned we aren't the only direct descendants of Captain Henry Stafford. Grams wrote a surprising story in her journal."

Many folks in the crowded room gasped out loud, their eyes wide.

Alex continued to explain, "We learned that our great-grandfather, Henry Stafford, had an affair with a young woman from the Wampanoag Tribe in Aquinnah named Watameeto. Watameeto had a daughter named Aponi. Aponi had a daughter named Katari. And Katari had a daughter named Mika. Mika's daughter is Choluna."

"So, I would like to ask my sisters to come to the front, to help me present this beautiful memory quilt. If Dr. Mika Sagamore, her daughter, and mother could come join us here, we'd like to offer this gift."

Alex grinned as her six sisters came to stand with her. Dr. Mika Sagamore stepped forward with Choluna and her mother following.

Alex's smile widened at the surprise in Mika's eyes.

"As great-granddaughters of Captain Henry Stafford, we would like to present you, Katari, Mika, and Choluna with this memory quilt — our gift to you. This is but a small present, to show you we would like to start the journey to restore a relationship between our families." Alex handed the memory quilt to Katari, the eldest woman of the family.

Katari Sagamore had tears in her eyes as she took the offered gift.

Mika spoke into the microphone. "Well, this is an unexpected surprise for all of us. But we're grateful to be acknowledged as descendants of the Stafford family. Thank you for the gift of this quilt."

Alex couldn't stop grinning as the quilt and craft show came to an end.

Afterwards, Mika Sagamore walked up to Alex. "I've never been more surprised than today. That was a thoughtful thing to do. My mother told me years ago that our family was related to you, but we appreciate being honored as a family member in this way. My mother's heart was touched. Thank you."

Alex nodded. "You're welcome, Mika. And we really hope this will be the beginning of restoration between our families."

"I do too. Thanks again," Mika replied and walked away to join her family.

Sam came to stand next to Alex.

"You did well today, Alexandra. That was well done — offering the Stafford family memory quilt as a gift for Mika Sagamore and her family." A light of appreciation and respect shone in his dark eyes.

"Thanks, Sam. My sisters and I felt it was the right thing to do. Maybe this will be the beginning of a new friendship between our families." Alex sighed.

"I think it will be." Sam whispered in her ear, "But I wonder if we might go somewhere and talk. I have something personal I want to say and give to you."

She looked up, surprised by the intensity in his dark

eyes. "Sure. Should we meet on the beach a little later today?"

Sam grinned, "I look forward to it."

It was early evening when Alex arrived at the sandy beach.

The sun was beginning to cast its red-orange glow across the water. It had the stunning visual effect of a fireball kissing the blue water — heat meeting cool and embracing their differences.

Did that image represent her and Sam? Perhaps she was the fireball and he was the cool and calm one in their relationship.

As she stepped onto the soft sand, she looked up to see Sam.

He was waiting for her.

Her heart lurched madly at the sight of him.

He was so handsome, in his navy-blue short pants and white t-shirt.

As she stepped closer, his compelling eyes riveted her on the spot.

"Alexandra, you're beautiful as always," Sam whispered in her ear and slipped one arm around her shoulders. "I thought we could walk together."

Alex placed one arm around his waist. "I'd like that." She grinned. "But first, let me slip my sandals off. I want to walk barefoot on the sand."

Patiently, he waited while she took off her sandals, holding them in her other hand.

Alex grinned. "Oh, the cool sand feels so wonderful between my toes."

Sam chuckled. "I'm glad."

Together, they walked side by side, enjoying time spent together.

"This has been a very eventful week. So many things have been happening," Sam began. "First of all, I'm very glad you're alright. I have to say I'm surprised it was Dylan Hart all along who was terrorizing you. I'm grateful he'll no longer be able to hurt you, Alexandra."

She nodded, sighing in relief. "Me too. It's difficult to believe the weight of that stress is gone. I feel like I can breathe easy now."

His smile was almost apologetic for all she'd been through.

"Yeah. Then there was the big grand opening of your medical clinic. That's an important step." Sam squeezed her shoulder.

"It is. And surprisingly, we are already booked up with appointments for the first month. It's been a crazy busy." Alex sighed with contentment. "And don't forget my necklace and photo were returned."

Sam nodded. "I'm glad. Did Detective Sullivan ever tell you if they found anything on that gold lighter or the cigarettes or the black watch?"

"The detective called yesterday to tell me they didn't find anything on the lighter or those used cigarettes. However, the black watch had traces of blood. They were able to match the DNA to Dylan Hart," Alex explained.

"No real surprise there. We thought that might be the result." Sam sighed heavily. "Then everything is solved, except for the unanswered questions of what happened to your parents all those years ago."

Alex grimaced. "True. However, we did get a few answers from Captain Granger and from Mrs. O'Connor about what was going on years ago. However, Dylan said something interesting that only brings up more questions."

"What's that?" Sam stopped and turned to her, his dark eyes questioning.

Alex explained, "Dylan said his brother, Ryan, is hiding some big secrets that if anyone knew, Ryan would get fired from the police force. He said his father, Sheriff Hart, has big secrets too. Then he said, his twin brother, Ryan, is protecting his dad, so his father won't tell on him. Apparently, Sheriff Hart knows details about the boating accident that killed my parents. Dylan told me it wasn't an accident at all. All I need to do is ask his dad's good friend Bobby Sutton."

"Wow, that *is* new information." Sam's eyebrows lifted in surprise. "What do we do with that?"

Alex tucked a strand of hair behind one ear. "I think our next step is to talk with Ryan Hart and Sheriff Hart. After that we'll need to have a talk with my dad's old friend Bobby Sutton. Hopefully, we can get some answers from him."

"Yeah, hopefully," Sam replied with a shrug. "I never thought I'd say this. But it seems like the deeper we dig for answers, the more I get the sense we'll find answers we aren't going to like."

A tremor touched her lips. "I've been feeling the same thing. But now that we've got this ball rolling, I don't think we should stop searching for answers to this mystery."

Sam ran a hand through his hair, expelling a breath. "You're right, of course."

Alex looked over at Sam, noticing his brows pinched together.

"Hey, it will be okay, Sam, no worries. You and I are not doing this alone. My sisters are very committed to finding answers as well." Alex did her best to help calm his nerves, to help him find peace in her topsy-turvy world.

"Thanks for that. It helps to know we're not alone in our search." Sam pulled her close to his side and kissed the top of her head. "I just want to protect you, Alexandra."

Looking up at him, she saw the heart-rending tenderness of his gaze.

A tingling began in the pit of her stomach, growing upwards until it flooded her whole body.

"I know you do, Sam. And I really appreciate that." She really was grateful. This man had proved himself time and time again — going to great lengths to show her how much he cared.

Sam pulled her closer to his side. She breathed a long sigh of contentment.

All of a sudden, he stopped.

Turning towards her, he gently shifted her so they stood face to face.

"Alexandra, I have to admit, this week has been one of the most difficult weeks of my life," Sam spoke in a broken whisper.

Her heart ached at the raw emotion she heard in his voice.

Sam's throaty voice was low and husky as he spoke, "That day, when my daughter hurried home and said she saw a bad man had tied ropes around you, I've never felt such fear in my life. The relief I felt when I saw you, and you were safe, was second to none."

A sense of awe rippled through Alex, at the depth of his feelings for her.

"Oh Sam…," she replied with a shaky voice as all the emotions she held deep inside came bubbling to the surface.

"It's true, Alexandra." Sam reached out, and his fingers tenderly brushed a stray tendril of hair behind one ear. "It was at that moment, I realized I love you too much not to have you in my life."

Happiness flooded her soul as she listened to his heart-felt words of love.

"I love you too, Sam. With all my heart." His love wrapped around her like a warm blanket, filling her soul.

She felt the blood surge from her fingertips to her toes at the passion in his eyes.

Her heart took a perilous leap when suddenly he crouched down on one knee.

Without thinking, her jaw dropped open and her eyes widened.

A small gasp escaped her lips.

Dark eyes looked up into hers, and her heart thumped faster.

"Alexandra, I have loved you ever since the first time I saw you in grade school. You were adorable back then with your blond braids and cuffed jeans."

With a raw voice he continued, "But, here today, you're

more beautiful to me than ever before. And I love you now more than I ever did. Sweetheart, will you do me the honor of becoming my wife?"

Her knees went weak at his words of love.

Alex bit her lip to stifle the outcry of delight.

Throwing her arms around Sam, she whispered, "Yes, Sam. I will happily marry you. I love you so much."

He reached a hand into his pocket and pulled out a gold ring with a marquis diamond.

Slipping it onto her wedding finger, their eyes locked together.

Without warning, he pulled her into his arms.

Claiming her lips, he crushed her to him.

His kiss sang through her veins.

The thrill of being in Sam's arms was incredible. However, the realization that she would be in his arms for a lifetime flooded her heart with a happiness that she'd never known before.

Sam's love had transformed her.

Who she really was given a second chance.

She received all those things her heart longed for: *acceptance, belonging, and, most of all, love.*

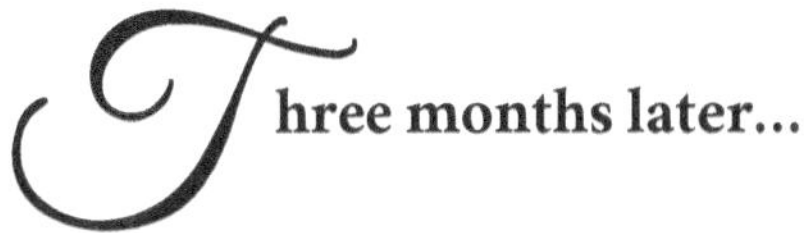

Three months later...

MESMERIZED, Sam smiled as his daughter walked slowly towards him.

Her pink dress flowed in gentle folds down her slender body.

Zoe's small hands carried a basket overflowing with red roses and baby's breath.

With each step his daughter took, she dropped rose petals to the wood floor of Lizzie's beach house.

Sam smiled proudly, as his daughter took her place to stand in front of Alex's sister Jane.

Beside Sam, was his brother Caleb, standing as best man.

Together they had decided on a small wedding with

family and a few friends to celebrate this magical day with them.

Alexandra's five sisters sat near the front on the bride's side.

His mom and his brother's wife sat next to Lizzie.

Tears shimmered in his mother's eyes.

When they announced their engagement to his mom, she was so happy.

His mother had whispered, "Son, I've waited for this day ever since your dear wife died years ago. I'm so happy for you."

A smile curved the corners of his mouth at the memory.

Sam's heart thumped loudly with the thought that today, he would marry his best friend and the love of his life.

Lizzie's large great room was the perfect place for a December wedding. It had been easy to set up two rows of chairs on each side of the room for the wedding guests.

Lovely red bows along with slender green vines graced each row of chairs — perfect for a Christmas Eve wedding.

Three months ago, he would never have dreamed that today he would be marrying the woman of his dreams.

In fact, he never thought he'd marry again.

But Alexandra had captivated his heart — much like she had years ago. If he was honest, he'd never stopped loving her.

He wasn't about to let her go. This beautiful woman would be in his life forever.

Sam waited with bated breath at the front of the room, next to Pastor Tim.

Gram's old pastor stood motionless, layered smile lines appearing by his gray eyes.

Sam's hands fidgeted as he anxiously awaited the first glimpse of his bride.

Then he saw her.

Sam sucked in a breath.

His stunning bride walked into the great room, looking like a vision in white.

She wore her grandmother's wedding gown, inter-woven with old lace and pearls.

Alexandra was a vision.

His smile widened.

Small steps took her down the aisle, bringing his future-wife closer with each step.

One slender hand was tucked into the crook of her brother-in-law Jonathan's arm as she glided down the middle aisle.

Seeing her walk gracefully towards him now with a wide smile, felt like he was looking at a little bit of heaven on earth.

Looking at her now, nobody would be able to tell that only months ago, she literally was fighting for her life against her attacker, Dylan Hart.

Alexandra had also risked her life to save his daughter.

He owed her so much.

To Sam, she was everything that was brave, noble and lovely.

He was so thankful that she'd come back to him.

Sam held out his hand and she reached for him. He tucked her small hand inside his own.

Leaning close, he whispered. "You are beautiful."

Alexandra's cheeks blossomed with pink, only adding to her glow as a blushing bride.

Pastor Tim spoke of commitment for a few minutes before asking them to repeat their marriage vows.

As Sam looked into Alexandra's beautiful blue eyes, he poured his heart into the words that would bind them together forever.

"I remember like it was yesterday, solving neighborhood mysteries, hand painting our t-shirts and walking the beach together at sunset." Sam breathed deeply of her flowery scent.

"I never told you, but I fell in love with you in middle grade, when we first rescued Mrs. Dillon's tabby cat from the tree." Sam grinned. "The more we saw each other, the harder I fell for you. Your courage, compassion and kindness won me over, since that first day I met you. I'm thankful for our shared memories, and I look forward to making many new ones together. I see you as perfect, pure and lovely, my beautiful bride. I love you, Alexandra."

His bride's blue eyes filled with tears, that stared into his soul.

In the beginning, he hadn't wanted to marry again.

But she had won him over.

No longer would fear hold either of them back. From now on, they would have a real marriage based on commitment and love.

Gently, he reached for her. Reaching for her waist, he

pulled her close. As he lowered his head, he touched her lips on hers.

The sweetness of her kiss intoxicated him. He breathed deeply of her floral scent, loving the way she clung to him.

Having Alexandra in his arms felt like coming home.

ALEXANDRA'S KNEES went weak and her pulse quickened as Adam's warm lips pressed against her own.

Her arms slipped further around his waist, holding tightly to her new husband. Love had melted her heart and turned her emotions into a hot mess.

She couldn't help but love every second of it.

The words her new husband spoke in his vows — words of respect, honor and love for who she was — only confirmed that marrying Sam was the best decision for her future.

For her, it had been a very long wait for a man who would love her like this.

A man who was safe. A man who was trustworthy. A man who was kind.

A man like Sam Chadsworth.

Believing she wasn't worthy to be loved because of past trauma, fear and shame — from what she'd convinced herself was her big shame — those had all been lies.

The lies had created a deep wound in her heart. They were the reason she had put up walls around her heart.

She could see that clearly now.

The hate-filled words from her attacker and the critical words from Lisa Cane had almost destroyed her. But, no longer.

Those were more lies that she now realized weren't true.

Sam really did love her.

He didn't reject her because of her terrible past.

He didn't feel sorry for her.

Instead, Sam gave her respect. He worked with her to solve the mystery of her missing necklace. He chose to help her at great risk to himself and his daughter. Most of all he trusted her with his greatest treasure — Zoe.

Now, Alex's longings had come true. She was a permanent part of a ready-made family.

For so long, she had felt lost, rejected and lonely. She'd been convinced that would never change.

Marrying Sam had shifted everything.

Now they were a real family.

She had been added to the Chadsworth family and now Sam was a part of the Stafford family.

It was the most wonderful feeling in the world.

Her heart overflowed with contentment.

As Sam ended the kiss, his eyes flickered with tenderness.

When her new husband released her, Alex sighed, missing his warmth.

Pastor Tim announced them to the wedding guests as husband and wife.

Her heart danced with happiness as loud applause swept the room.

Church bells in the distance chimed seven O'clock.

This time though, the bells didn't fill her with fear.

Instead today, the bells flooded Alex with faith, hope and joy for her future.

❦

"Let's walk along the beach for a little while." Sam whispered into her ear after they finished greeting each guest after the wedding ceremony.

Alex nodded and slipped her hand in his, "I'd love that."

Together they walked to where the sand touched the water.

The weather was cool, but being together with her new husband made Alex so happy that she hardly noticed.

"I'm so grateful you're my wife, Alexandra. Today, you made me the happiest man in the world." Sam whispered as he slipped his arm around her waist.

"Aww, Sam. We're a matched pair then, because I feel like the happiest woman in the world." She sighed, leaning close to him.

He chuckled warmly. "I'm also grateful that Dylan can no longer harm you." A crease formed between his brows. "Have you heard more about Dylan?"

Alex nodded. "Yes. Detective Sullivan said that Dylan Hart is now conscious, but he keeps babbling on about things that don't make sense. The doctors have decided to transfer him to the psychiatric ward. The detective told me Dylan seems unstable and incoherent."

Sam shook his head. "That's sad. However, he'll no longer be able to hurt you. I intend to do everything in my power to keep my beautiful wife safe."

Alex expelled a long sigh of contentment. "Thanks, Sam."

"At least your pendant necklace and photo are safely back in your hands. But it looks like we need to continue the search to find answers as to the cause of your parents' deaths' years ago." Sam ran a hand through his hair.

Alex reached up and fingered the necklace that hung from her neck once more. It was a reminder to her to have faith and not live in fear.

"It'll be alright, Sam. Remember, we have help. My sister Jane said she would talk with Matty's mother, old Mrs. Bellanger. And, my other sisters are determined to find answers as well. We'll also have another talk with the Sheriff and his son Ryan. See if they will tell us anything new." A new resolve flooded her.

Somehow, they would find the answers they needed.

"You're right. We have help. So really, we have lots to be thankful for." Sam nodded.

Her husband leaned close to whisper. "And best of all, now we have each other."

His words wrapped around her like a warm blanket.

"We do. And I'm looking forward to getting to know Zoe better, Sam. I already love her like she is my own daughter." Alex turned to him.

Sam smiled warmly, "And Zoe loves you. She's been so excited for this wedding. Ever since my first wife died, Zoe has longed for a new mother in her life. You'll be an amazing mom, Alexandra."

"Thanks for your confidence in me. For so long I've longed to be part of a family, and now I'm a part of yours,

Sam. I'm so happy." Alex felt like a breathless girl of eighteen again, at this second chance at love.

Her husband stopped. Gently turning Alex to face him, he spoke in a low voice. "I've learned how important it is to feel the love of family. You taught me that, Alexandra." He pulled her close, placing both arms around her.

They stood together in each other's arms for a long time, enjoying the sunset across the lake.

"We're close to the same spot I saw you months ago, when you arrived back to the island on the ferry." Sam's warm breath whispered against the top of her head.

Alex grinned. "I didn't realize you saw me." Alex frowned as memories of that day came back. "I was so convinced you were angry with me and that you would never forgive me for refusing your marriage proposal years ago. You didn't deserve to be treated like that. I'm so sorry, Sam."

"We've both had fears and misconceptions about each other. I'm grateful we've chosen to love each other instead." Sam moved closer to her.

Placing his hands on her cheeks, he tipped up her chin. "Marrying you was the best thing I ever did. I love you, Alexandra."

A single tear rolled down her cheek at his words.

She would never get tired of hearing him say those three little words.

Looking forward to reading Jane's love story?

Read *The Vineyard Mistletoe Christmas* when you go to Melody's BookShop: www.memorablefictionbooks.com

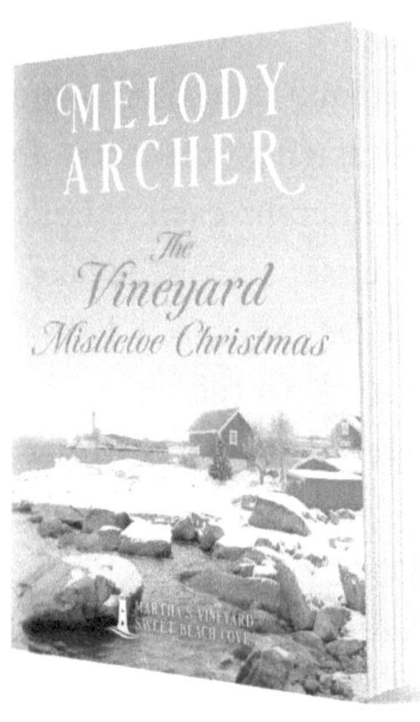

Jane Stafford has been on the run with her son, Noah, for over seven years, trying to escape the abuse of the man she believed was her husband.

**It all started on Christmas Eve five years ago.
One night she arrived home unexpectedly, and overheard Devon Hollingsworth in conversation with a woman, asking her how the children were and telling her that he loved her.**

The man who was supposed to be married to her... had a family.

Shocked, Jane confronted him. When she asked Devon

for the truth, he tried to lie... then finally admitting the truth -- that they had never been legally married.

Jane told him, he needed to leave. But, Devon reminded her that he was paying for the house.
So in the middle of the night, Jane took her son and escaped.

Ever since that day, she hated Christmas Eve.
Jane had lived in five different cities since escaping with her son seven years ago. Each time Devon seemed to find her eventually.

She was so tired of running.

When her beloved grandmother leaves Jane a very generous inheritance of heirloom jewels, she decides maybe it's time to move back to Martha's Vineyard.

Could she finally find a safe place? Would her family support her?

Was it possible for her -- or was her life too tainted by past mistakes -- that she would be forced to run the rest of her life?

Would Jane ever find a way to put a stop to Devon coming back into her life... bringing pain and trauma?

ABOUT THE AUTHOR

Melody Archer lives in Alberta with her husband and
their four young adults.

Recently, her oldest son married his new wife from Brazil.
Their family has been enjoying getting to know their new
daughter-in-love.

She loves new and classic romantic movies, green
smoothies and going on adventures with her family.

Melody would love to connect with you :)

facebook.com/memorablefictionbooks
instagram.com/memorablefictionbooks
bookbub.com/authors/melody-archer
pinterest.com/memorablefictionbooks
youtube.com/@memorablefictionbooks

ACKNOWLEDGMENTS

Thank you to all the wonderful people who helped me with this book.

To my cover designer, Wilette from Red Leaf Book Design, thank you for designing this gorgeous book cover.

Thank you also, to my very helpful proofreader Michaela, who patiently read through each chapter, helping me make this story so much better.

A big thanks to all my wonderful Advanced Readers (my ARC reading team), who faithfully read this book.

Lastly, a huge thanks to two of my young adult children who read through the manuscript, giving me all kinds of great suggestions on how to make this a better story.

Thank you everyone. I really appreciate you!:)

www.ingramcontent.com/pod-product-compliance
Lightning Source LLC
Chambersburg PA
CBHW030752310726
48969CB00005B/1380